ARIZONA GUNMAN

G. WAYNE TILMAN

WOLFPACK
PUBLISHING
— EST 2013 —

WOLFPACK
PUBLISHING
— EST 2013 —

Published in the United States by Wolfpack Publishing, Las Vegas

Wolfpack Publishing
6032 Wheat Penny Avenue
Las Vegas, NV 89122

wolfpackpublishing.com

Paperback ISBN: 978-1-64734-028-5
eBook ISBN: 978-1-64734-030-8

ARIZONA GUNMAN

ACKNOWLEDGEMENTS

My sincerest appreciation goes to Denise Kearns and
Rebecca Thomas Payne for their careful scrutiny of
the manuscript as the Beta readers, and to noted
survivalist
Teal Bulthuis for helping with high desert survival
techniques.

DEDICATION

This book is dedicated to my three daughters,
Heather, Holly and Ann Lee.
They would be the lights in any father's life.
They surely are in mine.

1

ARIZONA TERRITORY
1903

Arizona Ranger Sergeant James Duncan rode the blue roan into the town of Salome. He wondered if it was named for the Biblical reference, but looking around, did not see anything of interest to God. The only thing about it interesting to the ranger was Tonopah Creel may be here. He had a Dead or Alive warrant for Creel in his left saddlebag. The saddlebag also held several less fatal warrants, two fifty-round boxes of .45 Colt rounds, and four twenty-round boxes of .30-40 rifle rounds for his 1895 Winchester rifle.

Acrid, reddish dust stirred under Ace's hooves. The day was almost painfully hot and dry. Duncan didn't wear a coat. Just a vest and shirt. The blue bandanna with the small white dots tied around his neck signified he had been one of Teddy Roosevelt's Rough Riders.

Duncan entered the rutted street from the north, riding slowly. Before reaching the center of town, he loosened the Colt's revolver in its holster. He had a .38 S&W break-open in a deep leather vest pocket on his left side in case the five shots from the .45 were not enough. Like anyone with any sense at all, he carried the big Colt's single action with the hammer down on an empty chamber. Well, not quite empty. He followed the old cowboy habit of keeping a rolled-up twenty-dollar bill in it to pay for his burial if his draw was not fast enough or his shot was not straight enough. So far, in seven years of lawman and cavalry experience, he had been fast enough and straight enough. But every time he pulled and fired he figured his probability of remaining unscathed diminished.

He usually rode into a town with the solid silver, ball-tipped Arizona Ranger sergeant's badge pinned inside his vest. Today, he chose to pin it on the left lapel of the vest in plain sight. He was not sure why.

The ranger pulled up the roan when he reached the hotel, such as it was. Looping the reins over the hitching rail, he took the rifle out of its saddle scabbard and carried it in left-handed. He always kept his strong or shooting hand free. It had saved him more than once.

He walked up to the false front hotel's front desk. The wood was scarred. There was a guest register facing out and open to the current day's page.

Duncan glanced at the names on it before saying anything to the person standing behind the desk. The name Creel did not jump out at him.

"You need a room, Ranger?" the brown-toothed man in the dirty celluloid collar shirt asked.

"It depends," Duncan said. "Do you happen to have a man who goes by the name Tonopah Creel here?"

"I might. Why?" the man asked.

The sandy-haired ranger leveled cold blue eyes at the man, glaring and saying nothing. Just boring into the man's soul. He watched sweat form on the man's forehead. The man's right eye developed a slight tic.

"I got serious ranger business with him," Duncan said. "And, mebbe with anyone who hides him or holds back on my questions about him."

The man reached over to the book, as Duncan's hand dropped instantly and suggestively to the walnut grips of the .45.

The hotelier flipped back a couple of pages. Scrawled almost illegibly, T. Creel was written in the middle of the page. Duncan noted Room 205 was in the column adjacent to the name.

"Where might Mister Creel be right now?" he asked the man.

"Probably two doors down at the Silk Lady Bar. He goes there for lunch, a beer and cigar. Mebbe a game of faro or cards."

Duncan gave an almost imperceptible nod, the brim of his Stetson Boss of the Plains dipping less than an inch.

Walking back to his horse, he chanced the heft of his expensive issue rifle and put it in the scabbard, butt-forward and under the fender.

He had been told Creel was a big man, well over six feet and two-hundred forty pounds. And his size did not hamper his speed with a gun or a Bowie knife. Creel wore his black hair long and, unlike most men of the day, did not often wear a vest.

Duncan again lifted the 5 ½ inch barrel .45 slightly and let it settle loosely in the El Paso Saddlery holster as he walked to the bar.

Except for the bartender, nobody was standing. A group of men sat at a round table for six in the corner. The one facing the door was a large man with long, dark hair and was not wearing a vest.

Duncan walked to within twenty feet of the table. His

spurs clanked on the wooden floor covered with sawdust. His purposeful walk, somber expression and the silver star brought a hush over the bar.

"You'd be Creel," he stated to the man with whom he locked eyes. Two men with their backs to the ranger moved out of the way, knocking over their chairs and leaving them lie.

"Who in hell wants to know?" Creel asked.

"James Duncan, Arizona Ranger. I got a warrant for you. Dead or alive. Don't matter much to me either way. Your call. Smart or stupid. But, don't take too long considering since I'm already real impatient," the ranger said, his voice scary and hardly above a hoarse whisper.

He could see the big man figuring his odds. The eyes may be the windows to the soul, Duncan knew, but the hands are what killed you. He watched the hands.

Creel popped up to his feet amazingly fast, and his hand went down to a revolver at his left hip.

Duncan pulled and fired simultaneously. His .45 never moved more than inches from his hip, pointed instinctively at the big man's belt buckle by the ranger's body orientation. His second shot rang out almost before the sound of the first one cleared. Both two-hundred fifty grain rounds hit the shirt button just above the belt buckle, causing the man to suck in his gut and bend forward at the waist. Then, the Ranger extended his right arm, aimed and fired once again. A half inch black dot appeared on Creel's forehead. The outlaw crumpled unceremoniously and fell. His legs twitched a couple of times, but he had been dead before he hit the floor.

The ranger swept the Colt's revolver around the bar, scanning everyone there.

"Any of y'all want to join Creel in hell?" he asked. Apparently from the silence and motionless hands, nobody did. Knowing he had two rounds left in the big Colt and six in the small revolver, Duncan holstered the big gun with an intentional flourish.

He walked over to the prone outlaw. The man's eyes were open but rolled back in his head. A dark stain covered the front of his pants and a red stain was covering his gray shirt, pooling behind his back and under his head.

Quietly, Duncan asked the barkeep, "Is there a photographer in town?"

There was and a boy was sent for him. In the absence of a lawman in Salome, Duncan needed proof he had fulfilled the warrant.

He told the barkeep to sell Creel's gun and rig and add it to any cash on his person. He should then use the money to pay for a burial. The man asked what to do with the rest, since Creel had a valuable horse. The ranger just shrugged and walked away. The barkeep grinned.

Later, Duncan left with a picture of himself with the body, in a cardboard folder. It was signed, dated and the location noted by the barkeep. It certified the deceased was actually Tonopah Creel. Duncan rode out of town in the direction he had come. He decided he may have worn out his welcome in the lawless town of Salome and would sleep more comfortably in the desert tonight. He pulled the nine-pound Winchester from its saddle scabbard and laid it across the horn of his saddle, or the hull, as Arizona cowboys often called it.

Ten miles out of town at dusk, Duncan found a spot he liked on the side of the road. It was over a rise, so it was not obvious to passersby.

He unsaddled his big blue roan and hobbled him near some sweet grass. The tough, fourteen and a half hand horse grazed contentedly, but was as good as any watch dog.

From the right-hand saddlebag, Duncan withdrew a small side of bacon and some coffee beans. He gathered kindling and some bigger branches. He made two holes connected by a shallow, scooped out, tunnel for a low-smoke Dakota fire pit. He lit the fire from the steel sparker in his vest pocket and the blade of his pocketknife. The fuel and cooking grill were placed over the larger hole. Heat from it sucked air from the smaller hole and made the fire burn hotter and with less smoke. An hour later, he had bacon, store-bought biscuits, and strong black coffee for dinner. Maybe tomorrow he would soak some beans to go with the rest of the bacon. The ranger still had several warrants left in the saddlebag. No more Dead or Alive, but you never knew when any fugitive might get stupid and start shooting or slashing.

He stretched out in his bedroll and propped his head against the saddle. Lying the Winchester across his knees, he draped his wool Army blanket over it, pulled up the canvas tarp against the weather, and tilted the brim of the Gus-creased Stetson down over his eyes. Without a thought to what had occurred mere hours before, he fell asleep and slept soundly until just before dawn. He got up before the sun, warmed the vestiges of last night's coffee and hit the trail again. No rest for the wicked...or the manhunters.

2

PRESCOTT
ARIZONA TERRITORY
1889

Ten-year old James Duncan rode into town in the back
of his family's buckboard to join the crowd gathering to
watch for popular Sheriff Buckey O'Neill and his small
posse of Jim Black, Carl Holton, and Ed St. Clair to bring
prisoners back from Utah. The fugitives had robbed a
train in Diablo Canyon of fifteen hundred dollars and had
exchanged shots with the posse. Sheriff O'Neill had led
the chase and his hat was ruined and his horse was killed
as he was the lead rider chasing the robbers and rode into
the gunfire. But he, his posse men, and the outlaws escaped unscathed otherwise.

Most of Prescott and the surrounding area turned out
for the arrival of the lawmen and prisoners. The capture
further enhanced the popularity of the sheriff, and he
would quickly be elevated to mayor.

The boy was tall for his age, taking after his father, a
Highlander who had emigrated in his twenties with his

wife. He was blonde and blue-eyed like his mother, a Scot whose Viking heritage showed clearly. He climbed onto the seat of the buckboard to have a better view, smiling broadly as he watched his hero.

As Sheriff O'Neill rode in on a replacement mount, holding his holed hat up in salute to the cheering crowd, his badge glinting in the Arizona sun and the shiny walnut grips on his Colt's revolver prominent in a carved El Paso Saddlery holster, young Duncan's world changed. The boy knew what he wanted to be. A lawman. Just like Sheriff O'Neill. He did not say so. But his mother watched his expression and knew what he was thinking. She knew his resolve eclipsed the resolve of other ten-year olds'. She did not say anything either, but her lovely face changed from smiling to a grim expression.

Outlaw William Sterin was one of the four men tied with riatas in the absence of iron shackles or "nippers". His name would reappear to the Sheriff and the boy in the future in a most unexpected manner.

***

James shared what his mother already knew during the ride home.

"I want to be a sheriff, just like Sheriff O'Neill," he exclaimed with the enthusiasm only a ten-year old could muster."

"Well, son, we'd better be training you now, I ken," his father said, his Scottish brogue still present in his everyday conversation.

"Must you, dear?" James' mother asked, still with the worry lines on her lovely face.

"Yes, Ann. What I'll show him will help him as a hunter, rancher, farmer…about anything he grows up to be other than a store keep or accountant. And, if he still wants to be a law officer in eight or ten years, he will be ready," he responded in the quiet deep tone his son would develop as he grew.

James had tagged along behind his father for several years hunting for meat to supplement the odd cow they slaughtered, and he had helped work his mother's vegetable garden for the rest of their sustenance. But he had done this as a kid, not a student. Bright, he had picked up some things on his own. But, this, he knew was going to be different.

His father had him carry the 1873 Winchester carbine in .38-40 caliber. It was a revolver cartridge primarily, but in the longer barrel of the carbine, it could drop a deer at close range. Angus Duncan carried it instead of a revolver. He was fast and deadly with it.

They walked about a mile and his father selected a log. They sat on it and the lesson began. The first part surprised the young man, as family secrets were shared.

"Laddie, being a law officer is a fine calling. But you have to remember, sometimes people do illegal things to survive, not because they are bad. Sometimes governments and the people who represent them are bad and do things or make rules which cause good people to be classed as outlaws. The first thing a bad government does is to disarm its subjects like the English did to the Scots so we could not resist. I was declared an outlaw on land we had once owned. It's why your ma and I came to America. I became an Army scout, but after a while could not stomach what the Army was getting ready to do here. One day, I will tell you more about my decision.

"I will commence teaching you how to trail and avoid capture. It's something I know firsthand. But it was important to tell you this first. Now, there are sure enough bad men in this world, so don't neglect your instincts for your safety when you come up to a man. It you have to fight, win and win as quickly and violently as possible. The only rule in fighting, son, is to win. There is no dishonor in knocking a dangerous man down and leaving the area either, because the one who is still standing, even if he walks away, is the winner."

"I want you to become one with your surroundings. Like the Indians do. Be aware of every sound and listen for sounds which are not natural to the area. Danger can come from any direction, even above, in the case of a mountain lion. Or, an ambush. Make circles before you bed down for the night. Wide circles to see who may be in your area. Remember you have a nose. We have forgotten it's there in this modern world. But, use it. Blow out air when you begin to track or are looking for sign. Sniff though fresh nostrils, boy. Concentrate enough and you will detect more than just a cigarette or pipe, you will be able to smell a man or a horse."

In this first lesson, Angus taught his son how to detect signs and how to age them.

"Son, you can tell whether the man or beast was walking or running from how far the prints are apart. Whether, from the depth of the impressions on one foot or hoof, your quarry was limping." Pensive, the boy nodded and filed away the knowledge. James learned to look at shoulder height from the ground and on horseback for signs someone or something had passed by, looking for broken twigs or branches at shoulder height, afoot or on horseback.

"It is important to remember when it had rained in order to age tracks," Angus told his son, "as well as to look in the tracks for bits of dirt or leaves blown in over the passage of time. Are the tracks wet or dry? These things help tell you when who or what you are after was there."

On successive trips, he taught the boy how to make fuzz sticks from a branch and catch the spark from his steel or a match in the fine shavings attached to the stick in order to kindle a campfire.

"Take the driest pine twig you can find, not always a hard thing in the high desert of Yavapai," Angus Duncan said. "Start shaving off a piece, but leave it attached at the bottom of your knife stroke. Do as many as you can to have a plume of wood on the stick to catch a spark and begin to burn. It will be like a wee torch to put into your kindling to light a campfire. Remember, build as small and sheltered a fire as you can get by with. A small fire means gathering less wood and it does not give away your location to others."

He taught James how to build a shelter with as little material as possible to stay warm and or dry, noting "while it's easy to use all natural evergreen boughs, carrying a light tarpaulin on your horse and a roll of thin rope will allow you to run a line between two trees, hang a quarter of your tarp over it, then use guy ropes on the front and stakes on the back to make a more weatherproof lean-to than boughs would be, son. If it's gonna be stormy—rain or snow—put more tarp over the line. And tie the line lower to the ground to give you more protection. When there aren't trees to make a lean-to, you can roll up in your blanket with the tarp on the outside and sleep pretty dry on the ground."

He showed the boy how to set snares to capture game to eat without the sound or expense of firing a shot. Angus taught his son how to brew coffee and cook bacon and beans and make skillet fry bread and Dutch oven biscuits. He did this on a campfire at the ranch and the family always had the product for the night's dinner, and the young boy became proud of his culinary undertakings.

From a father who had lived off the land, often wounded, he learned how to make poultices from spider webs or ground herbs.

"If you make decoctions of brewed herbs, son, with the liquid strained out, you can cure many ills."

"What's a decoction, Pa?"

"Think of brewing tea. Take the bark or herb and use your knife to grind or chop it up as much as you can. Put it in cold water in your Dutch oven pot and boil it with the lid on. Let it boil twenty minutes to an hour. Check to see the water is darkened by the contents. Let it cool down to drinking temperature and strain the bits of bark and or herbs out. Sometimes, you can save them for another decoction later. The leftover liquid, like a tea, is your medicine. Make it strong enough and you can mix it with a grease to bind it and make a salve for bites, or wounds, too."

"Pa, why do you start with cold water instead of boiling it first?" the boy asked. "'That's a real good question, son. Somehow with cold water, the medicinal qualities start leeching out at the right speed. If you boil it, the material tends to seal up and the medicine is not as strong or good."

Angus showed him black walnut and white oak trees. He taught him black walnut and white oak decoctions and honey by itself could cure many things from gastrointestinal issues to coughs to fever. And, perhaps more importantly, wounds. Even everyday ailments like diarrhea could be helped with easily made curatives like a charcoal or ash slurry or sore throat with tea from slippery elm bark or wild licorice.

Though the father had learned from his own father and grandfather thousands of miles away, he told the boy the same knowledge had been practiced by Indians in the New World for centuries. Indians who had been his friends when he was an Army scout a decade and more before...a part of his life he had not shared with his son until this training began.

By the time Duncan was twelve, he was an accomplished woodsman. By fourteen, he could track man or beast over uneven terrain in any weather. He learned to be a deadly rifle shot, each costly round dedicated to a dinner target instead of an inanimate one.

The tough ranch work in hot summers and snowy winters toughened the boy as he grew into a young man. He made a point to stop in on sheriff, then mayor, O'Neill every time he was in town and remind him he wanted to be a deputy. O'Neill watched him grow and toughen with some interest. He was patient with the boy and spoke with him as he would any other adult. O'Neill shared what he was doing as either lawman or politician. He decided early on young James Duncan would be a good choice as a deputy. He liked the boy and was pleased at the man he was becoming.

***

When Duncan was fourteen, he was on a several day hunting trip with his father when they saw several Indians appear from scrub pines. As he began to raise his rifle, Duncan's father gently pushed it down.

Angus Duncan transferred his rifle from his son to his own left hand and carried it without threat by the balance point in front of the trigger guard. He raised his right arm, open hand facing the men as they stared at him and said, "Mhamka, Mastava."

The tallest and most muscular of the men returned

his salute and said, "Mhamka, Duncan," and smiled in greeting his friend.

The son watched the father and this impressive man with fascination and surprise.

They met and shared food and talked about hunting and weather, things important to both men. It was clear to the boy these men were old friends and held one another in high esteem. They spoke easily, but in a formal way, respectful, with few words and no contractions. James learned the Yavapai hunted for meat and grew the three sisters: maize, squash and beans. Duncan was to find those three vegetables would be an Indian staple virtually everywhere, and one he would come to enjoy.

The man who Angus Duncan first addressed as Mastava was known as Noah Piyahgonte. His son, who sat beside and slightly behind the father out of respect, was called Aaron. Both men had been given those called-by appellations by missionaries, while Piyahgonte was their Indian name. Aaron was the same age as James.

"Noah, I have something at the ranch I want to give you," Angus told his friend. "It is a young steer and would be fine eating for your band of Yavape. I propose to meet halfway between your camp at Fish Creek and my ranch at the large clearing on the Hassayampa River. You know the one. It is near Wolf Creek Falls. I will bring the steer there." The agreed upon meeting would be seven days hence. The Yavape men arose and left without further words or ado.

Angus also rose, and his son followed.

"Pa, if the man was named Noah, why did you call him 'Mastava'?" Duncan asked.

"He is of the Yavape band of Yavapai Indians, like the name of our county. The Yavapai do not have elected chiefs. They just follow strong leaders. Most are proven warriors. Mastava means 'warrior' and I called him Mastava as a sign of respect."

"For future reference, you can tell them from Apaches, with which they are closely associated, by their moccasins. The Yavapai have round toe mocs, the Apache have pointed toes. And, the Yavapai seem taller to me," he continued.

"Son, we, especially the Army, have treated them worse than the cursed English treated us Scots. The slaughter of bison in the seventies was not about meat for the railroad or fur. It was to kill off the Indians. When this group was herded into reservations many died. Colonel Crook is looked upon as a hero for bringing the Indians in this area under control. I'd use 'slaughter' instead of control, James. Crook killed over sixty Yavapai at Skelton Rock or Cave—it goes by both. The Army not only shot them, they rolled boulders down and crushed them.

"Crook," Angus continued speaking as his son was absorbing this history voraciously, "who just died four years ago, was an odd man. He never wore a uniform in the field, had funny looking mutton chop sideburns hanging way down from his jaw, carried a shotgun and rode a mule. Before you were born, I was one of the few white scouts for the US Army hereabouts. It did not take me long to figure out what they were up to and I quit. The Indian scouts knew why and respected it, so word spread back to the tribes I was a friend. Being fair-minded and a friend to the Indians has held all these years, James. And, it's a tradition you should continue."

The fourteen-year old thought for a minute without answering. Finally, he said "Pa, this is new to me and thought-provoking. But I see what you are saying and I promise I will keep our family reputation about being fair to the Indians. Whether it's the English and Scots, the Yankees and Rebs, or the white man and Indians, it sure looks like good people can do real bad things to each other."

"You're right son. I am sure you will follow your dream to be a lawman. And, it's a fine one. But, also be a peace officer, too. Try to talk people down from anger. Like we talked about the first trip out years ago to train you to be a scout, sometimes it's the government makes good people outlaws. Just remember that and be fair. Keep the peace whenever possible, son."

***

Later the next day, the Duncan men rode into the ranch, hailing wife and mother before coming into sight. Their bounty from the hunt was small. They had killed six large jackrabbits and a dozen squirrels. There was no deer laid across the back of a horse. And, Angus had decided to share a head of stock with his friend Noah Piyahgonte. But he knew the band following Noah needed the beef and it was the right thing to do, and a good lesson to the son, of whom he was growing prouder each passing day. Angus had the boy carve a fuzz stick and assemble a fire pit. He lit it from a ferrocerium rod sparking as he dragged it along the spine of his Barlow knife. While the fire burned to cooking coals, James skinned and portioned the squirrels. His mother brought flour and vegetables. The boy dusted the squirrel meat with flour, then browned it in a cast iron pan over the fire. While it was cooking, he peeled and cut the vegetables and put them in water in a Dutch oven over the fire. Adding the meat, salt and pepper, he moved the iron pot onto the coals and shoveled more coals on its flat, rimmed lid. James banked the coals and walked away for an hour. By the time he returned, they had a stew to eat with fry bread his mother had fixed.

The younger Duncan thought a lot about his father's words and about the Yavape specifically over the next week. He looked forward to riding out with the young steer and maybe getting to know, Aaron Piyahgonte, Noah's son. Duncan had some friends at school, but none were interesting to him. He suspected learning about the Yavapai culture and their way of living in harsh country would not only be interesting but would be good knowledge for a lawman to have.

Angus and his son left a day early to be at the clearing on the Hassayampa River at the appointed time. They camped overnight under a waxed tarp lean-to tied between two scrub trees, guy-roped off in front and staked down in back as the older man had taught.

They rode into the clearing the next day, hobbled their horses. Angus tied the steer to a tree. Soon, the Yavape arrived. Noah was a proud man and would not accept a present without giving something in return. The something was two knives in beaded sheaths. They had long Bowie blades and stag handles. Like Jim Bowie's original knife, they did not have quillons or cross guards.

He presented one to Angus and one to the younger Duncan. Both unsheathed their knives and tested the sharp blades. Neither had to feign pride or delight at the gifts. The two older men looked at one another and nodded, slight smiles on their faces. "Noah, these are fine knives. The blades are sharp and sturdy. My son and I will carry them with great pride and remember our appreciation to our friend each time we take them out to use," Angus Duncan said, his son nodding agreement.

"I have brought some food and cold tea and loose tobacco. We can smoke the tobacco in this briar pipe after we eat. The men ate and talked and all, including the boys, smoked at the end of the meal. Noah drew hard on the pipe and blew smoke in all four directions, as a way of giving thanks. The two teens were sitting side-by-side discussing wood lore and their two cultures.

Aaron said, "I am to go to an Indian school in a place called Pennsylvania eventually, when a spot opens. There, I will learn the white man's way and to read and write. With this knowledge, I can write down the oral tradition of the Yavapai. Now it is only passed down in story form by the ancients. As they die off, we lose a little bit of our history," Aaron finished in an uncharacteristically long speech. Duncan decided the tradition would be something well worth reading. When the two small groups parted, he wished his new friend well and gave him his address with a scrap of paper and pencil nub he carried.

***

Duncan continued to perfect his riding and knowledge of the woods, mountains and deserts.

The two boys became fast friends. Living a day apart, they would ride half a day to meet in the middle to hunt and fish together. They talked a great deal, Duncan learning more woodcraft than even his former scout father could teach him. His father was a tracker; Aaron was a stalker. James perfected both subtly different skills. Aaron learned about the white man's ways from his friend, which he found more interesting than appealing. They discussed religion and the differences between the Christianity Duncan had grown up with and was pressed upon Aaron by missionaries. Duncan learned Indian traditions.

Duncan learned Indian beliefs about being stewards of the earth. Aaron said, "Kill only what you need or what is threatening you. If you kill, use all of the animal possible, his meat to eat, skin for clothes, bones for fishhooks or needles. If you do, you will honor the animal and absorb some of his spirit. There is a dignity in all living things, and we must acknowledge and respect it."

Duncan liked what his friend taught him and began to understand the bond between their two fathers. A bond of respect. The boys solidified their friendship with their own blood brother ceremony to bond them as brothers for life.

That winter, Aaron embarked on his big adventure, riding the train all the way to Pennsylvania and matriculating at an Indian school there. Not a year from their first meeting, Aaron Piyahgonte wrote to Duncan in a hand clearer than his own. The letter initiated a series of communications between Pennsylvania to Arizona. It seemed more convenient than meeting a day's ride from each one's home. The boys wrote for another year. Then, Duncan received a letter from his friend saying , as he suspected before going, he did not like the noise and number of people in the white man's world. He told Duncan the teachers' objectives were to "Make me in the image they want instead of being the Indian man it is natural for me to be. James, I have reached my objective of learning to write and organize words. I know enough to document the history of the Yavape. It is time to come back and begin the long task of writing down our history. I believe it is of importance to my people."

The school's master did not share his goal, so Aaron would leave on his own. Sixteen-year old Duncan went behind the unused bunkhouse and dug up a Mason jar with his savings of twenty-seven dollars. He sent it to Aaron Piyahgonte to help with his travel expenses home. When Aaron arrived, his friend was at the Santa Fe station to greet him and had a horse for him to ride on the way back to his camp with Aaron. The two rode to the Fish Creek summer encampment, best friends.

3

PRESCOTT
ARIZONA TERRITORY
1897-1898

Early in 1897, Duncan made a withdrawal from his life savings. It was in one Mason jar and consisted cash made for various tasks over the span of his almost eighteen years. He had checked at the Sam Hill Hardware and found two guns that fit in his limited budget. He needed them for deputy work. One was a well-used four and three-quarter inch barrel Colt's .44-40 caliber Bisley revolver. It came with a holster and cartridge belt from El Paso Saddlery. Duncan knew El Paso Saddlery not only made Buckey's holster, but those of many Texas Rangers.

The other was a Marlin carbine in the same caliber. It was well-worn, with a solid, but scratched up stock. He knew some sandpaper and linseed oil would make a lot of difference.

The younger Mr. Hill waited on him, noting that the Bisley frame was noted for target accuracy and the shorter barrel was "gunfighter length". Duncan had done his research and knew that being named after target match, longer barrels and better sights had given the Bisley its reputation for accuracy, not the frame or short barrel. He liked the feel of the gun though and decided to buy it after examination without Hill's words contributing to his decision.

Duncan had spoken with his father earlier and was surprised to find he was quite knowledgeable about revolvers and did not own one only because "he did not have any particular use for it now". He had carried an Army issue .45 as a scout and used it to save his life from hostiles several times. Angus told his son to cock the revolver and feel whether there was play in the cylinder or it locked up tightly. He further said to check the barrels of both to make sure they had been cleaned by previous owners and were not damaged by the highly corrosive black powder.

He did that and both guns were in better mechanical shape than their outward appearance might suggest.

He made his purchase along with three boxes of Peters black powder cartridges. That evening, he sanded the buttstock and forearm of the rifle and began the process of rubbing linseed oil in with his fingers, letting it dry overnight and repeating until several days later achieving the finish he desired. The Colt's Bisley model, with its odd downward sloping backstrap, had black hard rubber grips. They were almost indestructible, other than by wear on their checkering.

Once the two were ready, and with some initial pointers from his father, Duncan began his practice. He shot at inanimate targets such as tin cans for the first time. At varied distances, he perforated the cans with regularity from offhand and from fast draw. The rifle, acceptable for deer hunting, was sighted for fifty yards and he learned the elevation needed for longer range increments.

Two days later was his eighteenth birthday. He rode into Prescott, wearing a six-gun for the first time and presented himself to Chief Deputy Ev Masters and Sheriff Ruffner. As Duncan spoke with the two lawmen, Mayor Buckey O'Neill walked in and endorsed him.

"Men, I've known James and his family ever since first coming to Prescott. He has told me since he was a boy his dream was to be a lawman. I say let's give him the chance. If he does not become the finest deputy in all of Arizona Territory, blame it purely on me. But I don't think such a thing will happen. You'll see."

James Duncan was sworn in as a Yavapai deputy five minutes later and his badge pinned on the left side of his vest. As it was within a day of the start of the county pay period, he started immediately.

Duncan's first assignment was to work as a jailer with Ev Masters, who ran the jail and administrative aspects of the office. Masters did that to give himself time to teach the new deputy before turning him loose on the world.

Over the next month, Masters gave him a book of Territorial laws and made him memorize it on his own time and taught arrest procedures and when to use what he called "common sense enforcing" where he would not arrest a minor criminal for information leading to a major one and would decide whether circumstances dictated an arrest instead of a stern warning.

"Now Duncan," Ev Masters began, "there will be a lot of times you will need to take someone into custody and they will be drunk, mean or both. They may be bigger than you and have spent their wasted youth fighting saloon brawls." He taught the new deputy something he had learned from the Earps while observing as a bartender in Tombstone.

"This is the fine art of 'buffaloing'." He unloaded his

long-barreled Colt's Frontier Model and told Duncan, "Resist me. We will do this in slow motion, okay?" He reached for Duncan's arm. Duncan pulled away and grabbed for Master's left arm. In rapid motion, the senior deputy drew and swung the barrel of the revolver towards Duncan's head. At the last minute, he slowed it and lightly tapped Duncan on the flat of his skull above his ear.

"You are now unconscious and falling into the sawdust, blood and beer," he said.

Other lessons, repeated until they became rote, included how to take ahold of a suspect's wrist, raise and twist it to take control. From that position, Duncan learned how to put them on the ground if he chose.

"Protect your hands, especially the gun hand. Don't punch anybody with it in a hard place, like their skull. Hit only soft spots, like stomach, kidney or crotch. You hit the wrong hard place and you will be unable to use your gun for weeks. And, Duncan, that could be the death of you."

***

Duncan rode into town months later. He held the reins of a horse with a restrained prisoner. His Yavapai deputy sheriff's badge glinted in the sun. The seven-pointed silver star had "J. Duncan, Deputy Sheriff, Yavapai County" on its face.

Lean and six feet tall, the deputy was still growing. He went about his work quietly and professionally, attracting as little attention as he could, but quickly gaining more respect than he knew.

He dismounted in front of the jail, tying his and his prisoner's horses with loops across the hitching post before assisting his prisoner down. The man was still under the influence of rot gut whiskey even after the forty-two-mile ride from Camp Verde.

Once the man, Oscar Wills, had both boots planted somewhat firmly on the dusty street, he uttered, "Sumbitch." He spat at the deputy. Duncan ducked and put a hard fist into Will's solar plexus, doubling him over. Wills retched and vomited all over his boots, as the deputy stepped back just in time. Duncan took the man's floppy, sweat-stained Stetson off his head and walked to the watering trough, where he filled it. He then splashed the tepid water on Will's boots before walking him over to the trough and dunking him in to his shoulders. The young deputy held him there long enough for Wills to begin choking, then lifted him up for a few seconds and said to anyone who might be listening, "What the heck," and pushed him back under for another fifteen seconds. He pulled Wills out gurgling and retching, and, grasping the rear waistband of the man's pants, frog-walked him into the jail. Wills was still sputtering and cursing.

Ev Masters, watched the whole episode from the door. He held a hand up to Duncan, stopping him on the way to the cell block.

"I'm thinking this piece of garbage got drunk, punched some people and maybe shot up a bar, right?" he asked .

"Pretty much it, Boss. Plus, he roughed up a lady of pleasure. Might have broken her nose. I'm not real sure. She was holding a rag on it and I didn't get a good look," Duncan responded.

The chief deputy got close into the prisoner's face, blowing the first whiff of the drunk's bad breath back at him. "You ever spit at, talk back to, or strike a law enforcement officer in my county again, Wills, and I will personally deal with you in a manner you will not like… if you live through it. You understand me?"

The drunk was a slow learner and spit in Master's face. In a blur, the chief drew his seven-and-a-half-inch barrel Colt's revolver and slammed the side of the barrel across Will's head. The man went down like he had been poleaxed.

"See, like that," Masters said referring to the lesson months ago. He and Duncan each reached under an arm and dragged him into the nearest empty cell and propped him against the cot. Masters took his boot and moved the thunder mug bucket over beside him in case his stomach was not yet settled. He closed the door and locked it with a large iron key, which he then hung on a nail well out of reach of the cells. He shook his head as he walked back to his desk.

"Did he give you any trouble at the bar or upstairs with the soiled dove?" he asked the young deputy.

"He resisted. He was wearing boots, hat and his union suit backwards with the flap open. He was pretty proud. While he was bragging, I buffaloed him with my gun like you just did. His hat saved him from getting his head split. The blow just slowed him down enough for me to twist his arm like you showed me and put him on the floor."

"James, what are you charging him with?" Ev Masters asked.

"I was thinking drunk and disorderly conduct, resisting arrest and aggravated assault. You agree?" asked.

"Yeah, I guess. He's in here at least once a month. He's gonna kill somebody one day, but he never seems to do anything bad enough to get serious time. You sure he did not rape the lady?"

Duncan grinned. "Probably did, but he paid her two dollars first, so it may not count."

The chief deputy walked away shaking his head.

Duncan walked out of the door, washed his hands

more or less in the watering trough, and sauntered down the street to a café. It was late for lunch, and he had not even had a breakfast yet.

He ordered fried chicken, biscuits, green beans, and sweet tea. He did not feel bad about the large lunch—which he followed with apple pie—or the steep seventy-five cents. It would likely be his last meal for the day and well into the morrow. He still had the second half of his large assigned patrol area to ride before a good night's sleep.

The afternoon found him riding slowly through Chino Valley and up to Ash Fork and Seligman. The former had been the original Territorial Capitol. He followed the Santa Fe Railroad tracks much of the way.

At Seligman, a merchant stopped him and reported kids had been stealing items from his storehouse in the rear of his establishment. When asked what was missing, he said, "Them boys got some candy, ammunition—.22 cartridges—and some hats. Just what you'd expect some dumb head kids to take," the merchant reported. On the way back, Duncan heard some sharp cracks of a small caliber rifle.

He pointed the dun towards the shots. After a mile, he found two boys, approximately fourteen years old, shooting a single shot Stevens .22 rifle at a couple of tin cans set up by a creek bed.

"You boys having fun?" he asked, catching both off-guard. The boy shooting the Stevens jerked the trigger at the sound of the deputy's voice and the bullet careened off a rock and disappeared across the creek.

"Yessir, deputy," they answered almost in unison.

"Y'all sure seem to have plenty of ammunition. Hell, when I was your age, I was lucky to walk out with ten cartridges in my jeans. You look like you got a couple of boxes of Winchester brand. Where 'bouts did you get them?" he asked.

The two boys looked at each other, then up at the sky. Perhaps divine guidance was forthcoming. Duncan looked up with them, but he found no guidance either.

"I am investigating thefts from Attleboro's General Store. I always get my man, so it's just a matter of time. You have anything you want to share with me?"

"Iffen the person who took the cartridges was to return the rest, could he escape getting locked up?" one of the boys asked.

"I suspect so," Duncan began. "Especially if he never took any cartridges again and returned his unused ones in good faith to Mister Attleboro. He, or they, should offer to pay with some chores. Might be smart to tell him the deputy had a long talk with you and you already received your punishment."

"You mean we're gonna get a whuppin' now, Deputy?" the shorter of the two boys asked.

"Nope. Your punishment is gonna be more mental than physical. You are going to remember for a long time I know who you are, and I am watching you. You won't even know it, but I'll be there. Watching. And, if there was a next time, I would surprise you when you least expect it and whale the living tar out of both of you. Do we understand each other?"

"We do, Deputy. We understand just fine. We gotta be going now. To see Mister Attleboro."

Duncan watched the boys pack up and leave. He suspected they had learned their lesson. But you never know for sure. So, he would keep an eye out for them, but on a very low priority basis.

He pulled the left reins and nudged the cow pony lightly with a spur and trotted off, heading back to Prescott and, hopefully, a hot meal and soft bed at his folk's ranch.

***

Deputy James Duncan spent the rest of 1897 honing his skills as a tracker and investigator, training now on real fugitives. He practiced daily with his revolver and his speed and accuracy became unerring, both aimed and drawn fast from his holster. Some folks, he opined, shot for recreation. To him, it was more serious. It was life and death in untamed Arizona Territory to a man with a badge.

***

Duncan rode into Prescott on February 16, 1998. He had his hat pulled down and wore a heavy canvas duster over his shirt, pants and vest. It had been a long, cold trail. He had three men, one shackled and two tied, trailing behind him. He noted crowds in the street, odd for the time of day and the weather. Something was afoot, he thought.

He took them into the Sheriff's Office and signed them in to one cell and marked the warrants for submission to the Yavapai County Court for trial.

"What's going on, Boss?" Duncan asked Ev.

"Big doin's. The Spaniards sunk the US Battleship Maine in Havana Harbor. There's talk of war already," he responded.

"Where's Havana?" the deputy asked.

"Cuba. An island south of Florida. Buckey is trying to get a bunch of fellers to form a militia to volunteer if it comes to war."

Duncan perked up at the mention of the charismatic Prescott lawman, journalist and current mayor, whose ride into town so many years ago solidified how the young deputy wanted to spend his life.

Once the prisoners were settled in the cell and the paperwork completed, he walked out and joined the crowd outside the newspaper office, listening to O'Neill.

"I have asked President McKinley for his support in raising a brigade of two-hundred fifty rough riding cavalrymen from the Territory and anywhere else we can attract the best from. Of course, you and I know the fastest riding, best shooting riders will come from right here in the Prescott area." The crowd, including one young deputy, began to clap and cheer loudly and did so for a full five minutes, as Buckey O'Neill waved and smiled.

Before many weeks passed, O'Neill had gotten authority from President McKinley to muster his two-hundred fifty "rough riding soldiers", a term O'Neill had coined before the speech. The men trained in cavalry formations, and military protocols at Ft. Whipple, just outside of Prescott.

On May 4th, amid much music from several bands, cheers and tears, and young girls kissing the handsomest strangers they could, a train with the Arizona Rough Riders of the First Volunteer Cavalry, headed by Captain Buckey O'Neill and others, pulled out of Prescott en route to San Antonio.

On the train, brand new Colt's .45 revolver and belt, toiletries, and a clean union suit in a carpet bag, was a tall, blond young man with cold blue eyes and a wispy mustache. Former Deputy James Duncan was off to war.

4

The train arrived at Ft. Sam Houston in San Antonio for three weeks of training. Colonel Leonard Wood, an Army surgeon who had won the Medal of Honor fighting Apaches a decade before, greeted the troops. His friend, a Lt. Colonel was second in command. He was former Assistant Secretary of the Navy Theodore Roosevelt. Roosevelt was in Washington finalizing materiel for the troops. Another Prescott man, Alexander O. Brodie, was the major.

Duncan was assigned, to his great pleasure, to Company A commanded by Captain O'Neill. O'Neill's friend, Lieutenant Tom Rynning, a famous Indian fighter, was the number two officer in Company B. Both companies were largely Prescott area troopers who knew one another. Roosevelt arrived shortly, making his presence well-known to all the troopers.

The lt. colonel was a personable former rancher and

hunter. He would spend more time talking about the West with a mixture of officers and enlisted than other hardened former officers might have. Roosevelt knew and liked Duncan's mentor, O'Neill. So, the young former deputy was able to spend some campfire time in the presence of the quiet, brave Wood, the charismatic Roosevelt, Brodie, O'Neill, and Rynning, a man whose stoic, firm temperament paralleled of Wood.

Even at his age—almost nineteen—Duncan realized he was privileged to be in the company of greatness. He drank in the talk, the ideas, and the integrity each time he was in the presence of any or all of these men.

Outside of the two Arizona companies, there was another man who would become a brief but powerful influence on Duncan. He was a short, stocky Dane who was chief quartermaster sergeant. When Duncan found he was among the Rough Riders, he sought him out and was not disappointed at the reception and conversations they had.

The man, Chris Madsen, was a legend among Western lawmen. Chief Deputy US Marshal, under Marshals Nix and Grimes in Oklahoma and Indian Territory, he was one of the Three Guardsmen of Oklahoma. These three deputy US Marshals captured or killed three hundred of the worst outlaws ever to plague the lawless territory. Madsen, Bill Tilghman and Heck Thomas. The dogged administrator, the handsome fast gun, and the Georgian who was arguably the best manhunter in history. Madsen spent time with the young Arizonan, sharing stories— some even true—of fighting with Garibaldi, the French Foreign Legion, being on the US Army marksmanship team. He also spoke at length of ending the reign of the Doolin-Dalton Gang or Oklahombres, with Tilghman and Thomas.

"Boy, I was not a good young man," Madsen began one evening as he drank a warm beer and reminisced, his Danish accent still strong after twenty-two years in the United States.

"I took the easy way, conning people and writing bad checks. I ran to the Legion to hide and dropped my last name. Madsen is my middle name. The Legion straightened me out, but I knew there was going to be no peace for me in Europe outside the Legion and a nom de guerre. So, in Seventy-six, I came to this country and joined the Fifth Cavalry. Soon, I was what I am now—a quartermaster sergeant. An Army with no food or materiel is no good Army at all. But I wanted to settle, so I homesteaded a section in Yukon, Oklahoma, not too far from Guthrie. Marshal Grimes swore me in, I met Bill and Heck and we raised some Cain for the bad fellas."

Duncan noticed Madsen, contrary to Army procedure, wore his revolver in an open cross-draw holster. The single action Colt's revolver was not a pretty piece, its full walnut grips scratched, and the bluing worn from holster wear on its frame and barrel. The case hardening's mottled purples and grays were worn almost to bare metal. The older man noticed Duncan's glance and drew the revolver and ejected the five .45 cartridges before handing it butt-first to him.

Duncan rechecked the cylinder to make sure it was empty. The Dane nodded approvingly, saying nothing.

He slowly cocked the hammer, listening to the four clicks spelling C-O-L-T. Holding the gun skyward, he pressed the trigger. It dropped the hammer well before he expected it to. The trigger pull was very light, almost a hair trigger. He smiled broadly and handed the revolver, again butt-first, back to the sergeant.

"Smooth," he said as Madsen reloaded.

"I learned how to hone actions and slick up triggers on the Army marksmanship team. Leave me your gun tonight, and it will feel like mine before you have chow in the morning," Madsen offered. Duncan emptied his revolver and proffered it to the former lawman. Madsen checked it again, then tested the stiff action. "You just got this one? What did you have before?" the former deputy US marshal asked. Duncan told him about the Bisley and how he wanted to step up in power a bit to the .45 so he traded the old one in.

"Sergeant Madsen," he began, "tell me about the Dool-in-Dalton Gang and how you brought them to justice."

Madsen smiled and patted the reloaded revolver in his holster. "This brought some of them bastards to justice, but Tilghman probably kilt more of 'em than the rest of us."

"How?"

"He was fast. Most pistoleers draw, point their arms out straight as they cock their guns and then shoot. Not him. He would square up with the guy, angle a bit left. When he was ready to draw, he pulled and fired from his hip, not wasting time to extend his arm. His stance and angle made the bullet go straight from his waist to just above the belt buckle. His man always folded up and went down immediately. Hot-damn, he was fast. I never saw the like and doubt I ever will."

"How did the draw work for people farther away?" Duncan asked.

Madsen grinned. "'Why you think we have rifles?"

"Heck was like a dog on a trail. He would never give up. Nobody could track like him. Not an Indian or nobody. Heck come after you, you are gonna wear the nippers on your wrists or come back dead across your saddle. No doubt about it."

"What a threesome, Sergeant. How many did you bring in? Or take down?" Duncan asked.

"Some say three-hundred. But it was more. A lot more. You get some rest now, boy. Come back after grub in the morning and get your 'new' revolver, okay?"

Duncan nodded and left, still deep in thought about the history he had heard firsthand from a legend.

The next morning, after mess call but before the first cavalry drills, he sought out Madsen. He could not believe the slick action on his single action, or the light trigger. Madsen also shared a trick with him. The lawman told him to get some petroleum jelly and put powdered graphite into it by shaving lead from a pencil. Once the jelly was darkened visibly, he told the young trooper to rub it into the inside of his holster. The resulting finish, "Would make the gun come out as fast as crap outta the goose," Chris Madsen promised.

Duncan quickly found the proven gunfighter was right, as near as he could tell, not having a goose handy.

The drills were mildly interesting to beginning cavalrymen and boring to experienced ones. The horses assigned were purely cavalry steeds. The horse issued to Duncan was oblivious to having a high velocity rifle shot from his back and used to the parade grounds. He was sure he would not be a good horse for patrolling the frontier, as he had done for slightly over a year as a Yavapai deputy sheriff. The animal was more a piece of equipment, what the Army regulars referred to as "materiel", than the partner his deputy horse had been.

Duncan had grown up shooting break-open shotguns and lever action rifles. The .30 caliber Krag-Jørgensen bolt action carbines were a novelty to him. They were handy and accurate, though he was to find they were not as accurate as the 7mm Mauser bolt actions the Spanish troops carried.

Buckey O'Neill made a somewhat startling discovery as he got to know his men better. One trooper, a school-teacher named Henry Nash, was a spitting image of William Sterin. Sterin was one of the train robbers O'Neill and his posse had captured slightly over a decade earlier and ten Duncan had seen being led into Prescott under arrest. After long and harsh questioning, by the captain and boy-turned deputy, O'Neill decided the similarity was probably happenstance and the matter was dropped. But he was never sure. Nor was the young rough rider who had been ten at the time. Bank robber turned schoolteacher or not, Nash accounted for himself well in the ensuing weeks, survived the war but went on to die of illness at age thirty-two, teaching in the Philippines.

Duncan watched everyone and learned. He was particularly impressed by Lieutenant Tom Rynning. Rynning, of Norwegian descent, had been a cavalryman in the 8th Cavalry. He had fought the Cheyenne then transferred to Arizona. Rynning been present for the capture of Geronimo under his current leader, Leonard Wood. His last action was against Sitting Bull during the Ghost Dance War. He was an experienced cavalryman and Indian fighter. His superior, and a friend of both Rynning and Roosevelt, was Major Alexander Brodie. Brodie was a West Point graduate and yet another rough rider cavalryman who had impressive Indian Wars credentials. Much of his experience had been fighting the Apaches and the Nez Perce.

A singular part of the cadre was comprised of the Harvard, Princeton and Yale sons of the scions of American industry...men who Roosevelt knew. People with names like Tiffany. They mingled with surprising comfort with the rough and tough Westerners, Roosevelt being the common denominator.

The young rough rider realized he was among proven men who had witnessed much of the history of what Buffalo Bill called the "Wild West", what he did not know yet was the fact many would go on to even more positively affect the growth of the Nation.

Over a thousand rough riders and twelve hundred mounts rode a steam train from hot San Antonio to an even hotter Tampa, and one of the most disorganized messes in US Army history.

While seeing Florida was of some interest to the Westerners and Northeasterners alike, their pleasure soon diminished with the heat, profusion of mosquitos and lack of preparation for their arrival on the part of the US Army. The troopers camped out as they would during their tenure in both Florida and Cuba, sleeping on the ground on bedrolls and covered only by an open shelter half of waxed canvas when it rained, which was often in both places.

As they made camp one night in Tampa, a rough rider commented to Duncan, who was unrolling his gear next to him. "I'm from Tucson. It rains about a month a year, all at once it seems. Here, it rains all the time." Duncan commented, "Prescott has four seasons, but it rains a lot in the mid-to-end of summer. But I won't miss sleeping on these thistles and around these snaky palmetto bushes." He finished unrolling his blanket, laid his shoulder bag, hat and Mills belt on the ground. After walking away from the camp to empty himself of several cups of remarkably bad coffee, he returned and took off his boots. He laid on the blanket, shoulder bag as a pillow, rifle beside him, hat over his eyes and pulled the small tarp over himself and everything else.

Later, the Florida weather got hotter. Duncan stood in full uniform with flannel shirt, tan trousers, leggings, suspenders and white Western-style hat. In the Tampa sun, he was drenched with sweat in what was basically a winter uniform sans coat and gloves. And, they were expected to wear their leather gauntlet gloves when doing the mounted exercises.

He looked at the trooper next to him, beads of sweat rolling down his face. Further down were the black Buffalo Soldiers in their all blue heavier weight uniforms.

The trooper followed his gaze to the Buffalo Soldiers and then commented, "Them poor guys is going to pass out from the heat dressed in those duds, Duncan. And, we'll be right there behind them on the ground. Cuba is further south. Which means it's gonna be hotter. This ain't gonna be no party with dancing girls and hard likker. Nope. Not at all."

Duncan nodded. "My pa was a scout during the Indian Wars. He said the problem with the Army was at the top. Up to mid-level officers like Buckey, the leadership was good. It was the generals who made the big, bad decisions. They were the ones who got folks killed. He couldn't take dealing with it anymore, so he quit. We can't do that, Ken, 'cause we got one simple mission to finish first. After that, the regulars can have their Army back as far as I'm concerned. I heard the top fellas of the rough riders talking the other night. They did not expect this war to account for much time. I hope they are right, because the planning couldn't have been much worse." Ken, a former Texas Ranger, nodded his assent

It began to rain torrentially that night. Like the thousand others, Duncan was rolled in his tarp on the ground. Though his body stayed relatively dry, his collar and socks got wet as did the back of his head. He uttered a Scottish curse and rolled over. It was the beginning of a number of miserable Tampa nights. The officers were billeted in Henry Plant's Tampa Bay Hotel, but Roosevelt, Brodie, O'Neill, and Rynning walked the bivouac area after taps each evening in Tampa to check on and chat with their men.

Much of their time during the day was spent sitting on the sand in palmetto and sand burr-filled fields listening to regular Army captains conduct training lectures or the chaplain preaching to them. Neither was appealing to action men of the West or to the Harvard and Yale graduates whose prior lectures had been a bit better delivered.

As time to sail for Cuba neared, it became clear the Army had not secured a way for the troops to go from the camp in Tampa to the Port of Tampa. Wood and Roosevelt commandeered a coal train, had their troops climb aboard, and backed it the nine miles to the Port of Tampa. They found even more confusion at the port regarding ship transport to Cuba. One third of the rough riders, including Chris Madsen, and all of the enlisted men's horses, had to be left in Tampa due to insufficient transport. They were now cavalrymen afoot. Once aboard their assigned ship, the Yucatan #8, they sailed twenty-five nautical miles from the port, past the forty-year old Egmont Key lighthouse, and into the Gulf of Mexico for the almost seven-hundred mile sail to and around Cuba to Daiquiri, near Santiago de Cuba.

Duncan stood on the top deck, staring over the rail near Lt. Rynning and Capt. O'Neill as the ship Yucatan pointed its bow towards the southeastern tip of the island nation.

The voyage itself was not bad, food and water notwithstanding. He liked the salt smell of the wide water and the movement of the ship. But he had some concerns over battle. How would he respond? Both officers turned to leave the rail and stopped to say hello.

"Tom, if you have not yet met him, this is James Duncan of Prescott. I have known him since he was a small boy. His father was a scout early in the Indian Wars," O'Neill said.

"Angus Duncan, the Scotsman?" Rynning asked.

"Yessir, Lieutenant. He is," Duncan said.

"I never met him, but have heard of his exploits, son. He was one of the best the Army in Arizona Territory ever had. Didn't he resign because he disagreed with policy?" the lieutenant asked.

Knowing he could be stepping onto thin ice, the trooper answered simply and truthfully as his parents had taught. "He felt the policy was moving towards just killing off all the Indians. He thought it was wrong." The two officers waited to see if he had anything to add before Rynning went on. "History will be the judge, trooper, but I suspect it will show the policy was way wrong."

"Tom, I have known Angus Duncan for nearly twenty-five years. There is no braver, nor finer man I could name, present company excepted. And, James here has been a Yavapai deputy sheriff for a while. He's a good one and his pa taught him well, particularly when it comes to cutting sign."

"With respect, sirs, may I ask a question?" Duncan asked, having learned the protocol required in military speech.

"Sure, son. Ask away," O'Neill said.

"What can we expect when the battle comes? I have had to shoot a drunk who was waving an axe at me and knock down people resisting arrest, but this is the first time for me with a lot of folks shooting back."

"Every skirmish, every battle is different, James," Rynning began. "Despite planning, nothing ever seems to go to plan. It feels like a lot of confusion. You will be shooting and hear the 'pop' as a round sails by. The people you are shooting at will experience the same. It gets real when you see a friend become a casualty. I can't tell you how you will feel. We all handle it differently. Some puke or soil themselves, some turn and run, some get madder than hell and try to kill every enemy on the field. It depends. I'm afraid you'll just have to wait and see. When it's over, let's have this conversation again, okay?" Rynning said quietly.

"Yessir. I'd like to. I appreciate your words." He snapped a smart salute to the captain and the lieutenant. They returned his salute and walked off.

Duncan turned to the rail and looked at the blue Gulf. He grasped the rail hard and gulped. His knuckles turned white he was gripping so hard. For the first time in his life, he was scared. One on one, even three on one, he could deal with. But a hundred people or more, all shooting at you at once? A whole different thing, he thought.

Duncan spent the rest of the trip on the top deck, enjoying the roll of the steel hull through the waves. It was unlike anything he had ever experienced. Other than a couple of storms, it was good weather to be transiting from Florida to Cuba. Duncan even stayed topside during light showers. Getting wet beat the smelly, dank humidity below decks where the men were assigned.

The lack of preparation aboard made the eating and drinking part of the trip intolerable; the canned meat for the trip and the war was neither corned nor salted. So, it was tough and vile. Duncan opened a can and barely made it topside to spit it over the rail into the Gulf of Mexico. Much of the water was bad and undrinkable. The troopers who had anything other than hardtack and water they brought, were sick. Dry hardtack did not satisfy even

the most experienced trooper for three-meal-a-day sustenance. Duncan carefully apportioned his canteen of good
water to last the duration of the voyage.

Duncan, like many of his ilk, observed this confusion
from San Antonio all the way to Cuba with some equa-
nimity. There was nothing he or the sergeants or officers,
including Roosevelt or Wood could do about it. "Hell, if
the Yankee Army had been this messed up thirty-some
years ago, we'd have won the war," one older Texan noted.
The career military officers aboard who heard him held
their responses. But they knew he was right.

Things did not improve upon arrival in Cuba. The port
in Daiquiri did not prove to be a port at all, just a village
on the water with a pier insufficient to land ships. Men
and materiel had to be transported ashore by small boats
from the transport ships anchored out.

Duncan climbed down a rope net ladder from the rusty
sides of the Yucatan and stepped onto a rocking twenty-foot skiff powered by a sailor with long oars. The climb
and step onto the small boat were treacherous, but nobody
on his skiff fell. Duncan had been able to swim since he
was six; whether he could do it in rolling seas with a rifle
slung around his neck and full gear was something he
was glad not to have found out.

One skiff with Buffalo Soldiers capsized and four of
the brave black troopers drowned, despite O'Neill and
several other officers jumping into the strong current trying to save them. Their gear and heavy Springfield rifles
pulled them down quickly, whether they could swim or
not.

Duncan, already ashore, waded in and helped pull the
victims onto the beach as several doctors rushed up and
tried unsuccessfully to resuscitate them.

Once all were ashore at Daiquiri, they moved inland

to set up a hasty camp. The still wet Buckey O'Neill addressed his company quietly and personally.

"Men, this has been a mess and both I and Cavalry leadership know it. But, now is the time to concentrate on why we are here—to drive the Spanish into submission. We hope to begin starting tomorrow. Get as much sleep as you can tonight so you'll be ready."

As they had every night since they left San Antonio, the troopers slept in the open, their blanket bedrolls covered by shelter halves to protect them from tropical rains. Duncan was hot as hell and soaked with sweat, wearing the heavy winter weight long sleeved shirt. One morning, they were called to assemble ready to march and, in formation, marched fifteen hot grueling miles.

The following day, on June 24th, the Rough Riders saw their first action at the Battle of Guasimas. It was a battle in thick woods, where they flanked the Spanish and caused them to retreat. The First Volunteer US Cavalry lost seven men with thirty-four wounded. In the firefight, it had been virtually impossible to know whether one hit an enemy soldier as a barrage of .30 caliber bullets was launched down range as fast as the bolts could be worked. The 7mm Mauser bullets showering them were fired by unseen Spaniards who, in turn, could not see the Americans.

At the end of June, they rolled out at dawn after only coffee and hard tack to fill their stomachs and moved along a road that was virtually little more than a jungle path under a hammock of foliage. Presently, they began to hear buzzing noises. Experienced military men quickly identified it as small, high velocity Spanish bullets whizzing overhead.

The shooters were obviously shooting from height, probably trees. O'Neill sent Duncan and two other

Prescott troopers ahead to try to identify and neutralize the snipers.

Unlike the .45-70's chambered in the Buffalo soldiers' single shot Springfields, the Rough Riders' cartridges were loaded with smokeless powder like the Spanish Mausers used.

Even when he climbed a tree, Duncan could not see any puffs of smoke when a sniper fired. As he settled in at his perch, he began to see a slight movement in several trees two hundred yards distant.

The slight movements were probably the shock waves of rounds moving leaves as they passed from the sniper's position, or his rifle barrel moving branches as he aimed. The Spanish did not worry about Americans seeing them yet, as they thought none were close enough.

Duncan changed those imperceptions with his first shot. Not as familiar with the trajectory of his Krag as he was with his Marlin back in Arizona, Duncan guessed some Tennessee elevation and fired a foot high at the point where he had seen the last movement. There was a scream, and a wounded man fell forty feet from his sniper stand, hit the ground, transitioning from wounded to dead. Duncan heard the buzzing sound as a bullet went "thwack" into the tree near where he sat.

Having already operated the Krag's bolt, he fired at the second tree with similar results. He felt a burn in his left bicep as he heard the buzz of another shot. He instinctively shot at the same height in the third tree in his field of vision. He thought he heard a rapid exchange of words. Then, silence. Nobody fell from the tree. Had he hit the sniper and the man was caught in the crotch of the tree? Had he gotten away? Duncan dropped to a lower branch and put the tree trunk between him and where the shot had originated.

Repositioned and still no shots coming in, he took a bandana out of his right rear pocket and blotted the wound, then tied it tightly around his upper arm. He thought it was a graze, not a through and through wound, but would check it when he was less likely to be in a line of sniper fire. He waited through twenty minutes of silence. Now, he just wanted to stop the bleeding and protect it. He climbed down and went back to his company, as did the other two troopers.

He reported back to Captain O'Neill.

"I got two or maybe three snipers in treetops. Things seem to have quietened down for now. I 'spect they'll pick back up again eventually," he said.

"Good job, Trooper. Tell me about the wound on your left arm," the officer asked.

"Haven't really looked at it, sir. Think it's a graze, not a through and through."

"There's the beginnings of a field hospital being set up down the path here," he gestured the direction, which Duncan already knew. "Go down and get it looked at. We are going to have more men die of infection and disease and bad food here than by Spanish bullets," O'Neill prophesized correctly.

"Yes, sir." He did a rifle salute and winced as he brought up his left arm.

A mile later, walking against military traffic and what he considered to be way too many Cuban civilians, he arrived at the hospital. Most of the patients seemed to be sick, though a few had bullet wounds.

The surgeon glanced at his wrapped arm and tossed him one of the new Johnson bandages, sterilized and wrapped in paper. "I got iodine, trooper. I'd highly recommend it, but it's gonna hurt like all hellfire."

"No, sir. I'll find some honey to put on it or something. Maybe a black walnut shell poultice."

The surgeon had already turned back to the sutures he was tying off. Duncan walked away, the bandage still in its wrapper and placed in his messenger bag. He remembered a village of sorts about half a mile further on and went there.

Seeing some women, he asked where he could buy some honey.

"¿Donde puedo comprar algunas miel, por favor?" Surprised at the trooper's use of her language, one woman motioned for him to follow her. She pulled a jug of honey out from some stores she had and began to look for something to put a bit into. Duncan shook his head "No."

He took off the makeshift bandage and dropped it. Taking the wrapper off the Johnson bandage from the company soon to become Johnson & Johnson, he held out his right palm, cupped and nodded towards it. The woman poured about two tablespoons into his hand. He applied it to the wound, which he could now see was a deep furrow. It would leave its telltale mark as long as he walked—or rode—the earth. Seeing how sticky his right hand was, the woman wrapped the bandage around his bicep and tied it off with some degree of practice. She motioned him to a pan of water and some lye soap to wash his hands.

Duncan realized something as the water turned pink with blood. He now had blood on his hands literally and figuratively. For the first time, he had taken a human life. Probably three. He shrugged and reconciled it was his job. And, they had tried to shoot him. He gave the woman a nickel for the honey and smiled at her surprise and pleasure. He walked back toward gunfire. It had restarted. Apparently, he had more work to do.

***

"How's your arm?" O'Neill asked as Duncan walked up.

"It will be fine now, sir. Give it a day or so and I'll just have a scar to show the girls back in Prescott."

"You got a girl back home?" Buckey O'Neill, who had known him virtually all of his life, asked.

"No, sir. I haven't had time to locate one. To my Ma's disappointment, I'm afraid," Duncan responded.

"Well, 'afore you and I go back to Arizona Territory and you start looking for some winsome lass, I want you to go towards the front line, climb another tree and kill some more snipers. Near as I can tell, you spilt some of the first proven Spaniard blood in this nasty, ill-planned little war. Lieutenant Colonel Roosevelt was here a while ago. He said scouts had gone forward and found this jungle clears after about a mile or so. Beyond lies Kettle Hill and the San Juan Heights. The Spaniards are dug in and well-protected. We gotta do something about tomorrow. So, you go hold the sniper fire down and keep our guys alive so they can do some hill-climbing tomorrow," O'Neill said.

Duncan headed back out, picking up some more .30 Krag cartridges for his ammo belt first. Rifle slung across his shoulder he found a slightly taller tree about fifty feet from the one where he had earlier success.

He climbed the tree more painfully than earlier as his left arm had stiffened from the wound. Duncan found a wide crotch in the tree and settled into a position that afforded him a good view of the trees fifty to several hundred yards distant. After about ten minutes, he saw a movement in the branches of a tree about seventy-five yards away and heard the whine of the .28 caliber or 7mm bullets whizzing by, followed by a "crack", as it broke the sound barrier. The phenomenon was a scientific fact about which he had no knowledge.

Duncan aimed several feet to the right and fired, immediately seeking shelter behind the main body of his tree. He heard a scream and a man toppled from his target tree. His body hit the ground and flopped like a rag doll. Duncan was pretty sure it was a kill. Several shots hit his tree trunk and branches around him, but he was not struck.

He climbed further up and found another sniper position and waited. Soon, he detected movement, heard the whine of the bullet and a crack. This tree was at least one hundred fifty yards away. Duncan pointed his front sight at the point of movement, swung it two feet right and elevated a few inches higher than he estimated the man's chest would be. He pressed the trigger and his Krag recoiled against his shoulder. Another kill. He quickly moved again; his shot now being answered by several rounds being fired back at him.

Those shots were answered by one from a nearby tree, fired by a Rough Rider Duncan did not even know was there. Another Spaniard fell from a tree. This one did not seem to be hit, rather injured by the twenty-foot fall. He began to hobble towards a thicket, but Duncan aimed for center of mass and fired, dropping him where he stood. He tried to get up, but the other Rough Rider fired again, ending his efforts.

The two Americans spent the afternoon alternating fire, hitting snipers, then moving. Together, they accounted for eight kills, five of which were Duncan's and one was joint.

As the sun started to drop, he heard someone below calling his name. It was Buckey O'Neill.

"Up here, Captain O'Neill," he answered in a low voice.

"C'mon down, son. I will get Nichols from further on. That'll do it for today," the former sheriff said.

Duncan climbed down slowly as his captain moved silently down the trail to call in the other Rough Rider sniper. As he got to the ground, he threw up. His stomach had been churning increasingly all day. Nausea and diarrhea had been rampant among both the volunteers and regulars. As the canned meat had caused problems in Tampa before they sailed for Cuba, he had checked some of the water in the barrels being loaded on shipboard. It had an odor indicating it was bad. He reported it and was told he was wrong. He knew he was not and bought two extra canteens from the Rough Riders who were being left behind and filled them with well water at the Port of Tampa. Today, he needed to replenish his water supply. Again, he eschewed the water brought with them and filled from a stream. It tasted good and he drank a lot, sweating from the hot uniform in the tropics.

As his stomach gurgled and he threw up again, he determined the stream water was not good. He had only eaten hard tack, beans and some of the canned fruit Buckey O'Neill had bought his company from his own resources, so he narrowed his nausea down to stream water. The coffee water had been boiled for five minutes to purify it before the coffee was added, so it likely was not the coffee causing his discomfort.

Back at the camp, he thought back to the old time remedies his father had taught him during the bush-craft lessons. He boiled his stream water vigorously for ten minutes. After it cooled to hot coffee temperature, he added charcoal he ground from gray ash in the cook fire. He made a thick slurry in a coffee cup and forced himself to drink it all. It was not tasty, but it worked quicker than he expected. He filled and emptied his three canteens with boiling water several times each to clean them, then refilled with boiling water. Once it cooled, it should be safe to drink, he thought. Oh, to be back in Arizona, where he could drink freely from most cool, flowing streams.

5

CUBA, NEW YORK
AND ARIZONA TERRITORY

The Rough Riders moved forward, beginning at dusk. This morning, the feeling in the pit of Duncan's stomach was not from bad water nor food. This was going to be the day of battle. And, maybe the next day also.

Each man had recovered his pack from camp and was issued a folding shovel. A field was selected beyond the thick jungle-like foliage they had been in once they had left the port. They were ordered to dig four-foot-deep trenches parallel to their enemy and filled burlap bags with the dirt they removed. Those bags were arranged as bunkers for cooking, supply and medical purposes as well as placed along the enemy side of the trenches for protection and aiming rests.

As the sun came up on July first, they saw Kettle and San Juan Hills in the distance. The soldiers of the 10th Cavalry were beside them, young white First Lt. "Black Jack" Pershing was one of their officers. A line of Spanish riflemen was spread across the immediate horizon some several hundred yards in front of them.

It was the first time the Rough Riders could actually see their enemies. Shooting commenced as the sun first came up over the horizon, each side using the elevators on their rear sights set to three hundred yards. It became readily apparent the Mausers fired by the Spaniards were superior weapons and were more accurate than the Krags at an extended range.

During the exchange of long-range firing, charismatic Captain Buckey O'Neill paced upright through the trenches, talking with his men and building morale. He stopped by Duncan.

"James, you ready for the big run when we get the command?" O'Neill said, pointing towards the hill with the line of Spanish regulars.

"Sir, you make an awful big target standing up like that," Duncan said as O'Neill lit a cigarette. He looked back out again towards the Spanish line as he took a long drag on the cigarette.

"There hasn't been a Spanish bullet cast can hit me, James," the captain said.

Then, the former sheriff was struck in the mouth by a Mauser bullet, which exited through the back of his head. He fell dead beside the young trooper to whom he had been a hero since he was a child. O'Neill was on his back. Duncan and another trooper rolled him over and seeing the exit wound, did not bother to look for a pulse. Blood on his hands, Duncan began firing until his magazine was empty and kept reloading and shooting until the barrel was too hot to touch.

Lt. Rynning had run crouching, along the trenches from his Company B, upon hearing what had happened to his friend. He had two Rough Riders carry Buckey O'Neill's body off the field and looked at the tall young man firing mechanically. He patted Duncan on the shoulder.

"Son, save your ammo for the charge up the hill. I think it's gonna come soon. You will need all your rounds," Tom Rynning said, seeing tear tracks through the powder coated face of Duncan and surrounding tough Company A troopers, to all of whom O'Neill had been an old friend as well as boss. Duncan checked his Mills belt. He moved back to the bunker and refilled it. He knew he had not fired his newly-tuned Colt's revolver and had a full belt of cartridges for it.

The war had just become very personal for Duncan. Up until now, it had been a succession of badly planned moves and bad meals and vile water. Even the Spanish snipers shooting at him had been unseen, as he was to them. The exchange had been neither terrifying nor very personal. He was shooting at movements by guess, not at human beings. Now, he was mad and determined to kill as many Spaniards as he could before they got him. He became focused and quiet. His mouth was a thin line across his face and his blue eyes ice cold.

James Duncan's life leading up to several minutes ago had been a mere rehearsal. In the moments after, he had become the man he would forever be. A gunfighter to be reckoned with. And, his legend with a six gun and Bowie knife would begin to grow this day.

The troopers saw Lt. Parker move up his battery of Gatling guns and began to fire the hand-cranked .30-40 caliber machine guns. Soon, they got their range, the Spaniards on San Juan Heights began to fall, or to rise from their trenches and run from the withering fire. In the next ten minutes, they would fire eighteen thousand rounds up Kettle Hill on the San Juan Heights, enabling a charge that would go down in the annals of American history. Duncan smelled the cordite from Gatling rounds as they rained down on the Spaniards and he heard their distinctive chatter as the cranks were turned.

Seemingly without an officer's order, the Buffalo Soldiers and the Rough Riders arose and began to run the first hundred-fifty yards, yelling and firing their rifles. Some fell as Mauser bullets hit them. The preponderance charged on.

Lt. Tom Rynning was in front as the First US Volunteer Cavalry, Rough Riders, and the 10th Cavalry's Buffalo Soldiers, ran up what the Americans called Kettle Hill.

Duncan saw the standard bearer for the Rough Riders get hit and fall. Before the lance with the colors hit the ground, Tom Rynning scooped it up and charged on, colors in his left hand, a Colt's .45 in his right.

Duncan almost caught up with him as they approached the first Spanish skirmish line. He saw a Spaniard rise from the trench and Rynning shoot him dead with his revolver. Duncan passed Rynning and was ten feet to his right. Another Spaniard stood aiming his Mauser at the lieutenant, who clicked an empty gun at him. Before he could fire, Duncan jerked out his Colt's .45 and thumbed two shots into the man. The Spaniard crumpled. Rynning looked over at him and nodded appreciatively as he reloaded his revolver. Others who saw Duncan's fast draw and deadly accuracy spoke of it around campfires long after. These were Western men who had seen gunplay before. And, so it had begun.

An officer Duncan did not recognize called for the men to stop charging, as they were running almost into the Gatlings' suppressive fire. He signaled for Parker to stop firing the machine gun battery and, when it stopped, he pointed his sword towards the Spanish and yelled, "Charge."

The men, white, brown, red and black, sons of former Yankees and Rebels, outlaws, lawmen, former slaves, and Indians charged. It was the most diverse Army ever fielded by the United States. Roosevelt appeared in front and led his men on to the main skirmish line.

There, the Rough Riders fought with pistol and Bowie knife and fist against Spanish rifles.

Duncan saw a Buffalo Soldier kill a Spaniard with a vertical butt stroke of his heavy single shot Springfield. Duncan, his empty rifle slung, fired his revolver until it clicked. A Spaniard ran towards him with a bayonet on his Mauser. Duncan stepped right, brushed the long rifle away with his left arm and rammed the ten-inch blade of his Bowie knife into the man's midsection. As taught in San Antonio, he twisted it as he pulled it out. The man was disemboweled. Rather than let him die a horrible slow death, he thrust the big knife into his heart and moved on.

As he reloaded the Colt's six gun, a Spaniard ran at him with a bayonet. The man dropped five feet away. Duncan looked and saw Lt. Pershing, of the Buffalo Soldiers, nod and turn his smoking cavalry model revolver to another target.

A Spaniard, larger than him, jumped on Duncan and the two went to ground. The Spaniard grabbed his knife hand and tried to wrestle the Bowie away. As they rolled in the dirt, Duncan punched him in the Adam's apple and, as the man clasped his own throat, the young Rough Rider jabbed him with the knife and ended the fight. The hand-to-hand fighting lasted ten minutes. When it was over, a number of his compatriot Rough Riders and Buffalo Soldiers lay dead on the field. A greater number of Spanish defenders were casualties.

He heard Roosevelt's odd voice yell out, "C'mon, men. Onward to the blockhouse at the top of San Juan Hill.

Follow me. Charge."

Men who were used to going everywhere by horse were winded and bloody, but they rallied and charged. Duncan, his rifle and revolver reloaded, ran behind the newly designated full colonel. He saw the long legs of Tom Rynning go past him, as well as a 10th Cavalry sergeant, George Berry, and Pershing. Roosevelt, wheezing slightly, ran at a good pace. Duncan determined to run beside his Colonel to protect him as much as he could.

There was a blockhouse at the top. Parker poured Gatling fire into it until his own troops got too close. Then, the Rough Riders, 10th Cavalry and 3rd Cavalry began to fire and to engage the troops at the top. Berry and Pershing, Rynning and Sgt. Norton of his company were the first to the top. Duncan saw a Spaniard take aim at Col. Roosevelt. Duncan fired his .45, hitting the man dead center and his target crumpled. Roosevelt turned and nodded appreciatively at Duncan. He saw Duncan raise the big Colt's revolver in his direction and felt the air move as the slug sailed past. He spun and saw two Spaniards. One was falling dead from Duncan's second shot. Roosevelt killed the other one himself with four shots from the revolver recovered from the sunken ship Maine. Both Rough Riders, colonel and sergeant, ran on. They were loading and firing their revolvers all the way to the top. The few Spaniards left in the buildings there were dead, wounded, or all the fight was gone from them. The surrender was assured.

Remembering the two Spaniards Duncan had killed, saving him, Col. Roosevelt asked Maj. Brodie to have Duncan's new captain, Frank Frantz from Prescott, fill an empty sergeant slot the next day with the young Rough Rider. Roosevelt came to pin the chevrons on himself, an honor the young sergeant cherished lifelong.

Sgt. James Duncan. He liked the sound of it.

The next month included a siege, then a full surrender by the Spanish. The war was over. Many Rough Riders were dead, wounded or sick with malarial fever, which they called "Cuba Fever", yellow fever, infections and every gastrointestinal complaint then known to medical science.

Once the terms of surrender were signed and ships loaded and ready to sail for Spain, Col. Roosevelt wrote a scathing letter to Secretary of War Alger. He elaborated virtually every shortcoming in planning, medical care, transportation, weapons and materiel which had hampered his brave men. Roosevelt's letter was not well-received and delayed him being awarded his well-deserved Congressional Medal of Honor posthumously a century later.

In August, the men boarded a ship and sailed north. At sea, they were advised they were going to an Army base at Montauk, Long Island, New York. There, they received medical care, since most were sick, and were mustered out a month later. The Ivy League contingent was familiar with Long Island. The Westerners may as well have been deposited on the moon. But, stalwarts, they gave up their issued weapons and gear and shook hands with the Colonel. To a man, they respected him. Brave men shed tears of respect at the parting. Roosevelt clasped Duncan and said, "Thank you again, Sergeant. But for you, I would not be here now." Duncan, filled with pride and accomplishment, could only smile and nod his head. The colonel understood and nodded, clasping the young sergeant's hand in his, the older man's left hand squeezing Duncan's shoulder.

Most of the Westerners had carried their own revolvers, so they were armed for the trip home. Some spent a few days in New York City, others went to Boston or caught trains to places from which their families had migrated to Arizona Territory, Texas or Oklahoma Territory.

Duncan travelled to New York City and bought civilian clothes. He wore a suit home and a new Stetson. By a circuitous connection of trains, Duncan went to Texas.

At Houston, using some of the accumulated pay, he bought a powerful blue roan with a black mane and tail. Though broke, the horse, who he named Ace, was still wild and tended to buck once or twice when first saddled and mounted. On the ride back to Prescott, Duncan found him to have great speed and endurance. The perfect lawman's horse, he thought.

He rode into Prescott in November 1898. He had a few gifts for his mother and father from cities along the way where trains had connected. He had bought French perfume and cloth for his mother, in New York City, and a new burly pipe and sack of tobacco for his father. He stopped only for a few minutes at the Sheriff's Office to check in, see Ev and the acting sheriff, Jim Roberts, and advise he was available if needed.

"So, how was the war?" Ev Masters asked.

"Ill-planned. The majority of us suffered more from weather and bad food and water than Spanish bullets," Duncan responded.

"Tell us about Buckey," the taciturn Roberts said, spoken softly even for him.

Duncan gulped and gathered himself for a moment.

"We were at the last trench before the charge up the hill. We were all hunkered down firing and bullets were cracking overhead. Buckey was walking upright along the trench, cheering everyone on. Being Buckey. He stopped to check on me and lit a cigarette. Before he could take a draw on it, a Mauser round caught him. He fell right beside me."

"Did he suffer?" the chief deputy asked.

"No, it was immediate. The way he was hit by that high velocity round, he was dead even before he fell. Lt. Rynning got there fast and had two troopers move him behind the lines to the field hospital. After that, I emptied a whole Mills belt of ammo at the Spaniards. The lieutenant had me go back and get more cartridges because the charge was coming up shortly," he said.

"The charge. How did it go?" Roberts asked.

"It was long, Sheriff, and uphill. We were already tired. But, about halfway up, the fighting got fierce. Hand-to-hand. You forgot how you felt and just fought for all you were worth."

Masters spoke again. "It said in the papers you saved Rynning once and Roosevelt twice. And, that you killed several Spanish soldiers with your Bowie knife."

"It was hand-to-hand, Chief. Everybody was close in and shooting to save themselves and anyone on our side. That's all that matters," Duncan said.

The two men lived and understood the Western way and accepted the answer as given without pursuing it further. They had each read the whole story. Much of America had. Certainly, all of Arizona Territory.

"You now have a reputation as a bad man to buck against, James. Just keep that in mind when you pin this badge back on," Roberts said as he handed it to him. "I know first-hand what it means to punks who think they are fast with a gun. Keep your wits about yourself at all times," he said.

"I will, Sheriff," Duncan said. "I'll see y'all in a week, if that's okay," he said and shook with both lawmen, turned and left for his folk's ranch.

Duncan rode on to his family's small ranch and surprised his parents. The homecoming was a happy one. Both parents saw the war had changed him, made him more serious, quieter. He helped his father around the ranch, getting in feed for the livestock and moving outlying cattle in closer to avoid loss to wolves or mountain lions. Knowing it was better to talk than keep it in, the elder Duncan pressed his son about the war and his actions. He was filled with pride as the young former sergeant related everything with simply stated facts, showing emotion only when speaking about Buckey O'Neill's death and Teddy Roosevelt pinning on his sergeant chevrons.

**

Most cowhands matched their Colt's revolver and Winchester in caliber so the cartridges would be interchangeable. Duncan had originally done that when he started as a deputy. But Duncan liked his .45 revolver and there was not a matching Winchester in the caliber. He went to Samuel Hill's Hardware and traded for an 1894 Winchester in the relatively new .30-30 smokeless caliber to carry in his saddle scabbard. He had learned in the Rough Riders more than one canteen was a good idea, so he added two canteens to his purchases at Goldwater's Store. He purchased clothes suitable for patrolling, a new heavy waxed canvas trail coat lined with wool, a bedroll with wool blankets, and heavy and a light tarp. Some cast iron cookware and utensils completed his purchases and finished his bankroll.

As promised, he presented himself to the sheriff and chief deputy a week later and was sworn in again as a Yavapai deputy sheriff. For the second time, Duncan pinned on the seven-point star.

Duncan spent most of his time riding the wild country

between Yavapai's small towns and Prescott. He had to use his gun several times in the next several years and his reputation as a man-tracker and fast gun grew. Duncan perfected the Tilghman-style quick draw and used it to good advantage against dangerous men. The word about his speed and unerring accuracy spread throughout the Territory and to Nevada, New Mexico and Texas. Even his old mentor, Chris Madsen heard tales of his gunfighting in Oklahoma. The new century came and went with not much more than a few celebrations, which just meant more drunks to wrestle into the jail. And, more hours in a courtroom, waiting to, then testifying.

***

In August 1901, Burton Mossman was named the first Captain of the newly reconstituted Arizona Rangers. The group was closely patterned after the Texas Rangers. A famous cattleman, Mossman had run the Hash Knife Outfit in Northern Arizona. He successfully recruited and organized the Rangers. Duncan watched this with interest but took no action other than continuing to ride as a deputy in Yavapai.

In September 1901, President William McKinley was assassinated.

Vice President Theodore Roosevelt became the youngest president in American history.

The following year, he appointed Major Alexander Brodie of the Rough Riders as the Governor of Arizona Territory. Mossman considered his job done and resigned to go back to ranching at the famous Hash Knife Outfit.

Brodie and Roosevelt unanimously agreed there was only one man to replace Mossman. The man was Tom Rynning. In 1902, Rynning was appointed to be the second Captain of the Arizona Rangers. He moved the ranger headquarters to Douglas, on the Mexican border.

Rynning heading the rangers did it for Duncan. He sent a telegram to the man whose life he had saved at San Juan Hill.

"Need ranger? Interested. Five years deputy Yavapai. Sergeant Rough Riders. Wire Duncan at Prescott." The operator added the requisite "stops", and it was gone. Two days later, he received his answer: "Come Douglas to be sworn. Need you Western AZ. This area for couple months. Rynning."

Duncan resigned from the Sheriff's Office once again and told his folks what he was doing. There was no girl to tell. He packed Ace, for a tough, cold ride and headed southeast three hundred miles to Douglas.

***

Duncan had found Ace to be smart, and often thought the horse understood him. So, to pass time he talked with the horse on the trail. Every now and then, Ace would shake his head, whinny or grunt. Duncan took those to be responses. On the second night, he stopped at the Tonto Natural Bridge and found a site with water near. He put a hobble on Ace so the blue roan could move around and graze. It was cold and he built a fire before setting up camp. He never made large campfires and was careful to use low smoke wood whenever possible. A cold rain portending sleet and maybe snow had started, so once the fire was going and a night's supply of wood was laid in, he built a low lean-to with the heavier of his tarps, putting fully half the material on the front side of the support line to give a more protective roof. He would use the other, smaller waxed canvas tarp to wrap around his wool blanket once he retired.

The lean-to was up against a rock wall. Duncan made a small shield of rocks on the opposite side of the campfire to reflect heat back into his sleeping area. He positioned longer than usual small logs so he could push them in to stoke the fire without much movement so he would not spill body heat from his bedroll. The only thing he put on the fire was his wrought iron coffee pot. He supped on strong black coffee and biscuits. He would replace the latter tomorrow when he rode through the pine-fringed valley below the Mogollon Rim to Payson.

After two mugs of coffee and one large biscuit, which he knew would not hamper his sleep after two days of long, hard riding, he prepped the fire for the night and dragged his Winchester into the bedroll down his left side, Colt's revolver on his right. He had seen bear scat on the trail as well as mountain lion tracks. But it was more two-legged critters of concern to the young lawman.

Part of the reason the Rangers had been formed last year was rustlers and robbers. And, the Mogollon was rife with them.

The next day, he got more supplies at Globe and spent the night at a rooming house. Driving sleet slowed his trip, and the roan struggled a bit crossing Picahaco Pass. Duncan gave him his lead and let the big horse set the pace. He rode head down against the weather, looking side to side and front and back enough to assure himself there were no threats looming. He patted the big horse on the neck. "Ace, buddy, do it at your chosen speed. I don't want you falling and breaking a leg. Pick your trail and I'll give you free rein." He got a whinny in acknowledgement.

They skirted Tucson, stopping over the next several days at Benson and Tombstone, where the famed gunfight had occurred twenty-one years earlier. Tombstone was the most cosmopolitan place he had been except for passing through New York after leaving Montauk. He treated himself to a good dinner after instructing the livery stable to take special care of Ace's grooming and feeding. He had some salty Smithfield ham from Virginia, sliced and wrapped in waxed paper and a dozen biscuits for the trail. Knowing he would need it with the ham, he filled his canteen from the first ice cold stream he passed.

Duncan made several more similar camps as he paralleled the mountains and rode to Douglas. The town was directly north of Agua Prieta, Mexico and about fifty miles from Tombstone.

Late in the afternoon of the fifth day, covered from the rare two inches of snow, he rode into Douglas. He should have been exhausted and cold, but he was not. This was what he did. Whether a wool tunic in the tropics and bad water or a biting cold wind blowing sleet and snow so hard it hurt when it hit, it was what it was. He accepted it without equivocation, the fortitude of his Highland blood and frontier upbringing showing.

He knew one thing though, as surely as the sun would come up and set every day, his life afield with danger around every turn, beat working in a store or granary. Or a factory like those poor guys back east. Duncan grinned to himself and hitched the big blue roan in front of a likely looking hotel. He secured a room, then carried his gear in before walking Ace down the dirt Main Street to a livery stable.

Once he knew his partner would be brushed, fed and watered and was safe in a stall for the night, he walked back towards the hotel on the wooden path optimistically called a sidewalk.

There was a restaurant along the way, so he stopped for dinner. A big T-bone, corn bread, and potatoes, with copious amounts of strong black coffee filled the void in his stomach.

Duncan walked back to the hotel, looking unintentionally like either a lawman or a gunman. He saw his reflection in a shop window, thought about it, and guessed he was really both.

He had lucked out on the room; he did not have to share it, as was the case so often in the West. So, he would not have to shoot a man for snoring too loudly like John Wesley Hardin had. Not something he would be likely to do. Throw him out the window. Maybe. Shoot him? Probably not...

He hung his cold damp clothes on hooks in the wall of the small room and climbed into a single bed, asleep almost as soon as he became prone. He slept with the .45 under the feather pillow. The pillow smelled suspiciously like cheap hair pomade.

The next morning, he returned to the restaurant and had bacon, eggs and biscuits. He ordered a dozen more of the latter to go. Finishing his coffee, he went to the livery and ordered Ace to be saddled and ready to ride in an hour.

The stable owner seemed to Duncan's peace officer experience to be a respectable fellow. He asked the man where the Ranger post was and got directions without any queries addressed to him.

He checked out and left his gear, except for the Winchester, which he carried in hand, in the lobby. Retrieving Ace, he led him back to the hotel, loaded up and made the direct, short ride to the ranger camp.

Two miles down a trail passed for a road, he spied the camp. There was a cabin or cottage for headquarters. He suspected, correctly, Rynning also lived there. Surrounding it was a series of permanent wall tents with stove pipes sticking out, an open shed he surmised was the cooking facility and a corral with some fine-looking horseflesh in it. There was a line of four privies a hundred yards behind the dwellings. A number of men were ambling around, finishing breakfast, and working on tack or cleaning guns.

He rode Ace up to one group. He noticed the men eyed him as a threat and kept their hands near their Colt's revolvers.

"Howdy, would I find Captain Rynning up there at the house?" he asked.

"Who wants to know?"

"James Duncan," he responded.

"That mean anything to the Cap?"

"I 'spect it does. He there?"

"We will take you there." The man didn't directly answer Duncan's question.

Duncan noticed two men flanked him and one was directly in back. Though not a threat, he assessed the situation. He was leading Ace by the reins. He could spin, kill the man behind him and turn, firing at the other two before they cleared leather, he suspected. Probably. But he did not really know how good these rangers really were. He was pretty sure he would find out soon enough...

The ranger on his left opened the door and walked in after knocking. The one behind Ace moved up to his left, so Duncan would continue to be flanked. He knew they should have stood a bit behind him, not directly beside him. They lost tactical advantage the way they repositioned.

Rynning came to the door, a bit heavier than his Rough Rider days, but still a force to be contended with. He glared at Duncan for effect, as his rangers watched and waited.

Stepping across the threshold, he broke into a big grin and stuck out his hand. Two men, whose relationship had been forged in battle, shook. Rynning grasped the younger man's shoulder with his other hand, coming as close as the two would come to a bear hug. But the meaning was not lost on the three rangers.

"Duncan. You are older. And tougher looking. Though you probably killed more Cubans than any other single man in the Rough Riders as a mere boy. And, saved my butt on the Hill."

"Cap, I didn't mean to hit the guy in front of you. I was aiming for somebody else," he lied.

"Boys, meet James Duncan, sergeant in the Rough Riders. Saved me. Saved Colonel Roosevelt twice. Was one of the first with me to the top of San Juan Hill. His Colt went dry and he gutted two Spaniards with his Bowie knife. He patrolled Yavapai for five years total, wearing a badge before and after the war."

With this introduction, each of the three proffered his hand in welcome.

"Thanks, boys. Duncan and I have some serious talking to do. Y'all get ready to go on patrol. Take two more and slip along the border. Keep your eyes peeled and your guns loose, okay?"

"Will do, Cap," one of the rangers responded.

"Duncan, come in. It's cold out and there's a pot of coffee on. The water's a sight better than when we last shared a cup."

6

ARIZONA TERRITORY
1902

The two sat at Rynning's desk, sipping strong coffee in chipped mugs. After a brief catch-up, Rynning began to outline his vision of changes he wanted to make to the overall ranger operation.

"Mossman did a good job of recruiting. I still don't know all the fellows well enough to have full trust, but so far, so good. I do disagree with his idea of these uniforms. They are based somewhat on the undress uniforms of the Northwest Mounted Police up in Canada for some damn reason. Thank God he did not opt for the red jackets. What targets."

"I am changing the uniform of the day," the tall captain continued, "to what riders wear on the trail, and dressing it up a little around town. So: dungarees; shirts with bandannas on the trail; ties in town; Western boots, and Stetson hats. I suspect most fellas will add vests like yours for the extra pockets for makins' or a hideaway gun like I see printing on your left. What is it, by the way?"

"It's a break-open Smith & Wesson .38 backup," Duncan replied. Rynning nodded approvingly and continued.

"They are issued an 1895 Winchester lever gun in .30 government and, if they don't already have a serviceable one, a Colt's Single Action Army in .45 Colt caliber. I have gotten funds to add Sheffield, England-made high-quality Bowie knives. I have a case of them. They just came in. Seeing you on the Hill in '98 influenced my decision."

Duncan just nodded his head and listened.

"But, Duncan, here's the big thing: the early Texas Rangers went out to fight Indians and later rustlers in troops. I want these boys to patrol alone, unless they are after a gang. That way, I can cover all of Arizona with the number of rangers I am allotted. And, the evildoers won't know where we are or necessarily who is a ranger."

"It sounds like a fine plan, Cap. How can I help you the most to implement it?" Duncan offered.

"Well, Duncan, some of it's already in motion. I have all but one of my allotted sergeant slots filled. Sergeants are in three regions around the Territory, each with two to five men to supervise. I have one lieutenant, who is off on personal leave back east with sick parents for a bit. He works out of the capital in Phoenix. Eventually, the territory around Prescott is where I logically want you. You know it from patrolling it for five years. Plus, you grew up there and have roots. What I don't have yet is an allotment of five men to send with you when you go back. But you will be here for a month or two to get used to the ranger way and to conduct some training," Rynning said.

"I want you to be a pattern for the new ranger. You already look the part, the way you are dressed and equipped. I have followed your deputy career. Your wire to me only beat the one I was writing to you by days. You went on patrols, sometimes with warrants, sometimes just to enforce the law. You tracked people. You used woodcraft to live in the wilds. I want you to share those procedures and skills. Now, mind you, many of these fellows were peace officers or cowmen who know a lot of it. So, you have to instruct by doing and showing, not lecturing. Not preaching like those regular Army captains did to us at Tampa before we left for Cuba.

"To give some credence for your role, you will start right off as what you quickly became in the Rough Riders: Sergeant James Duncan, my final allotted sergeant."

Duncan was surprised and pleased. "Thank you, sir."

"Don't thank me, boy. You will earn it hard. And, I might have just put a bigger bullseye on your back with it. But I know it's the right decision to move this change process along," the captain said.

He stood and reached into a file cabinet and took out a silver sergeant's badge. "Raise your right hand and put your left on this Bible," he said. "Do you, James Duncan, swear to uphold the Constitution of the United States and enforce the laws of the Territory of Arizona, so help you God?"

Duncan answered "I do," without hesitation.

"Congratulations, Sergeant. Sorry, I don't have the same fella to pin it on as last time, but I suspect President Roosevelt is a mite busy at the moment." Duncan grinned at Rynning and said nothing.

Rynning walked over to a crate and took out a knife and sheath, both wrapped in waxed paper. The blade, when shown, was eleven inches of glistening Sheffield steel and sharp enough to shave with before being stropped at all.

"Here. This first one's for you. Check it out."

Duncan fully unwrapped both blade and sheath and hefted the knife, turning it slowly in his hand. He felt the blade, unbuttoned a sleeve and shaved a small amount of hair off his arm dry. He looked at the captain and grinned.

"She'll do, Boss," he said. And he threaded the sheath onto the left side of his belt.

The tall captain rose and went to a closet and withdrew a carbine length Winchester rifle with no tube under the slender barrel. It was an 1895 lever. The advantage was it had a magazine. Other Winchesters, and most lever guns, Duncan knew, except for the 1899 Savage, had a cartridge tube where cartridges were lined bullet tip to the primer of the cartridge in front, so only round or flat nosed bullets could be used to prevent recoil from having a pointed bullet next to the primer of the cartridge in front igniting it in the tube. This gun could use more ballistically efficient pointed or boattailed bullets. It fired the same .30-40 round as his former Rough Rider Krag bolt action issue rifle. It was a mid-power cartridge a bit more powerful than the .30-30 carbine in his saddle scabbard.

"It's a good gun. Teddy ordered them for us for Cuba, but like everything else related to the war, it got screwed up. Only fault I have with it is with the built-in magazine located where it is in front of the lever, it's a bitch to hand-carry very far if you are tracking someone on foot. But, how many times did you actually do as a deputy?"

"Only a couple times in five years," Duncan replied. "'What I like about my Model ninety-four is perfect balance, less weight and almost the power and range."

"No reason you cannot have two scabbards on your blue roan," Rynning responded with a wink. Duncan took the drift and said nothing, grinning. On longer patrols, he used a packhorse in addition to Ace anyway.

"I am going to call a meeting now before those five take off on patrol. I want you to start training once they return, so I'll give them a target time to get back," Rynning said.

"Any idea what you'd like me to hit first?" asked.

"No. Your curriculum, Sergeant."

"I've got some ideas about equipment I'd not leave camp without and using a Dakota fire hole to keep smoke down and make it easier to disguise your camp to start off."

"Good. There's a smaller wall tent with a stove, smokestack and wood floor I've been saving for the final sergeant. The old one went back to his ranch for good. It's halfway between the other wall tents and this head-quarters cabin. Might want to move your duffle in and move some firewood over. Head into town to the Levy Dry Goods Store and get whatever you need to set up housekeeping…though most of will be on the trail, I'm afraid," the captain said, giving him a voucher for up to twenty-five dollars.

Duncan complied and went to the smaller tent, still eight by twelve feet in size and with a wood plank floor. It had a musty, canvas smell, and he opened it up to let the cold wind air it out. He took a pencil nub and back of an envelope and noted what he needed: oil lamp, oil, pillow and blankets for the cot, small table and a lockable footlocker for possessions and ammunition. He knew he'd need some trail food, though most of the meals would be with the other rangers and cooked by a camp cook. He would pick up an axe, and small shovel for the trail when he had a pack horse, and a hatchet and trowel for when he was living out of his saddlebags. He knew many men would use their Bowie knives to dig camp holes.

Angus Duncan had taught his son to use the right tool for the right job, wherever possible. "Boy, the big knife Noah gave each of us is a weapon. Keep it clean and sharp for fighting. Digging and chopping with it will dull it and make it less effective when your life depends on it."

By the time he had gotten back, it was almost dark. He found out two things: he had missed dinner and the captain had a couple of Rangers pile a week's supply of stove firewood beside his tent.

He sliced some bacon he had bought for the trail and built a Dakota fire pit outside, using the new trowel and his hands. Setting up his trail tripod for a coffee pot and a small cast iron grill for the bacon, he soon had the area around his tent smelling wonderful.

Several rangers wandered over and he explained the benefits of the fire hole to them and promised more in subsequent training. He shared some of the bacon and put his on a large biscuit from the dozen he had picked up on the way out of town. Supping on a bacon biscuit and good, strong coffee was normal for him and enjoyable. Maybe one day he would have a wife and family and more normal dinners, but that day was not yet in sight. It was not even on the horizon.

By the end of his first week, he had taught many trail-craft skills, how to perfect a fast revolver draw and shot, recommended essential equipment for short and long trail rides and had begun training how to track with help from some older rangers who had been Army scouts. He also talked about emergency medicine, showing the long bullet crease on his arm and telling how he had kept it from getting infected.

In teaching the draw, he said, "Men, I was taught the Bill Tilghman draw directly from his good friend, Deputy US Marshal Chris Madsen. Bill, Chris and Heck Thomas cleaned up Oklahoma and Indian Territory not ten years ago. Bill would square himself off against somebody who might draw and angle a bit to the left, seeing as he was right-handed. When he drew, he kept his gun hand close to his holster as he cocked and fired. It was the orientation of his body which aimed the gun at the man's gut, not extending his arm and aiming. Extending takes valuable time. Time you could die in. I want each of you to unload between now and the next instructional period and practice. See if it's for you."

Duncan slowly drew his .45 and shucked five cartridges into the palm of his hand and handed them to the captain. Rynning watched as his sergeant drew and clicked the empty revolver twice even faster than he had saving Rynning's life on the Hill. The lawman had never seen someone draw and fire so fast. Nor had the rangers watching. Some were former Texas Rangers who had seen the best.

Rynning continued to quietly watch the training and was pleased at the increase in abilities shown by the twelve rangers assigned to HQ, within few short weeks. He knew rustling and robberies were heating up on both sides of the border. Which led to his next plan. He planned to introduce himself and his new sergeant to the flamboyant head of the Mexican Rurales and negotiate a mutual aid agreement with the Rurales without the knowledge or interference from the State Department or Mexican diplomats. The two men had already communicated by letters which hinted their intentions but did not divulge them in legally enforceable terms.

***

Following rollcall and dispatching several teams of rangers out on missions to conduct surveillance—and if necessary, punitive action—against a band of horse rustlers operating on the border, Rynning motioned Duncan to the headquarters cabin.

"There is someone I have not met with, but information I have suggests he could be invaluable in our activities. Those activities are against rustlers from both sides of the border, criminals who duck back and forth over it to escape us."

He immediately had the young sergeant's full attention.

Rynning continued, "He is the head of the Mexican rural patrol, or Rurales. He is a Russian who worked his way up to Colonel in the Mexican government. His name is Emilio Kosterlitzky. He and a couple of his men have offered to meet us just across the border. His note says we will see him before we get to Agua Prieta. He will turn west, and we should follow him slowly at a distance until he stops. He has a private place in mind where we can have a confab. Since we don't know each other, he asked we each wear a red bandanna around our necks. Got one, I presume?" Duncan nodded affirmatively.

"Cap, do you think it's an ambush? I mean, who is to say it's really Kosterlitzky? Couldn't it be the head of one of the rustler gangs?" he asked.

"Could be, Duncan. But I think it's worth the chance. If we were to come to some sort of mutual aid agreement by-passes the damn bureaucrats and diplomats, think of how much easier our job will be. Oh. There's one other thing. He claims he's going to bring us a present to show good faith."

Duncan was pensive for a minute, then asked the Captain, "What do you think 'present' might be?"

"Well," Rynning began, "it could be anything from a bottle of tequila to the head of some rustler. These are tough men and they have the authority to try and execute offenders on the spot."

Rynning continued, "Since I'm assuming you don't speak Russian, how is your Spanish?"

Duncan grinned. "Passable Spanish. No Russian. Maybe a wee bit of Gaelic. Nobody'd mistake me for a native Spanish speaker, but I can communicate."

"Good. Mine is okay, too. But I am going to take Ranger Torres with us. He is a native speaker and we might need him for some sort of nuances in words," Rynning said and Duncan nodded affirmatively.

The three red-scarfed rangers rode out after mess call the following morning. As usual when a ranger went anywhere, they took extra ammunition and a kit to allow at least one night's camping.

They rode south towards Agua Prieta. Several miles outside of town, they spotted four horsemen. One raised a pair of binoculars and viewed them before raising his sombrero and circling it over his head. He then spun a white stallion in a circle and rode off at a gallop. The three other horsemen followed, as did the Rangers.

A half hour's riding took the two groups to an area of rock formations. The front group stopped and awaited the rangers.

"Captain Rynning. I am Kosterlitzky. Let us seek the protection from both the sun and those who might wish to harm us, under this rock outcropping," the man on the powerful white horse said.

At the protected site, they dismounted and shook hands, introducing themselves.

Kosterlitzky was a striking man; his presence and charisma were powerful, and Rynning and Duncan both liked and trusted him within the first ten minutes of conversation. His uniform seemed to not have a speck of trail dust on it, nor did the large white sombrero he wore.

He told the Arizonans about growing up in Russia, his military experience and moving to Mexico. Kosterlitzky was aware of Rynning's Spanish American War role and even a smattering about Duncan saving the President. Clearly, he was a man with broad intelligence contacts and not just one who rode the back country looking for outlaws.

The men agreed informally to exchange information and prisoners without using bureaucratic channels. They knew it was an illegal, but efficient way to deal with a growing criminal situation.

Once logistics about where exchanges could be made and lines of communications were set, one of the Rurales rode off about a mile into the desert and built a fire. He piled brush on it to make smoke rise into the blue Mexican sky and be seen several miles off. Within fifteen minutes, the group under the overhanging rock saw several horsemen riding from the southwest approach the single Rurale. Within minutes, the group rode towards them. As they got closer, Rynning, and Torres could see one horseman was wearing a Stetson instead of a sombrero like the Rurales wore.

As they rode up and dismounted, the Arizonans could see the man in the Stetson was an Anglo, his clothes dusty and smeared with blood from a broken nose at the very least. He steadied himself against his horse as well as he could with his hands tied behind him.

Kosterlitzky said, "If you do not recognize this man, his name is Frank Moore. He is wanted by Phoenix authorities for murder, rustling horses and cattle, and for sexual assault. He is in good shape for a felon captured by the Rurales. I give him to you under our new agreement. There will be no extradition, or papers involved. This is the way I would like for our agreement to work."

Rynning thought for a moment. He was tempted to comment on the fact the man had been beaten but thought better.

"Thank you, Colonel. I concur and look forward to re-ciprocating with you by bringing you someone of interest to your judicial system very soon." He reached out and shook the handsome Russian's hand.

"Captain, inasmuch as a moving target is harder to hit, let us part and ride. Adios, mi amigo." He turned the white stallion and rode off at full gallop, his men follow-ing at speed.

The rangers remounted and rode off towards the bor-der, this time Moore riding with them.

"Do you need water?" Duncan asked the prisoner. He replied affirmatively and Duncan handed him his can-teen. As he was riding, his hands had been tied in front. So, he was able to down almost half before returning the canteen.

"No need to look too uniform, so let's get these red bandanas off," Rynning suggested.

At the ranger camp, a ranger was sent to the town telegraph office and Moore's identity and warrants were verified with the Territorial Attorney General. Duncan made his first arrest as an Arizona Ranger, charging Moore with rustling, murder and forcibly undertaking carnal knowledge. Moore was fed, allowed to clean up and Duncan took Torres with him on the prisoner transfer to Phoenix the following morning.

Since Moore did not have a coat, the rangers gave him a wool blanket to wrap up in. Knowing he was gal-lows-bound, he was sullen the entire two hundred-thir-ty-mile trip. Instead of getting scarce hotel rooms, they camped along the way, Moore with his iron nippers pad-locked to a chain, which was, in turn, padlocked to a tree. The two rangers slept on the other side of the larger than usual fire, out of the reach of the chain and its felon, who could walk in an eight-foot circle, eat, drink and relieve himself behind his tree. The three had biscuits, ham or bacon and coffee for breakfast and dinner, beef jerky and water for lunch.

At dinner on the second night, as the men crouched cold around the campfire, Torres asked Moore about his offenses.

"I ain't gonna tell you nuthin', Ranger," Moore responded.

"Why not? Won't do you no harm. We're going to drop your sorry ass off with the sheriff and ride on. It's not like we are going to use what you say on the trail to testify against you. Who was the woman you assaulted?"

"She was just a bitch married to a rancher we borrowed some cattle from. No big deal."

"Did she have children?" Torres asked.

"Yeah, but they didn't watch. She was in the bedroom when it happened, they was in the other room, where the fireplace is. She wasn't all good."

"So, she was not worth hanging for?" Duncan asked, receiving no answer.

"Did you kill her?" Torres asked.

"Naw, but she died after," was all Moore would say.

The two rangers looked at one another with disgust at the man's unwillingness to take responsibility. In Duncan's experience, when a subject changed the person from first person to a more vague or indirect person, they were lying. Always.

Duncan wanted to unshackle him on horseback the next day, hoping he would run.

A fleeing prisoner was fair game. But, he didn't, thinking Moore's contemplation about getting his neck stretched would be more punishment than a bullet.

It was Friday before they got to the Maricopa County Sheriff's Office and turned over their prisoner. The sheriff asked if it was a tough capture. They just shrugged. Torres asked how the woman who Moore assaulted had died.

Sheriff Cook said Moore had beaten her in front of her children before dragging her into the ranch house's bedroom and raping her. He said she had succumbed from her injuries.

The two rangers left and began the ride home to Douglas. Torres' mount was as trail-worthy as Ace and the trip back was at a faster pace without the prisoner.

The snows became heavier and the winter months passed quickly as Duncan took the headquarters rangers through training.

The captain watched with satisfaction as the men learned more and more daily about how to be a better ranger. Tracking, tactics for making an arrest alone, shooting skills, living on the trail, writing brief but comprehensive status and arrest reports.

Duncan worked more frequently, too, with the head of the Rurales, and developed a great deal of respect for the Russian. Had he known Kosterlitzky would go on to become an American operative spying on German spies in a great international war over a decade away, he would not have been surprised. The man knew how to work sources and deal with people. Even ones who did not wish to be dealt with.

Frank Moore stayed in jail for over a month awaiting trial. The trial was fast, and he was found guilty on rape and the subsequent murder. The court did not bother with rustling as he already had a death by hanging verdict. The date was set for three days from the reading of the verdict. A day before, Moore strangled a jail guard to death, stole a broom handle Mauser automatic pistol and a horse from the Sheriff's Office, and rode west as fast as four legs could carry him. He angled into Mexico and resumed his criminal rampage.

Always on the lookout for Moore, Duncan continued to train his men in trail-craft and shooting and rode patrol alone and with them. He participated in arrests weekly and firefights at least monthly. He did not mention the latter in his letters home to his folks. Rynning noted but did not comment upon the fact Duncan rode out each time with the short, fast 1894 Winchester .30-30 in his saddle scabbard instead of his issue Model 1895, which was heavier and only slightly more powerful.

The captain turned a blind eye, not wishing to alter the approach of a young man who was the best and most successful man-tracker he had seen, even contrasted with the Indian Wars scouts he had commanded before the Spanish American War.

With the saloon drawdown on Tonopah Creel in Salome, Duncan's reputation as a bad man to draw on had soared.

But he was not one who sought fame or fortune. Just a good man with a fast gun hand. He approached his job with clarity, efficiency, and a love of the outdoors characterized all of his days. He practiced drawing daily and marksmanship weekly. He kept his revolver oiled and his holster slicked inside with petroleum jelly mixed with powdered graphite. He still had no reason to disbelieve Chris Madsen's goose story.

Since the action Madsen had smoothed was so light, he never held a man at cocked gunpoint. He feared the hair trigger might go off unintentionally. Besides, he knew he could thumb the single action's hammer and touch the trigger in a split second if needed. He had a local gunsmith in Douglas smooth the action on his Winchester carbine, but wished he had geographic access to the older Dane, who lived in Reno, Oklahoma and still wore a badge.

Even after the turn of the century, the Three Guardsmen were still active lawmen and ones to be reckoned with.

7

RICHMOND, VIRGINIA, AND WICKENBURG
ARIZONA TERRITORY
1904

Miranda Hancock walked down the sidewalk away from
the Victorian house on Church Hill where she lived with
her husband Riley Hancock II. It was late winter in the
former capital of the Confederacy. She wore a coat and
carried a carpet bag with meager belongings for the wife
of a successful post-Reconstruction Richmond businessman. Her fine gowns, a necessity to the wife of a Hancock
wife, were left hanging in the wardrobe at her house.

She had not seen her husband for several days.

The last time was when he staggered in drunk at midnight, lipstick on his collar, and smelling to high heaven
with cheap perfume. She became infuriated.

"You were going to your club with college friends," she
began. "It is obvious the friends you were with never saw
the inside of Richmond College, Riley. I seriously doubt
any of your school chums wear lipstick or perfume. You
hang out with harlots and want to come home and bring

diseases to our bed? You can forget that. Ever again," she said.

She knew what would happen next. He balled his fist, screamed, "Damn you, woman. What I do is my affair and none of yours," and swung at her. Prepared this time, she ducked and stepped back. The swing was more than his drunken lack of balance could handle and he staggered back. She brought the fireplace poker in her right hand up between his legs hard. He doubled over in pain and she gave him a push against the chest. Riley Hancock fell onto the Persian carpet in their bedroom. Once down, he looked at her with surprise, and still grasping his groin, rolled over and commenced snoring.

Miranda pulled his shoes off and draped the duvet over him. Let him lie there on the floor, she thought. If he throws up and chokes to death on his back, so be it. She knew she would smile behind a black veil at the philanderer's funeral.

Though his blow did not connect, this attempt to beat her was the final act of violence she could take. It was the first time she had defended herself. Miranda was not concerned about repercussions. He regularly became black-out drunk and did not recall anything that transpired while he was in a drunken state.

She had already arranged for the sale of the home her parents left her, with a Petersburg lawyer. The only thing left was to sign the power of attorney for him to handle the closing in her absence.

Miranda packed a riding outfit, several dresses, some under garments and toiletries and put her winter coat, a hat and some doe skin gloves out for early the following morning.

She awoke early and walked down the street to Broad, where she took a streetcar to the train station on Main

Street. Once out of the residential area, she could see and hear the bustle of Richmond, now just beginning to come back after the war. She smelled the tobacco smells emanating from the warehouses at Shockoe Slip, near the James River. Though an old part of town, the warehouses were new, replacements for ones burned by the Confederates as they retreated from the city just before federal troops took it.

When she thought of her husband, it was as an abusive, drunken bastard. She had married him at age twenty, a year and a half earlier. It had seemed like a good match. She was a beautiful brunette who had flashing eyes, a pleasant temperament and comely figure. He was dashing, from an old Richmond family and sought after by many available Richmond ladies from sixteen to forty. But, appearance, she learned, often belies reality. He beat her savagely within the first month. The Richmond police did not seem to want to get involved, saying what was between a man and wife was not their affair. While their reluctance may have been the status at the time and place, she thought the real reason was their reticence to go against the family whose patriarch was Colonel Riley Hancock, Senior.

So, she avoided her husband whenever possible, traveling home to Petersburg by train more often than he liked. She was sure he frequented off-Broad Street brothels to satisfy his more prurient needs, all the more reason to avoid his bed. It was an uneasy life. She knew if she left and went to her late parents' home in Petersburg for any extended period of time, either he or the sheriff would bring her back.

Miranda's ace up the sleeve was unknown to Riley. He was so wrapped up in himself and his own family he had failed to ask about hers. He was unaware her older cousin was a Spanish American War hero and the Territorial Governor of Arizona, Alexander Brodie. Their nicest wedding gift, a sterling tea set in Miranda's bag to hock to help fund her life in the West, was from "Cousin Alexander". Riley was so disinterested in anything not about himself or the Hancocks, he never questioned who the cousin was.

She had written her distinguished cousin in desperation. He had secured a teaching position for her in Wickenburg, Arizona Territory, and had sent a personal check to cover her train and other expenses. He had also included a Remington two shot .41 Derringer for her protection on the arduous trip West. Once she exited on Main Street, Miranda sought a pawn shop. She hocked the silver tea set for a surprisingly good amount of money at a reputable pawn establishment and walked on to the new Main Street Station, not far from the James River. She spoke with the man at the ticket window and he sold her a progression of tickets which would get her to Phoenix several days hence. From there, she visited with Cousin Alex and his wife Mary. The Governor promised to take her to Wickenburg by buggy after the visit. From his bully pulpit as a Governor and as a close personal friend of President Roosevelt, he had already had the papers prepared for her divorce from Hancock. Spade work by a Pinkerton detective showing adultery on the part of the husband would facilitate the process.

Miranda had several hours before the southbound train to Atlanta, her stepping off point to the succession of westerly trains. She walked down Main Street and stopped at a diner. Not knowing how food would be on the train, she bought several bottles of Hires Root Beer, a bottle opener and several cheese sandwiches. She thought they would last in the heated car better than beef or ham.

She had some experience traveling, having attended Randolph-Macon Women's College in Lynchburg, Virginia for two years, taking education courses before her father's illness and subsequent death. The death had caused her to return to Petersburg for financial reasons and to care for her mother, whose health was also failing quickly. Shortly after her mother died, she moved to Richmond, where she met and married Hancock.

Miranda looked at this trip as both an adventure and an escape. She was truly scared of Riley Hancock and his family. His ego would be bruised by having a wife leave him and having his dalliances appear in the Times Dispatch society column. The Colonel would be furious. She was glad to have someone of the luster and power of her cousin to stand between her and the Hancocks, though up to now, he had been several thousand miles away.

Miranda boarded the train and was shown to her seat and temporary home. The steam whistle blew, and the wheels started to move slowly, steel on steel. Forty minutes later, the train stopped at her hometown, Petersburg. She had time to quickly run to her bank across the street and close out her passbook savings account, and to assign the authority to sign in her behalf to an attorney who she had previously retained to sell her parent's home. The property had been left to her. When it was gone, all of her remaining previous life and connection to Virginia was gone with it. When the house sold and closed, the cash would supplement her war chest of the money from Brodie and the sale of the silver set. She felt some sadness.

Miranda reboarded the train. A few people got on and went to their seats. She settled in with a small, leather bound copy of Sir Walter Scott's The Bride of Lammermoor.

Before the first stop, Miranda found the tragedy romance so depressing she left the book in the dining car for some other poor soul to read. Devoid of reading material, she stared out of the window, watching the Carolinas pass by, then northern and central Georgia. Over the next several days, she stopped at Birmingham, on to Dallas, then across the wide expanse of Texas before ultimately getting to Phoenix.

Miranda arrived in Phoenix somewhat bedraggled, stiff, yet uplifted in spirit. Her cousin and Mary Brodie met her at the train depot and took her back to the house in a buggy. After a bath and nap, she joined them for dinner. The next day, Mary took her shopping for all she would need in the smaller town of Wickenburg to begin teaching school in two weeks.

Brodie had received several wires from the attorney he had retained in Richmond. The man was a fellow West Pointer who practiced with a reputable Richmond law firm after serving in the Judge Advocate General's corps in the Army. The lawyer, named Smith, advised the Hancocks were furious local papers had jumped on the matter and painted Riley Junior as a philandering cad. Her lawyer had dropped the hint during contrived drinks with a reporter from the Times Dispatch. Smith thought the judge might be disposed to grant a quick divorce and some sort of financial settlement to Miranda.

After the visit with the Brodies, Miranda went to Wickenburg and began to teach at a one-room school. The previous teacher had not done a very good job, and she had her work cut out for her bringing each child up to where she thought they should be for their age level.

Weeks passed. Miranda received weekly letters from either her cousin or, more frequently, his wife Mary Louise. The two had become close in the few days they had spent before Miranda departed for Wickenburg.

Wickenburg, Miranda realized, was a rough and tumble mining town and living proof the Wild West was not dead. She decided she would teach with the small Derringer in a pocket she had sewn into several dresses and could hide under an apron. The fact she was pretty and vivacious was not lost on the local men. She would have been a standout in any town. But here there were virtually no young women, so she felt like a large goldfish in a small bowl.

The teaching position came with a small cottage adjacent to the schoolhouse. She decorated it and, unlike the Western custom, locked the doors when she was both away and at home. By the end of the second month, she took her paycheck to the bank and deposited the larger part and used the cash to buy a used single barrel shotgun and box of shells. She practiced, bruising her shoulder, but liked the feeling of empowerment. The used Harrington & Richardson scattergun found a place in the corner of her modest bedroom, near the bed.

The days, then weeks passed. Miranda did not hear a thing from Richmond. Each time she heard a horse, she feared it was either Riley Hancock or someone he had sent for her. Then, a letter came for her at the post office.

It was from the lawyer who had been her cousin's classmate at West Point. It contained a brief agreement for her to sign in the presence of a notary public. She had seen a sign stating "Notary Public" on the desk of one of the men at the local bank.

Miranda carefully read the agreement. It said for a sum certain—ten thousand dollars—she would relinquish any claim on the house, furnishings, monies, or artwork associated with the home on Church Hill in Richmond, as well as not making any claims now or hereafter for financial support from her husband or the Hancock family. It was agreed if both she and Riley signed without amendment the judge would grant an immediate divorce.

Miranda walked down the wooden sidewalk from the post office to the bank and went in. The older man in the guard's uniform spoke to her as he always did. He had a brass name badge on his dark blue uniform identifying him as Officer Wilson. His ready smile reminded her of her late father. Possibly because of, when she decided to bake an apple pie, she baked two and bought him one. His grin reminded her of a little boy getting a Daisy BB gun for Christmas. She had made a friend.

Within thirty minutes, the document was signed, notarized and on its way back to Richmond. She felt as if a heavy weight had been lifted off her, and walked the half mile back to the school and her cottage with a new spring in her step and humming.

Several months passed with her checking the post office every day. Finally, a letter came for her. She opened it and found the promised check drawn on the escrow account of the Hancock family lawyer. It was for the agreed upon ten thousand dollars. Included was the final divorce decree signed by a judge.

She was free, and by her own estimation, well off. Not the kind of large home on Church Hill like she had in Richmond, but sufficient money for her needs, a place to live and a job she liked.

Miranda put the check and the divorce decree in her purse and immediately went to the bank to deposit her check. As she went in, she stopped and chatted with the guard, who asked her if she had any baking planned. She laughed, patted him on the arm and promised him she would make him a pie within the week.

Miranda walked up to the cashier's window, the check

still in her purse. She had forgotten to take it out because of the conversation with the guard.

All of a sudden, someone yelled, "Nobody move. This is a robbery." Miranda's blood ran cold.

She turned as seven men ran in, masks on and rifles in hand, except for the man in front. She saw the guard draw his revolver and fire, striking the lead robber. The man screamed out and grabbed his leg near the groin and collapsed onto the bank's floor. Another shot rang out from the robber behind the leader. In horror, she saw her friend drop his revolver, and clamp his chest. He looked directly at her and seemed to be asking for help. Then, he fell forward onto the floor.

The man who shot him ran over and kicked the guard's gun away. He then went to the cashier's window, shoving Miranda aside.

"Move, bitch." he exclaimed. The outlaw leader was trying to stand and finally did, using a desk for support. Miranda moved to the guard, knelt beside him and turned him over. He was still alive, pink froth on his lips. He tried to say something to her and could not. He died in her arms. She turned to the robbers and screamed, "You killed him, damn you."

Money in a burlap sack, the robbers were moving towards the door. Miranda looked at the guard's gun five feet away. The leader, though wounded, was still in charge. He saw her and yelled.

"Stay away from the gun or there'll be two bodies on the floor, lady."

Then, to his second-in-command, "Bill, grab the girl. We might need her."

The man called Bill roughly took her by her arm. She dropped the purse with the letter in it as he dragged her outside.

"Can you ride?" he asked.

Miranda nodded her head up in terror. Bill looked at the street and grabbed the reins of a strong looking dappled gray from the hitching post in front of a store adjacent to the bank.

"Get on. And, don't pull any silly side saddle stuff. Straddle the damn horse like your life depends on it, lady. 'Cause it does," Bill ordered.

Miranda complied and mounted the horse. She hitched up her skirt, baring her legs all the way to the knee. But, she thought, now was the time to stay alive, not to worry about exposing herself.

The leader, who one of the men called "Frank" once they were in the street, painfully mounted his horse and let out an expletive as his butt hit the saddle's seat. He took his bandana and tied it tightly around his thigh as his men scanned the area with eyes and rifle muzzles.

"Alright, boys. Let's ride," he said, his pistol in hand.

The bank president, who Miranda knew to be Mr. Stone, came out of the bank. She could see he was furious. He had a Colt's revolver in his hand and started shooting.

The leader aimed the odd looking pistol with which he had shot Mr. Wilson and he and Stone exchanged several shots, neither hitting the other. The wounded outlaw whirled his horse and took off as Stone fumbled in his pocket fruitlessly for more cartridges.

Miranda had ridden some, but never at more than a canter. This was full gallop and she squeezed her legs tightly against the horse. She was taller than most women of her time, so luckily the stirrups were at an acceptable height, helped her to stay on as they rode out of town and into rough country. The faster they rode, the colder she became in her street clothes and light jacket. It was going to get worse. A lot worse.

The man called Frank yelled at Bill: "Where is there a doctor in front of us? I'm hit bad and bleeding."

"I think there's one in the mining town of Bagdad. It's about sixty miles. Most of those mining towns have a doctor. The mining companies bring them in," Bill responded.

"Okay, we'll go there. But, watch I don't fall offen this damn horse, okay?" Frank Moore asked.

They rode on fast, one seriously-shot man, one terrified woman and six career criminals who only cared about their share of the money in the burlap feed sack tied on Bill's saddle horn.

8

Rynning sent a ranger to Douglas daily to check at the Western Union telegraph office for messages. He was beginning to use electronic and postal communications more and more to keep aware of goings-on throughout Arizona. Each ranger afield was now also required to mail a letter weekly to headquarters advising his current location and probable areas he would be in for the following week. He was expected to both report status of cases and include reports of cases closed.

When the ranger read the telegram, he knew he would have to spur his horse to a gallop. The captain would want a message from Colonel Kosterlitzky as soon as possible.

In the message, Kosterlitzky advised fugitive Moore had been seen south of the border a week ago, and the Rurales were on his trail. Moore was heading northwest. Kosterlitzky requested several rangers be sent to a small Mexican town to unofficially accept custody of the fugitive once caught.

But, before the ranger at the telegraph office could turn and leave after reading the message, another more compelling one came in. The telegraph operator stopped the ranger by holding up a finger, signifying "wait".

The new message read "Captain Rynning Stop Bank robbery in Wickenburg Stop Governor AO Brodie cousin Miranda Hancock kidnapped Stop Send Rangers Now End". It came from the Territorial Governor's Office.

Ranger Thomas rode at full gallop to headquarters, his fast arrival signaling something urgent to all, including the captain, who came out of the sole building. Duncan also came out of his tent and strode rapidly to where Thomas was dismounting.

Rynning read both telegrams, then handed them to his sergeant.

After Duncan read the two, Rynning spoke.

"Duncan, I have a sergeant operating out of Phoenix, as you know. He's a good man. But you are the man-tracker and gunfighter. I want you to go to Wickenburg and talk with the governor, who is going there. I don't know if he is in Phoenix or Wickenburg. Find him. Talk with the witnesses at the bank. Then, wire me and tell me your assessment of what ranger assets are needed. Get on the trail. I will come up with an alternative plan to take care of the Moore situation down here. Getting the Governor's cousin, who I know he brought out West and kinda looks after, is paramount. It is surely higher priority than one fugitive. But we do have to have to maintain our credibility with Kosterlitzky. With a little luck, his men will shoot Moore and we can just transport his lousy ass back to the States over his horse."

He paused for a minute, deep in thought. "It's over two hundred miles over to Phoenix and the train tracks are not finished yet. Get on Ace and ride hard for the capital.

Leave as soon as you can and keep me advised by card and wire."

"Yes, sir, Captain," Duncan said and unconsciously did a perfect military about face in the dirt, heading back to his tent.

Near the tent, he asked Torres to get Ace and saddle him. It was a job he always did for himself, but this was big, and time was of the essence. Torres ran to the corral seventy-five yards distant to get the big blue roan.

Duncan poured coffee from his pot into the small stove in the tent to extinguish the fire. He put a hatchet, trowel, a Johnson bandage and some black walnut first-aid salve he had mixed up and put in a screw-top metal container, and his cook gear in a saddlebag. He added a bag of pinto beans, salt, a side of bacon and a dozen biscuits he had just made in his Dutch oven. In the other, he put his handcuffs, a lot of revolver ammunition, some rolled up clothes, and a woolen cap his mother had knitted him. He could feel late winter snow coming in, if not a blizzard.

He thanked Torres as he saddled Ace and put the saddlebags, two canteens and his rifle scabbard on. Fearing he would need more power he selected the heavier 1895 Winchester .30-40 carbine issued by the rangers over his lighter .30-30. He added two boxes of .30-40 cartridges to his kit. His blanket roll was tied in one smaller and one larger waxed tarp on the back of his saddle. Duncan strapped on his cartridge belt of .30 caliber and .45 caliber cartridges. His Colt's revolver and Sheffield Bowie knife were already on the belt. A sweater and badged vest over his shirt, a heavy long coat and his Stetson on, he mounted and rode to the HQ building. As the long coat covered his Colt's revolver, he slipped the smaller .38 into the deep right pocket of the coat.

"You saved my ass in Cuba, son. It's a helluva lot more

important to save this girl. Ride, and God be with you." Captain Tom Rynning yelled as Duncan spun the big roan and galloped northwest, never looking back. Rynning had faith in his sergeant. He just hoped he wasn't sending him to his death.

***

Duncan let the big blue roan run.

The ranger sergeant did not have specific kidnap experience. But he knew from reading books on detecting written by America's greatest detective, the late Allan J. Pinkerton, as each day passed, it decreased the probability of getting the person back alive. He also wanted to know if she was at the wrong place at the wrong time or was targeted because of being kin to the governor. The latter may help her survival rate.

Two camps later, he arrived in Phoenix. He went directly to the governor's home.

Mary Brodie answered his knock on the door. Clearly, any servants the governor may have had left for the evening. Mrs. Brodie saw the ranger badge under the open duster and let him in, looking closely at him.

"Sergeant James Duncan of the Arizona Rangers, Ma'am," he said in introduction.

"Do you have a squad of rangers waiting outside?" Mary Brodie asked.

"No, Ma'am. Just me. Where is the governor?" he asked.

"My husband has already gone to Wickenburg," she answered, then asked, "What is your plan, Ranger?"

Duncan replied, "I will ride on to Wickenburg tonight, ask questions and get on the trail as soon as possible. Depending on what I find out, I'll wire the captain for needed assets to get the governor's cousin back. I know it's a strange question for a ranger to ask, but I left at a gallop as soon as the captain got your husband's wire. Did the regional sergeant or one of his rangers question anyone? Are they on the trail?"

"No, our information is they are a hundred miles away after a rustler gang and don't know about the robbery or kidnapping yet."

He thanked the woman and rode into town. Rousting the manager of the stable, he got grain for Ace and let the big horse drink from the water trough. The stable owner pointed him towards the road to Wickenburg and he rode off, tired but determined.

Duncan arrived late night and it was not difficult to find the hotel on a snow-covered main street. He rang the bell at the desk. A sallow clerk, still half asleep sauntered in from a room behind the desk. Duncan thought he could be the twin brother of the one in Salome. He got a room for the night and found where he could stable Ace. He did so and returned to the hotel desk.

The glint of his badge and a steely-eyed stare when he asked, resulted in the clerk advising him which room the governor was in.

Once he settled his gear in his room, he knocked on the Governor's door. It was midnight, but A.O. Brodie answered in his shirtsleeves.

Brodie remembered him from Cuba since Duncan had saved the lives of two of his good friends...now President Theodore Roosevelt and Captain Tom Rynning. In response to several questions about the robbery, Brodie insisted on the hotel clerk telephoning the house of the bank president right away to meet with them immediately. Then he said Duncan would have the background he needed before leaving early in the morning to track the gang.

Before the men arrived, the politician and lawman sat in the room and spoke in low tones.

"Was your cousin, Miranda Hancock, specifically targeted as a kidnap victim, Governor? Or was she just a bank customer who got grabbed? Also, I'd like a description of her and a picture if one is available," Duncan said.

"I do not think the robbers knew who she was. She was there to deposit a settlement check from her abusive piece of shit ex-husband's attorney. There were not many people in the bank. I am afraid she was the most comely. By far. Here is a locket with her picture. It was in the purse she left behind when they grabbed her. You can take the locket for identification purposes.

"You mentioned the husband or ex-husband. Could he be involved? You know, maybe from a ransom standpoint?" Duncan asked.

"No," the Governor said. "He is in Virginia and does not have the sober clarity to think of something like this."

"Before the banker gets here, do you know how many robbers there were? Were any identified? Anything distinguishing?"

The governor thought for a minute, remembering. "There were six plus the ringleader. The ringleader had a funny pistol. It was big and had a long skinny barrel. One of the cashiers said he thought it had a magazine instead of a cylinder. When he shot it, it sounded like a real fast little bullet—not like .44 or .45 sounds. The doc dug one out of the body of the bank guard he killed. Said it was like .30 caliber and not lead but coated with harder metal."

Duncan remembered the notice about Frank Moore stealing a big Broom-handle Mauser automatic pistol from the guard he killed. It had a magazine instead of a cylinder and was a small, but high velocity caliber. An odd gun in the US, Duncan had heard of them, but never seen one. It would be hard to find the .30 caliber cartridges, he thought. But it was too much of a coincidence. It had to be Moore. If so, it added a bad element to the case: Moore was a rapist as well as murderer.

The picture in the locket Brodie just handed him was of a beautiful brunette. Though just a bust shot, she had full lips, sparkling eyes and a well-rounded bosom. Duncan feared for the young woman.

"May I keep this for a while?" he asked, and the Governor nodded. Duncan buttoned it in a small vest pocket, above where he usually kept his backup revolver hidden.

At the governor's order, the hotel employee brought a pot of coffee and a plate with cold roast beef slices and some bread. A few minutes later, the banker arrived with his balding cashier in tow.

"How much money did they get?" Duncan asked the bankers.

"Two thousand eight hundred fifty dollars," the cashier of the bank offered. Continuing, he said, "The guard, Wilson, exchanged shots with the leader as soon as the robbers came in. Both were hit, but Wilson died right there. The robber limped out after they had gotten the money. They seemed to have grabbed Miss Hancock as an afterthought."

This corroborated Duncan's pressing questions, but it did not allay his fears for the young woman. He found she was almost twenty-two years old.

"Has anyone gone out the road looking for sign? If the leader, who I believe is a fugitive named Frank Moore, was hit in the groin, he may have bled out and died by now," Duncan asked.

"Nobody tried to pursue them, per se," the bank president said, "but, it is the main road northbound out of town, so lots of people have travelled it since. Nobody has reported finding a body, blood or anything. And, before you ask, there has been no sign of the girl."

Normally stoic, Duncan's lips formed a straight line under his mustache and Brodie noted the concern, which added to his own. The Territorial Governor had sent money to his cousin—more like a niece—to help her divorce her abusive husband in Richmond, then arranged for her to come live and work near him and his wife. He felt a great deal of responsibility for her welfare.

"Gentlemen, did the robbers enter with Colts or rifles?" the ranger asked.

Walter Stone, the bank president, responded with, "All had long guns…two short carbines, one full rifle and one short-barreled shotgun. Only the leader carried a handgun—funny looking one with the long, skinny barrel."

"Did their horses have bedrolls, canteens, and saddlebags?" asked Duncan.

"I got my pistol out of the drawer and went outside as they left. We exchanged shots, but nobody got hit on either side. But I saw their horses. They did have full gear behind the saddles. Six bays, but the leader was on a sorrel. They stole a dappled gray for the young woman. It was not a strong looking piece of horseflesh. Kinda old and bony looking," said Stone.

"Were all the horses about the same size?"

The bankers replied they were. could be important in tracking. It was agreed they were, except for the smaller horse the hostage was on.

"Anything else you gentlemen can remember?" Duncan prompted.

"No, that's about it," the bank president said as his cashier nodded in agreement.

"Oh. One last question addressed to all of you. Heading out the road they took, which is the first town with a doctor?" he asked.

"If they wanted to stay on the main road, it would be Prescott," Brodie said. He added, "If they wanted to veer west off the main road and head into wild country, I would say Bagdad would be the best bet. It's what I would do if I was them."

Duncan visualized a map of Arizona Territory before making up his mind on the matter.

"I believe you are right, Governor Brodie. We should send a telegram to the doctor in Bagdad to see if he has treated gunshot wounds in past couple of days," Brodie said. They drafted the telegram and Walter Stone offered to take it to the Western Union office on his way home.

Both the territorial governor and the lawman were shocked but pleased when a runner delivered a telegraphic response from the doctor at Wickenburg at two in the morning. Apparently, a late-night personal telegram from the Governor was something the doctor thought deserving of a prompt response.

It stated the doctor had treated a stranger for "an accidental, self-inflicted gunshot wound to the upper right thigh the previous day. The man insisted on leaving and was given laudanum for the pain and sent on his way. He was described as a white male, medium height and build, dark haired and wearing an odd-looking pistol butt-first in a right-hand holster shaped like a wooden gunstock. The doctor confided he could not imagine the man riding very long, fast or far on wound.

After discussion, Duncan and Brodie decided, even given the information early, it would be advisable to wait until first light to ride over sixty miles to Bagdad. They separated and Duncan managed two and a half hours sleep.

At five thirty the next morning, he prepared to leave

for Bagdad.

Duncan had asked the governor to send an update telegram to Rynning, stating he was on the trail and he strongly suspected Frank Moore was the gang leader and had evaded the Rurales and doubled back to Wickenburg. He advised Rynning he would provide a status at the earliest possible time, as well as what ranger help he needed.

He claimed Ace from the local stable and resaddled and packed the big horse. They took the road northwest into a virtual no-man's land, riding at a canter, eyes scanning and the Winchester across his saddle at the ready.

The dirt road was cluttered with many tracks. After several hours, Duncan noted the majority heading off towards Bagdad. Duncan had all the information he needed so it was not necessary to stop in Bagdad. He had passed the road to his hometown, and being in Yavapai County, he was on familiar land for most of the rest of the day. Eight sets of tracks traveling together continued northwest. He dismounted and crouched over the tracks.

He blew air from his nostrils, clearing them like his father had taught him. Duncan bent, nose close over several tracks. He smelled carefully and detected a faint animal smell. The tracks were distinct—not sullied by wind. He reckoned, he was within several hours of the eight horses and their seven dangerous outlaws and one scared rider.

One of the horses seemed to cast shallower tracks than the others. He memorized the wear and indents on the shoes, thinking this was probably the horse the girl was riding. It, according to the bankers, had been one tied to a hitching post down from the bank and stolen for the Hancock girl's use. But, if the horses were roughly the same size, the one described as "bony" with a hundred pounds lighter rider logically should be the woman's. All he had to go on, Duncan decided he would follow the group with horse's tracks if the larger group split anywhere along the trail. In his experience, especially after dividing the take from a robbery into shares, gangs frequently split and went separate ways.

He could feel the elevation increasing and with it, the temperature decreasing. He reached in a saddlebag and took out the woolen stocking cap and put it on instead of the Stetson. He had a braided chinstrap in the latter to hold it on during fast rides and used to secure it on the saddle horn. He already had woolen gloves over doeskin ones. Collar up and woolen hat pulled down, he rode on, always at the ready.

Duncan wondered how scared the young woman might be. He knew she had been wearing town attire with a light jacket and must be freezing by now. Used to riding the trails in cold weather, Duncan was already cold.

As darkness approached, he reckoned he had to stop. The big horse was fine, but he feared riding up on the outlaws unexpectedly in the dark and having Miranda, as he had begun to think of her, shot in the ensuing firefight.

Duncan saw a stand of trees beyond a rise next to the road. He rode over and saw they were scrubby pines. There were patches of grass for Ace.

He dismounted and hobbled the horse without unsaddling or unloading him. He still rode with the heavy carbine in his hand, so he carried as he circled his probable campsite with a half mile radius. Nothing. Nobody. High desert country. Barren. Just cold with a chilling wind.

He came back to Ace and took the bedroll, saddlebags, canteens and scabbard off him. There was no rock or hill big enough to serve as a windbreak. Searching, hatchet in hand, he found some branches and enough downed wood to start and maintain a fire all night. Tying his lariat between two trees, he threw the waxed tarp over it and staked it down in back, using his hatchet to fashion and hammer down improvised stakes. The rear ones were staked to the ground. On the front he tied lines to each corner and then staked tightly at angles in the front. Duncan moved his bedroll inside.

He figured he was still far enough back to risk a fire. He picked up a number of desert rocks, glad it was cold enough none of them hid a rattler. He made a small wall of the rocks and, using the trowel, began to dig his fire pit between it and the shelter. He used his trowel to dig a larger and smaller hole several feet apart, then used it to scoop out a narrow tunnel connecting the two. He built a fire in the larger hole. Placing a grill over it, he began heating water with coffee grounds in it for coffee. He also placed several pieces of the sliced beef on the griddle to warm. While the coffee was brewing and the beef warming, he built a stone reflector behind the larger pit to reflect heat back to his lean-to.

This was his standard trail camp. Without the time needed to circumnavigate the site to make sure nobody was nearby it had taken only fifteen minutes to build. Duncan ate, then taking his carbine, he walked to a tree one-hundred yards from camp and relieved himself. Returning, he stoked the fire hole and crawled into his blankets, drew the smaller waxed tarp over his head and went to sleep.

He awoke just before daybreak and broke camp. His breakfast was to munch on a biscuit and some jerky while tracking from Ace's saddle.

The town of Kingman was a couple days in front of him as he paralleled the Big Sandy. He still did not see any sign of the gang, except for the tracks of six horses. The hoofprints he had designated to the leader and Miranda were still among the scatter of prints. As the country got higher and higher, rising towards the peak of Hualapai, the tracks were harder to discern in the snow-covered rocks. But he was cutting sign from brush seemed much fresher. The wounded Moore and the girl must have been slowing the gang down. He saw a periodic drop of blood, still red instead of older brown. He knew he was closing in due to their slow progress with wounded Moore and the hostage.

Duncan levered a cartridge into the chamber on the .30-40 lever gun across his saddle and eased the hammer down to half cock. He knew he had to be ready for a firefight at any time.

His wrinkled and stained Arizona Territory map showed the Hualapai to be a bit over eighty-four hundred feet in elevation. He could tell the air was getting thinner. He was breathing more out of his mouth and becoming conscious of breathing in bigger gulps of air.

Large snowflakes were falling. He knew they would get smaller and more voluminous over time. Duncan was getting increasingly worried about the Hancock girl, improperly dressed for the terrain or the weather. He would have to kill seven men to retrieve her. The fact it did not worry him was not due to a false sense of his own invincibility. He knew the only thing which would save her was a violent and ruthless plan. He planned to identify the girl's blanket when sneaking up on the sleeping camp at four a.m. like an Apache. He would shoot the other blanketed forms as fast as possible. He did not ponder the morality of the plan. But, if he had, he would have reasoned that Moore had already been sentenced for death and killed two men since escaping, and the other four had likely committed capital offenses. His sole objective was to get Miranda Hancock back to the Territorial Governor alive and well. Capturing and attempting to deliver five prisoners over hundreds of miles alone while looking after a cold, scared victim would be virtually impossible. So, shooting hard and fast was the only answer.

So far, Duncan's pursuit of the band had gone unnoticed. But that was to change. Wounded and possibly psychotic, Frank Moore had survived over twenty of his thirty-eight years on the lam.

He was no fool.

As Duncan rode along, eyes alternately scanning one hundred eighty degrees along the Big Sandy, a shot rang out and a bullet tugged at his left shoulder hard. Duncan did not know immediately whether he had been hit or just his coat had. He slid off Ace, tripped, and rolling, he took cover behind a big rock beside the trail. He scanned the area where the shot had come from, knowing anyone Moore had sent was not likely to leave without either verifying a kill or finishing the job.

Duncan knew sliding off the horse and slipping gave every appearance of having been hit by the sniper's bullet. To perpetuate the ruse, he slipped off his boots and slid one on its side within sight outside the rock. As he did, he groaned loudly.

Carrying his rifle in the crook of both elbows, Duncan crawled on his belly away from the rock. He made his way from boulder to boulder, knowing his progress was unseen by the shooter. Going uphill, he found a commanding point and settled in, waiting for the outlaw to show himself. He waited ten minutes, hardly breathing. Something caught his eye twenty yards out from the rock he had hidden behind after sliding off Ace and planting the boot as a trap.

Duncan watched carefully as the form of a man in a duster coat and wearing a black Stetson appeared. The form was carrying a rifle and moving furtively. Clearly, he had seen the boot sticking out. So far, the trick was working.

Now, Duncan was faced with a decision. The rest of the gang may be close enough to have heard the rifle shot. They would hear his return shot at the man. If he used his Colt, the sound would not carry as far. Maybe. Either way, Moore's gang would either expect the man to return after killing Duncan or not return because Duncan had killed him. It was a no-win situation, so the ranger drew a bead on the man's chest and pressed the trigger of the Winchester.

The big Winchester boomed through the hills and the impacting bullet sounded like heavyweight champion Jim Jeffries had slugged the man in the middle of his chest with his massive fist. He went down, stumbling forward on his face, then rolling in the slight ravine.

He carefully observed the downed outlaw as he approached. The rocks were cold and sharp on his sock feet. The man's eyes were open and lifeless. Still watching in all directions, Duncan replaced his boots. The man had very few dollars, which Duncan took. He also slung the man's revolver belt over the horn of his saddle. Another gun and more ammunition were always welcome.

He dragged the man to a gully and rolled him in. Mounting Ace, Duncan rode, backtrailing the man's infrequent prints in the hard, rocky ground until he found the man's horse. He returned the man's 1873 Winchester carbine to its scabbard and fashioned his lariat on the bridle to lead the horse. He may need it for Miranda to ride when he freed her. The possibility he would not be able to free her did not enter his mind. "One down, six to go," he thought.

The shot and non-return of the bushwhacker definitely sent a message to the outlaw gang. Somebody was back there. They did not know who or how many. They would be watching their backtrail and may send another to ambush him.

Duncan decided to parallel the trail a half mile over to the left, checking the real trail once an hour to make sure the gang had not veered off. When he felt he was out of sight from the main trail, he galloped Ace to get closer to the gang. Duncan's speed was limited by the second horse, but he still made up valuable time.

Duncan spoke to Ace as they rode along, using the horse as a silent partner in thinking out plans and just passing the time on the trail. Today, his words were low and terse, and the horse felt the stress in the man who took such good care of him.

The snow began to fall faster and more heavily. Duncan knew this would spur the outlaws to build a camp quickly as the canyons darkened before the high desert mountains. He pointed Ace over to the original trail and once on it, slowed their pace to a wary one.

The low mountains and canyons took on an eerie appearance as the snow began to mask their reds and oranges. Duncan could smell the scent of the sparse trees, and something else. Smoke was wafting lightly in his consciousness. Soon, he spotted a single column of smoke in a valley a mile distant. There was a stand of trees, and the smoke column were all he could make out.

Duncan knew getting the young woman back as soon as humanly possible was his goal. would involve riding away fast as soon as he got her unless he left five more bodies on the ground. But he was worried the presence of Ace and the dead outlaw's horse might cause whinnying and signal the outlaws a rider was near.

Duncan found a draw, still almost a mile from the outlaw's camp, and hobbled Ace and the dead outlaw's horse.

There was some water and maybe a little grass not yet covered by snow. He put another box of rifle shells in his pocket, draped a dark blue wool blanket over his heavy coat, and began the stalk to the camp. It was both cold and dark by the time he arrived.

He selected a sniper's nest twenty yards uphill from the camp. Duncan leaned against a tree with the blanket drawn over his body, only his face showing and began his long surveillance as the men below went about building a fire and starting coffee and beans in cast iron gear hung from a tripod over what would be coals within forty-five minutes. His plan was to isolate exactly where the girl was sleeping and then hit an hour before dawn. His great grandfather had operated by ambushing English patrols in the Highlands, and the Apaches had done the same against wagon trains and the US Cavalry. It had worked for both sets of guerilla fighters…and it had to work for the ranger.

The coffee and beans smelled good to Duncan as he sat cross-legged against the tree. His coat and the wool blanket kept him warm, but he was hungry as hell. He gnawed a piece of beef jerky from his pocket, knowing the salty meat would make him thirsty for water he did not have.

The wind was both Duncan's friend and his enemy. It brought virtually every sentence spoken in the outlaw camp to his ears without straining but hurt his exposed face. They were all speculating about someone named Bill. It had to be the man he shot, Duncan thought. He saw one of them take a mug of coffee to a person bundled in a blanket. It had to be Miranda, because the only two who would be waited on were her and the wounded Moore. He had immediately identified Moore, near the girl, from his curses and groans. The wind swirled out of the small canyon and brought cold air twenty miles an hour right into his face.

Hours later, Duncan looked up, trying to find the moon so he could guess the time. If the moon was still up there, he couldn't see it. The skies were dark muddy black and snow flurries alternated between light and blizzard strength. By his best reckoning, it was time. He could hear snores, groans from the wounded outlaw chief and nothing from the girl. One man had been detailed guard duty. He was apart from the prone outlaws and hostage, and was sitting, leaning his back against a tree in a shadow. He appeared to be a man who had stood sentry duty before. It did not make what Duncan was planning easier. But he had no better plan and he began to circle around behind the sentry.

He crept behind the tree the man was leaning against, and gently laid the Winchester on the ground. He reached around the man and covered his mouth and nose with his left hand. With his right hand, the slid the big Bowie across the man's throat, twisting him away to avoid the heavy spray of blood. He laid the man face down, hand pushing his face into the snow and knee on his back until he stopped gurgling and moving. He knew he was dead. He left the outlaw's rifle on the frozen ground but removed the revolver from the man's holster and stuck it in his left coat pocket.

The sentry position was on a slight rise. Miranda lay just below him, not ten feet away. He could hear her teeth chattering. He feared the onset of freezing. Taking his rifle, he aimed at each of the five other bedrolls with a body in it and a succession of shots rang out in the night. He could hear the thuds as bullets hit men with what sounded like a punch and the movement of the prone bodies as the .30 rounds pushed the targets. Two were not killed immediately and Duncan's five shot rifle went dry. He pulled his Colt's revolver and the sentry's and began firing with both hands. Men jerked and screamed. Duncan heard a distinct high velocity sound and knew it was Moore firing at him with the Mauser. He felt the burn as a 7.63x25 mm bullet hit him in the right shoulder. He dropped his revolver but kept firing the other with his weak hand until it clicked.

Though wounded again, this time by Duncan, and in grievous pain, Moore grabbed the girl and shoved her towards the horses tied to a line between two trees. He carried a bag. Duncan's own gun had dropped in the dark and he only had the sentry's gun, a .32-20 for which he had no cartridges.

Duncan staggered towards them with only the bloody, wicked Bowie knife in his left hand.

Moore made the coatless, shoeless girl mount while Duncan was still trying to negotiate the field of dead. He was losing blood himself and dizzy. He stumbled over a dead outlaw and saw the man's revolver in hand. It was a S&W Schofield. Duncan pried it from the man's hand and, using his left hand steadied against a tree, shot at Moore as he rode by fifteen yards away. He heard the shrill scream of Moore's horse, which he had inadvertently hit hard in the neck. The horse stumbled and threw the twice-wounded outlaw. Moore landed with a thud in the snow. Miranda's horse reared up and she almost slid off its saddleless back. Duncan took careful aim at Moore and pressed the trigger. He got a dull "click".

Groaning, Moore grabbed the bridle of Miranda's horse and, still holding the bag, climbed painfully on behind her. He kicked the horse with his sock feet, and they rode off, leaving Duncan standing cursing the day of Moore's birth and promising God he would kill the man before another day had passed.

But, instead of killing Moore, Duncan collapsed in the snow amid the men he had killed and passed out cold in every sense of the word.

***

It was the shivering and chattering of his own teeth awoke James Duncan. He struggled to his feet, and promptly blacked out and fell back down. He opened his eyes and finally focused. The sky was getting lighter but was it still gray and a light snow was still falling.

Duncan reckoned from the light dusting on his clothes, he had not been unconscious for more than ten or fifteen minutes. He knew the men laying around him were all dead. Finally getting some balance, he slowly walked over to the dead horse. He did not feel anything about killing them. He felt awful about killing the poor horse.

There was no time to bury the men. Let them freeze into prone statues where they laid. In the dim light, Duncan found his Colt and reloaded it. He walked painfully back to where he had left his Winchester and reloaded also. He picked a likely horse to ride back to Ace on and freed the others of any manmade gear. Let them run wild and free.

The snow was still coming down as he entered the small draw and saw Ace and the bushwhacker's horse. Duncan opened his saddlebag and withdrew the metal jar of ointment he had prepared for wounds. He bared his right shoulder and smeared a palmful on it. He could not tell if the high velocity pistol round had penetrated his shoulder or was still imbedded. Duncan thought from the wet feel in back the wound was a through and through. At least he hoped so. He tried to put some of the ointment on the back and was not sure if he had been successful.

The horse he had ridden over from the outlaw camp seemed to him to be a better mount than the bushwhacker's. He unsaddled and unbridled the latter horse and gave it a slap on the flank and it galloped off. The slap reverberated through his body and the pain made him nauseous. He knew he could not stave off shock and the smartest thing would be to roll up in his bedroll and the tarp and try to sleep and sweat it off. But he did not have the luxury of doing that. There was the girl. And she was solely in Moore's hands. He had to press on. He had hit Moore with a rifle shot. Moore would have a serious close-range wound added to either a .44 or .45 near the groin from the bank guard. He had to be hurting. Duncan did not understand how the outlaw could be functioning at all.

Duncan had left Ace and the horse he released saddled and ready. He left the bushwhacker's saddle on the ground and made his lariat into a lead for the new horse, which he would use as a packhorse. He hoped to find a sawbuck pack saddle in the robber's camp. Unsteady in the saddle, he was nonetheless cautious as he rode back to the outlaw gang's camp. If he were Moore, he would have circled back for his boots, bedroll and a saddle.

The camp was deserted. The corpses were freezing quickly. Duncan grabbed more dry beans, coffee, flour and salt. There was also a side of bacon wrapped in cheesecloth. He did not find a sawbuck pack saddle and cursed roundly. Duncan then put one of the dead outlaw's saddles on to hold saddlebags. The pain of lifting the saddle and cinching it made him stagger backwards with vertigo and his head spun. Recovering, he filled the saddlebags with the foodstuffs. Looking around the camp, he picked the best two blankets, bullet holes were obvious, but both were devoid of blood. He tied them on the impromptu pack horse. He found one of the men's coats hanging near where he had died in his bedroll and added it to his survival plunder.

Lastly, Duncan picked a revolver caliber rifle and put it in the scabbard under the saddle's fender. It was a .32-20, like one of the gun's he had commandeered in the gunfight. He dug around and found the matching caliber Colt he had emptied and dropped and put it in a saddle-bag along with a box of .32-20 cartridges he found with further rummaging.

It was fully light now, though the sun was not shining through the falling snow. Barely able to stay on Ace, Duncan held the lead attached to his packhorse and began to follow the trail of Frank Moore and Miranda Hancock. He fought to focus and feared shock from the gunshot was setting in fast.

***

As Moore painfully mounted behind the Hancock woman, all he could think of was getting away from this hellish shooter—probably some sort of badge-toter—and making it the remaining ten miles to his initial destination with the gang. He had used a miner's cabin several times during his career in crime and had briefly hidden there after escaping the noose at Phoenix. Bill was the only person in his gang he had known prior to the bank robbery. Bill had lived periodically in Wickieup, and Moore had found him there while passing through to the cabin. He had told Bill to assemble a small gang to pull off a job he had in mind that would net each man at least a year's cowboy pay. He had bought a few supplies for the cabin and ridden on.

Moore met his new outlaw gang a week later and they rode on to Wickenburg and the bank.

The lawman had done him a favor. Moore had chosen the money bag over his boots at the ambush and now did not have to split the money four ways, or however many depending on who the lawman had left alive. As far as the lawman himself went, Moore had seen him fall. He was probably dead. Moore knew he had hit him with a shot somewhere on the center of mass. The Hancock woman was a looker and was icing on his cake. He had thought, through the persistent pain from the guard's shot, about retiring to the cabin with her and living the good life. Now, he just had to get there and hold up before they both froze from riding bootless in the blowing snow. Then, he could work on stopping the bleeding from a wound through his side. He had temporarily given up on the pain from the leg wound.

***

Duncan may have left thirty minutes behind Moore and Miranda, but the trail was easy to follow in the fresh snow. He knew he would catch them readily, since despite leading a pack horse, he was not riding double and bareback. Unfortunately, he was leaving a bigger blood trail than the man he was tracking.

In less than an hour, as pursued and pursuer climbed steadily towards the eighty-four-hundred-foot elevation Hualapai Peak, he heard them ahead. He slowed his pace, not wanting a gunfight with Moore and Miranda both mounted on the same horse. Duncan could not hear Miranda, but was sure she was suffering from the cold and the ride, since Moore continually and irritably cautioned her to shut up sobbing and shaking, they were near the cabin he had been riding towards since the day of the robbery.

It was good news to the ranger. He would kill Moore at the cabin, then use it for Miranda to thaw out and maybe tend him as he went through the shock and fevers he knew were starting already.

They were in high mountain desert. Forlorn country, except for a rise with a cabin just above a creek off the Big Sandy.

Moore fell off the horse and landed hard. The girl slipped off shaking almost uncontrollably and stood there, not offering to help her captor. She just stared, frozen by cold and fear. So much about the man reminded her of a more grizzled Riley Hancock. She hated him and knew she would hate him more each day if he survived his wounds. Her only salvation would be her powerful cousin would stop at nothing to get her back to safety as quickly as possible. She knew in her heart he had sent the lawman who ambushed the camp, killing all the outlaws except the leader, known only to her as "Frank", She saw the lawman fall and prayed he was only slightly wounded. Miranda knew he was her best hope of a speedy rescue. Likely, her only hope.

Miranda had managed to keep the derringer hidden the entire time, a weak two-shot last resort she would use on Moore when he tried to rape her. Until he tried to do , she knew she depended on him to survive. She had no idea where she was in this mountain wilderness or how to escape if she killed him. She had to find out things from him, if possible before trying to kill him. Like how to get back to Wickenburg. She had become turned around in the trip from the robbery.

Moore slowly raised himself and, using a stump for leverage, pushed himself to his feet. He and Miranda went to the cabin. He already had firewood set ready to light in the fireplace. He took a box of matches off the mantle and struck one, immediately lighting the seasoned wood.

He pointed to the bed and told the hostage to get in under the blankets. He unfolded another wool blanket from a shelf and draped over her. As the cabin warmed, he attached the holster/butt stock to the Broom handle Mauser, turning it into the only semiautomatic carbine extant at the time. He put it down next to the single chair, pulled the cork out of a bottle of rotgut whiskey and took a long pull as he sat in the chair. He then followed with another longer pull on the bottle.

Moore turned as the door flew open. A tall ranger stood there, a Colt in his left hand and unbeknownst to Moore, another in his fist under an improvised sling.

Moore grabbed for the Mauser, but he never heard the shots. They hit him in the torso and forehead. Duncan had shot the deadly Colt as fast as he could three times with his left hand. It was fast enough to anyone listening, the shots sounded as one. The fugitive outlaw slumped back dead in the chair the Mauser unfired in his hand. Frank Moore died as unceremoniously as he had ingloriously lived.

Duncan looked at the shocked woman under the blankets and softly said, "Arizona Ranger, Ma'am," before he collapsed unconscious onto the rough-hewn floorboards of the cabin.

9

ARIZONA TERRITORY
1904

Miranda knew the ranger was a Godsend. She just hoped she could nurse him through the effects of his wound. She struggled to help him into the bed where she had so temporarily been. For now, she covered him up, all but coat and boots on. She needed to get the outlaw's body outside as soon as she could. She dragged him by the ankles to the door, out into the front and around the corner. She took pains not to put him near the pile of firewood she would have to visit. Miranda heard Ace whistle and saw the other horses standing where they were upon the ranger's dismount. She saw a lean-to stall against the cabin and unsaddled the horses and put the tack inside. Finding feed, she fed them. Miranda found a bucket and used the edge to break the skim of ice on the stream in front of the cabin. She filled the bucket and made enough trips to half fill a watering trough inside the small corral she had ushered the horses into. Ace looked at her and whinnied. She almost got the feeling he was trying to ask her something. Without thinking, she put her hand on his neck and whispered, "He's hurt, boy, but I am going to make sure he pulls through, okay?" The big horse whinnied again. "Whew," she said, not quite understanding what had just happened.

Miranda picked up three split pieces of firewood and carried them into the cabin. Moore had left a box of matches on the table. She arranged the firewood and went back outside for kindling. She heard the ranger moan before she left, but knew he needed the warmth of a fire more than anything at the moment. She lit the fire within minutes and adjusted the logs to each catch quickly.

The ranger was twisting and turning and unconscious. She put her cold hand on his forehead. It was burning with fever already. Miranda had cared for her father in his last days, but her experience did not extend to wounds. She thought maybe he was in shock. Leaving once again, forgetting how very cold she was, Miranda retrieved the bucket and filled it from the stream and brought it inside the cabin. She extended the iron arm in the fireplace and filled the coffee kettle with water. Using a piece of her underskirt, she squeezed out water and used it to lightly blot the man's forehead. Miranda spoke to him softly. She did not know his name but owed him a great debt. All she knew was he was tall, sandy-haired and handsome. And, he was deadly with either hand based on her observations at the camp and cabin.

He shivered uncontrollably. Miranda realized he was wearing wet clothes and she immediately undressed him. She used her own skirt to blot him dry, then glancing up for forgiveness, stripped and got into the bed with him. She pulled the covers up and held him tightly to her. It took several hours for him to stop shivering.

She checked the wound. It was on both sides of his

shoulder, so she would not have to take the scary Bowie knife and dig out a bullet. She held him closely until first light, then dressed in his long flannel shirt and went through the collection of saddlebags she had brought in. She found coffee, bacon, dried beans and a jar in what she thought was the ranger's bag. It had some sort of salve in it. Instinctively, she rubbed a quantity on the entry and exit wound on the ranger's right shoulder. She also found a bandage wrapped in paper. She removed it and cut it in half with the Bowie knife, placing half on the entry and exit wounds. Miranda dumped a couple of handfuls of dry beans into an iron pot, added bacon, water and salt and let it simmer for the rest of the day. She made strong coffee for herself, drank it and took the shirt off. Miranda slipped back into bed to hold the ranger.

He spoke periodically, not to her, but to someone in his dreams. She hoped it was not a wife or lover. After tracking and killing her captors, and hours of her holding him in her arms, she was beginning to feel very possessive. Miranda did not try to analyze the feelings. There would be time for that later. By the next day, she was able to give him some water, though he was not yet fully conscious or coherent. She had some of the bean soup and kept it simmering away from the main fire.

By the time several days had passed since the fight in the cabin, the ranger was showing signs of improvement. He no longer had the long night sweats, tossing and turning. Nor did he moan in pain as he slept. The odd grease seemed to have had a positive effect on his wound. Holding him, bodies pressed tightly together, gave her something to which she could look forward.

***

Duncan groaned. He opened his eyes and fought for a full minute to focus. When he did, thought he was dead and looking into the face of an angel. He realized where he was and at whom he was looking. Miranda Hancock was far prettier than the locket photograph promised.

"Thank the good Lord you are awake. I have been so worried about you," she said in a soft voice. It had a smoky timbre. He liked the sound of it. A lot. She caressed the side of his face. Something else he liked.

"How long have I been out?" he managed, his voice hoarse and his throat feeling dry, despite the cup of broth in her hand and the spoon poised towards his mouth.

"Four days, in and out of consciousness, feverish. You finally cooled off and slept softly," Miranda responded.

"Where's Moore?"

"As dead as anyone I ever saw. Two bullets through the heart and one between the eyes. You must be a leftie," she noted. "I dragged him as far outside the cabin as I could. He's frozen and under a pile of snow now."

"Nope. I'm right-handed. Just lucky I guess."

Miranda Hancock did not buy his claim for a second and smiled at him.

According to his mother, Duncan was a handsome young man. But he never gave it much thought, knowing his mother might be a little prejudiced in his favor.

But as the woman studied him—he would never think of her as a girl again—Duncan prayed she agreed with his mother. Her blue eyes bored holes all the way through him. Much like Moore's bullet had. But, far less painful.

"Missus Hancock, I am Ranger Sergeant James Duncan," he said.

"So I figured from your feverish mumblings. I'm Miranda. No longer 'Missus' anybody," she responded.

He smiled weakly as she continued.

"I knew my cousin would send someone after me, but I thought it would be a whole posse. Seeing what you did to those men, including the one called 'Frank,' I guess one was enough," she said.

"Are you okay, Miranda? Did they hurt you in any way?" he asked hesitatingly, asking more than the words expressed.

"No, not physically or in any other way. I think other ways were in my future, until you arrived. Should I call you Ranger? James? Jamie? Jim?"

"James is fine," he responded as she fed him a spoonful of some sort of broth.

Realizing his shoulders were bare as she adjusted the blankets, he looked quizzically at her.

She knew what he was asking without words.

"You were drenched from the driving snow and shaking uncontrollably after the shooting stopped here in the cabin. So was I. After I dragged the monster out and dressed your wound front and back, I climbed in with you under the covers and held you. Body heat kept both of us alive. I got up only long enough to stoke the fireplace and try to keep the cabin as warm as possible. But it was really us keeping each other alive. I truly believe it. And, don't get the wrong idea. I was kinda dressed," she lied.

"Thank you, Miranda," he said eyes fixed unflinchingly on hers.

"No thanks are necessary. It was exactly what was needed at the time. And, we are both alive...something I would have never expected, especially after the shooting began at the camp and later when you came through the door."

"There is a little jar of black walnut ointment in my stuff. It will work wonders on lots of things, including a wound. If you have hurt or dry spots on your body, rub it on them, too," Duncan offered.

"When I checked you all over for wounds," she began

as he reddened, "I saw you had put gobs of a grease on the entry wound in your shoulder. I washed it off with water and replenished it. It looked like what you had put on, so I put it on the entrance and exit wounds both. Your wounds, while bad, were, I believe, helped by the bullet passing all the way through. That surely beat me having to try to dig it out with the large knife you wore. I noticed dried blood on the blade and cleaned it off. Did you kill one of the outlaws with it?"

He nodded. "The night sentry. I identified where you were, quietly killed him, then opened up on everyone else. Moore—'Frank'—was good and shot me in the melee. The rest died quickly. Did you unsaddle Ace and the other horse I brought for you?"

"Yes, James. There is a lean-to inside a small corral. You could not see it when you rode up. The three horses are ranging around in the corral and moving under the roof when it is snowing or sleeting. I broke the ice on the watering trough each day. There was a little feed in the lean-to, but it's running low."

"Miranda, I don't know what this broth is, but it's maybe the best thing I ever tasted," Duncan said sincerely.

"It's the liquid from bean and bacon soup I made with creek water and a little salt. Now you are awake, I think some of the solid part is in order. It will build your strength for our ride back to Wickenburg once the weather breaks."

"You mean we can't stay here forever?" he thought, not realizing he was thinking aloud.

She just smiled and did not answer. Instead, she brushed a sandy lock of hair off his forehead.

The protein in the bean soup helped both of them build strength. Six days after the firefight in the cabin, Duncan was outside checking the horses. Miranda had fashioned a better sling than the one he improvised when tracking her and Moore to the cabin.

They would have to leave soon, ready or not. The food for horse and human was dangerously low. It had stopped snowing. The accumulation, for now, was two feet. It was not enough to deter travel, only to slow it down.

Duncan and Miranda talked about food stores. While it may be possible to shoot a deer for more meat, they knew they needed staples such as coffee, flour, and vegetables. The horses needed more forage than was available, even if hobbled outside the corral.

They determined they had to leave the following day.

Though his shoulder was stiff, Duncan decided to eschew the sling and wear two guns until he had returned to normal.

They finished the remainder of the bean and bacon soup for dinner, as well as Duncan's last small portion of Arbuckles' coffee beans. There was not much to pack. They just had to load the bedrolls and tarps on the packhorse in the morning, saddle up and ride. Miranda would lift them up, which guaranteed Duncan would not open his shoulder wound.

But, ride to where? This was new country for both of them. Duncan thought Kingman was about fifty miles north of their current location. In the snow, they would probably be making one camp at dark on the day they left.

He remembered there was a train depot there. There was also an east-west line going to his home in Prescott. He was unaware of any line heading south to Wickenburg, where Miranda lived.

He presented his plan to her.

"I propose we push north to Kingman. Get two train tickets to Prescott. Board your horse and Ace on the train. Sell the other. We will use the horse money for travel expense. At Kingman, I will telegraph the Governor and my captain. I will tell them you are safe, and all five outlaws are dead. I will also tell him we are bringing back all the money taken in the robbery," he said. She listened and said nothing yet.

Continuing, Duncan said, "I think getting to Prescott is good. We can stay at my folk's ranch. I know you'd like my mother. Once we are both fully back to normal health, I will escort you back to Wickenburg. Then, the captain will probably station me back at Prescott. I…er," he stumbled on whatever he wanted to say next, so he just shut up.

Miranda Hancock locked eyes with him for a long time before speaking. He waited.

Finally, she spoke. "James, you seem to want to say something. Just go ahead and spit it out. We've been through a helluva lot together in a short time. I've stripped you and bathed you and slept with you, though I was partially dressed, and you were too weak to act up under the blankets. I 'spect we can talk out anything you have on your mind by now, my dear James."

His eyes widened at the "my dear" and he smiled. She knew why the smile appeared and was glad her signal got through. This man was a hero by anyone's measure. But he surely did not have much experience with women.

"Miranda, we have been pretty great partners. When I put this in my pocket"—he took out her locket from the pocket of his coat hanging on the chair where he sat. He handed it to her, causing her eyes to widen this time—"you became real to me, though we had never met. I knew I had to bring you back safely. I knew I would bring you back, no matter how many men I had to kill to do it. It was a duty when I rode hell for leather to Phoenix, then up to Wickenburg and saw Major Brodie again.

She interrupted him. "You already knew my cousin?" she asked.

"Yes, I was a sergeant in the Rough Riders under him and Colonel Roosevelt, but it does not matter.

"What does matter is it became personal—not a duty," he said.

"Getting to know you made it all the more so, Miranda. I know I have no right, but I'd be proud to get off the train and have you walk on my arm in Prescott…to introduce you to my folks…to personally deliver you back to the Governor and then back home. I guess I'm bumbling this up bad," he hesitated.

She reached over and took his hand.

"If anybody has a right, it's you. You rode your big horse through a blizzard to save me. You killed seven men dead. Then, you took a bullet for me, and killed the seventh. A man who planned to rape me and keep me a virtual slave according to what he said. My cousin sent the best person in the world to save me. I truly believe nobody else could have done what you did."

"I almost don't want this to be over, because we might never see each other again. I cannot imagine anything more horrible than that," she said.

For the first time since she was on the train West from Richmond, she broke down and sobbed.

Duncan took her in his arms and held her for a long time. His face buried in her hair, he whispered, "Don't worry about us not seeing each other. I won't let it happen. I'm not walking away from you, Miranda." She hugged him tighter, as a month of pent-up emotions poured out. He did not care how very much the tight grasp made his shoulder hurt, because of how happy her words made him.

Later, she said, "We need to get some sleep. How about you in your long Johns and me in one of your long flannel shirts and no messing around? We only have one bed in here and it's how we have been sleeping," she said, her fingers crossed behind her back with her white lie. "Would you turn away so I can get ready?" she asked not waiting for an answer. He complied briefly.

She walked to the corner of the cabin and shed her garments, back to him.

Her bare back, bottom and legs were smooth and beautiful. Miranda put on one of his flannel shirts before turning.

"Alright, I am decent."

She walked past him with a smile and a jiggle and climbed into the bed. He built up the fire, moved the Winchester by the bed and, union suit on, climbed in.

This time, she put her head on his left shoulder. He hugged her and gave her a tentative, then deep kiss. Duncan could feel Miranda smiling at him. The glow of the fireplace was not sufficient to give visual proof. But visualization was not necessary. They laid there thinking similar thoughts until drifting off to sleep.

The next morning, they saddled their mounts and loaded the packhorse. Miranda had Duncan's break-open S&W in the pocket of the coat he had brought her from camp, and the light caliber carbine in the saddle scabbard of her horse. Duncan wore his Colt under his coat and had the Colt's revolver matching her carbine in his left coat pocket for use until his strong arm had its strength and speed back.

The couple drank water from the canteens and saved the remaining dry stores for when they made camp. They covered the miles in good time, arriving to within fifteen miles of Kingman before stopping to set up camp.

While Miranda hobbled the horses and collected fallen wood, Duncan set up a lean-to with one tarp, spread out the other tarp and bedrolls and dug a fire pit. He lit the fire with nearby twigs and started coffee. These familiar actions took longer, using just one hand. Soon, Miranda returned with the light carbine in hand and food from the saddle bags and downed branches under the other arm. Duncan fed the wood onto the fire. They shared a mug of coffee, having only one mug, and then retired. As the night before, they pulled the blankets and tarp up and fell asleep in the firelight her head on his uninjured shoulder.

10

ARIZONA TERRITORY
1904

By mid-morning the next day, Duncan and Miranda arrived in Kingman. Duncan immediately negotiated a deal to sell the packhorse for half his value at the local stable. The funds would provide train ticket money and some clothes for Miranda. There was no town marshal or deputy stationed there, so Duncan led the two horses to the Western Union Office, tied them to the hitching rail and helped Miranda down. He took the pad and wrote a message for the operator to put in the requisite stops and end. Before the transmission edits, the message, to both the Territorial Governor and Captain Rynning, said: "Mrs. Hancock recovered safe. All money recovered. Duncan shot. Will recover. Frank Moore and six outlaws dead. Kingman to Prescott train. Need recovery time. Will deliver Mrs. Hancock and money Wickenburg less than week. Sgt. Jas Duncan.

Duncan also sent a telegram for delivery to his parents requesting a room be readied for a female guest.

Miranda went into a general store and purchased boots, doeskin gloves, several woolen shirts, riding pants, a long riding skirt, and a small men's warm ranch coat not unlike Duncan's, a hat, and some personal articles. By the time she was back at the wooden train depot, she was wearing a new outfit and carrying the rest of her purchases in a paper sack. Duncan had picked up ham biscuits and bottles of Coca Cola for the trip to Prescott. He had Ace and her horse loaded onto a horse car near the caboose.

Miranda Hancock now wore the .32-20 Colt's single action belted around her waist, the riding skirt, a small man's wool shirt similar to a Royal Stewart plaid, boots and a brimmed hat. She looked more the part of a Western woman than a daughter of the Old Dominion.

The train cars were cold, and she kept the coat on, the Colt hidden under and the derringer pocketed.

Steel on steel, the wheels began to roll slowly picking up speed as the steam engine built pressure. Duncan did not expect a response to the two telegrams until arriving at Prescott. The two sat side by side and held hands when not eating lunch. They chatted and got to know one another better. Duncan described his parent's ranch outside Prescott and a bit of Scottish history from the Rising of '45 through the Highland Clearances to when his parents immigrated to America, less than thirty years before. Miranda, a native Virginian, likened how the Scots were treated to the Reconstruction in the South following the War Between the States.

They were growing close without speaking about it. The man had not been around females and did not know how to act and the woman was coming out of a bad, abusive situation. But they had been through a lot together.

Each hoped those experiences be enough to make a relationship work.

Mid-afternoon found them rested from napping and famished. They ate the ham biscuits, and each drank a Coca Cola. Before they could finish, the train's wheels screamed in protest as the brakes were applied full on. Items flew off seats, including several people, who ended up in the aisle dazed.

"Must be a snow drift or a tree across the track," Duncan said as he released his protective hold of Miranda.

The next sound was shots. There were several, loud and close. Three men rushed to the car from the connector with the car ahead. All had bandannas over their faces and revolvers in hand.

Duncan pushed Miranda to the floor between the seats as he stood and drew his butt-forward Colt's .45 fast with his left hand. If the wound or weak hand had slowed him, no one seeing the draw and the flame emitting from the muzzle would have guessed.

The front outlaw pitched forward, clearing a shot at the second for Duncan, who had already thumbed the hammer back and pressed the hair trigger. The second man caught a 250-grain cast lead bullet in the eye and the back of his head exploded into the face of the man behind.

As the third outlaw tried to clear the gore blinding him, Duncan killed him, too.

Duncan knew he had two of the standard five cartridges left in his cylinder. He scanned in front, behind and out the window. All clear for the moment. He motioned for Miranda to stay down, noticing the .32-20 already in her hand. She nodded.

The Ranger stepped over the three dead men and moved swiftly to the connector between cars, reloading as he moved.

As he got to the connector, he saw more men coming, guns in hand. Worse, they had scarves over their faces. Outlaws. Not help. The one in front represented the largest threat. He had a double-barreled shotgun and the idiot was walking with both hammers cocked and a finger on the front trigger.

If Duncan shot him, the scattergun would go off, filling the narrow car with a cone of lead as it transited the length of the aisle. But there was no other option. He had to be neutralized.

Eschewing the Tilghman hip shot, Duncan extended his left arm, aimed and snapped off three fast shots hitting his intended target. The first hit the sidelock of the shotgun and sheared the right hammer. It careened off and struck the outlaw in the right chest. The second took his trigger finger off. The third finished the lock work of the gun. Miraculously, none caused the gun to fire. A fourth shot struck the outlaw in the mouth, ending his criminal career and his life.

Duncan had one cartridge left and several men barreling towards him. He shot one center mass and did a border roll, transferring the .45 to his less operable right hand as he drew his backup .38 with his left. He fired several snap shots as two men, one of whom was the man he had shot in the chest, crashed into him and all three toppled onto the aisle of the train.

The wounded man was big—Duncan's height and fifty pounds heavier. He threw an arm across Duncan's windpipe and pushed, his body weight cutting off the lawman's air supply.

He heard a succession of "cracks", and saw the man in

back fall from Miranda's shots. The man on top of him was aiming his revolver at Duncan's face. He felt movement as someone ran to his side. Still struggling against the giant on top of him, he saw Miranda standing over them.

She had a wild animal look in her eyes and snarled, "Hell no, you bastard. Mine," through a clamped jaw as she fired the .32-20 Colt point blank into the big man's ear.

He fell over and Duncan, gasping for air, pushed him aside. Duncan picked up both outlaws' revolvers. One was a standard single action, the other a handy, but fragile Colt's Lighting model double action. Checking, he found the .44 had been shot once and the smaller .38 had a full cylinder. He handed the Lightning to Miranda, kissed her hard on the mouth and asked her to stand behind the door to the connector while he checked the rest of the train.

She responded with a vehement, "No. I'm coming with you." The ranger was shocked, but had a wide grin spread across his face, not disappointment. He painfully got to his feet, feeling the dampness signaling his shoulder wound had opened. He was bleeding again.

He did not have time to bleed, so he ignored it and loaded his revolver as the two edged through the train, looking for threats. Duncan made sure his badge was clearly visible, not wanting to be mistaken and killed like Deputy Williams, accidentally shot and killed in Abilene by Marshal Wild Bill Hickok back in '71. Like him, Miranda had a different Colt's revolver in each hand and looked, he thought, every bit as dangerous as she actually was.

In a car near the engine and coal car, the two found the engineer, the uniformed conductor and a shaken postal guard. All raised their guns as Duncan and Miranda appeared, Duncan yelling, "Arizona Ranger."

The three diverted their eyes to the floor, where another outlaw lay. He was a mess. Duncan saw why. The guard was holding a ten-gauge shotgun, muzzle pressed into the floor. Such a weapon from mere feet was among the most devasting guns of this or any era.

"How many horses?" Duncan asked.

"Seven," the engineer said. "I saw 'em all ride up. Seven for sure."

"Then, they're all dead," Duncan said.

"Well, we got us one here. How did y'all account for the rest, Ranger?"

"She got two," Duncan said, nodding to Miranda as the shocked men noticed the second person, Colt's single action revolver in hand, was a beautiful brunette.

"And, my partner got four," she added.

"Sure as hell makes seven," the conductor concluded.

"I heard shots before we engaged the six coming down the train towards us."

"They fired some warning shots in the ceiling. Then, one shot was Albert here with his Post Office special scattergun," the conductor said.

"We need to check to make sure no passengers were hurt. Helluva lot of lead been flying around, gentlemen," the tall lawman noted.

"I will gather some of the male passengers and we'll check the whole train and move the bodies all to one place." All nodded and the conductor moved towards the back of the train to fulfill his plan.

"And, I'll get some fellas up this end to help me clear the logs across the tracks so we can get this train moving towards Prescott," the engineer said.

"How long to Prescott, once we get rolling?" Duncan asked.

"About an hour and a half."

"Do we have telegraph capability on this train?"

"Not yet, Ranger," the engineer said.

Duncan looked pensive, then his eyes rolled back, and he fell to the floor.

"My God." Miranda exclaimed, "He's been shot again."

She pulled his coat further apart. The badge could be seen on the left side of his vest and they saw blood seeping from the shoulder wound by Frank Moore, on the right. She felt him all over and did not find more blood. She ripped off a piece of her new petticoat and made a pad. Miranda pressed the pad to the wound and held it tightly.

"Should we lift him up into a seat?" the engineer asked.

"I don't think so. I will tend to him here on the floor where he can lay flat. Will you be here in case I need help?" she asked the postal guard.

"Yes, Ma'am."

The engineer left to assemble help to get the tracks cleared, while the conductor and his several volunteers checked the rest of the train cars.

***

Fifty minutes later, Duncan opened his eyes. As a week ago, he looked straight into the eyes of Miranda Hancock again.

"Hell no, you bastard. Mine?" he asked in a hoarse voice.

She nodded and said, "Yes," defiantly.

Miranda was still pressing down on his shoulder. He saw three blood-soaked pads laying on the floor.

Moving his head, he weakly gestured for her to lean down.

She did.

"I love…" and he faded out again. She got the message and kissed him while she was close. She straightened, tired but happier than she had ever been in her life.

The postal guard cleared his throat.

She looked up to his gaunt form.

"Who is he, Miss?"

"He is Arizona Ranger Sergeant James Duncan, sir."

"Damn. I figured it had to be him."

She looked at him quizzically.

Studying her expression, he asked, "You really don't know who he is, do you, Ma'am?"

"I know he is the man who rescued me by killing Frank Moore and his whole outlaw gang. The man who killed four more outlaws here today, despite having a bullet hole through his shoulder."

"Of course, he did. He's a legend in Arizona and beyond. Yavapai deputy. Ranger who killed Creel in the most famous Arizona gunfight since the OK Corral. Rough Rider who saved Teddy himself on San Juan Hill."

Miranda knew he was fast and deadly, but she had never seen a gunman in action. A legend? Yes, she could see how he would be. She knew he was determined and virtually without fear. Miranda decided to have a long talk with her cousin Brodie and find out more about this silent man who had become so important to her in less than two weeks. She was pretty sure she was not going to get it out of him…at least with the level of detail she wanted, given what the postal guard said.

The conductor came by again as the train was slowing for Prescott. Miranda asked if he could send someone for a doctor. He said that he would.

Duncan was stirring and she blotted the wound with another piece of her petticoat. The cotton came back dry.

She smiled. The lawman stirred at the sound of voices and tried to open his eyes. He did on the third try. Focusing took a bit longer.

He tried to sit up, realizing for the first time he was laying in the train car's aisle with Miranda kneeling beside him.

She firmly held him down and said, "You passed out after the shooting. The fight opened your shoulder wound again. On top of all the blood you lost this past week, you lost even more today. So, you are going to be weak and a little off-kilter. Let's take it slow, honey, and Mister Groome here"—nodding up at the postal guard—"and I will help you to your feet. I don't want your mother to see you carried off on a stretcher unless there is no other way."

"No," he began hoarsely, "it would scare her half to death. She certainly knows I'm a lawman, but she doesn't have any idea of the dangers."

Miranda rolled her eyes at him. Right. His mother would have no idea her son the lawman was also a fast gun, war hero and all those other things she wanted to learn more about? "In a pig's eye," she thought, but said nothing as the guard helped her bring Duncan upright, then to his feet. He helped by steadying himself on a seat with his left arm.

The conductor appeared.

"Ranger," he said, "I sent for a doctor to come check you and supervise getting you off the train. You will have quite a party greeting y'all. The Territorial Governor is here, the head of the Rangers, and your folks. On behalf of the railroad, I'd like to thank you for what you did when we got robbed. You, too, Ma'am. He killed four outlaws who could have killed my passengers and crew, and you killed two. The two of you are one dangerous couple to tangle against."

They heard one of the station crew telling people to stand aside for the governor and his party.

Territorial Governor Brodie, his wartime friend Tom Rynning, and the Duncans came in. An older man with a small black bag followed. Duncan assumed he was the doctor.

They all stepped aside for the worried mother, who immediately went to her son, propping himself precariously on a seatback as he stood in the aisle.

His coat was still off and his vest wide open so Miranda could tend his wounds. They had arrived so unexpectedly Miranda had not had enough time to make him more presentable. His gray shirt had an eight-inch diameter dark stain on his right chest and shoulder. He leaned down to kiss his mother and she steadied him on one side and a very protective Miranda did on the other.

"Are you okay, James?" his mother asked, her beautiful face furrowed with concern.

"Yes, Ma'am. I have had the best possible nurse. I would not be here but for her," he stated.

"A lot of people, me included, wouldn't be alive today if it wasn't for your son, Ma'am," Miranda added.

She smiled at her cousin, then at the ranger captain, winning him for life.

The doctor pushed through and, seeing the bloody bits of compress on the floor, asked, "Did you stop the bleeding completely?"

"Yes. But it might start again from the walk or buckboard ride to your office, Doctor. He has a through and through wound from a foreign pistol. He bled a lot at first and had fever until several days ago when it broke. I put black walnut ointment in and on both sides of the wound. It seemed to prevent it from getting infected," Miranda told him.

Upon seeing the young woman and hearing about the black walnut ointment, Angus Duncan said softly to his wife, "I ken this one could be a keeper, Ann." Miranda was the only other person who heard this big man who looked so much like the ranger. She gave him a dazzling smile.

"Boss," Duncan turned to Rynning, "this saddlebag has all of the money stolen from the bank in Wickenburg. Will you make sure Mister Stone gets it back? And, Pa, Ace and a horse we commandeered for Miranda are in the stock car. Would you please fetch them?"

"Aye, son," he said, leaving the lawman in the care of his wife and...whoever the lovely brunette was. She was clearly more than just someone James had saved, he thought.

Big Tom Rynning and the two women helped Duncan the short distance to the doctor's office after Brodie had exchanged kind words with his cousin. Rynning had brought two rangers with him and they took charge of the saddlebag of money and counted it to give Duncan a receipt.

Brodie split off from the group so he could wire bank president Walter Stone with the information about the bank's money being recovered. He had delayed telling Stone until he had the money under his and Rynning's control. Based on Miranda's count at the cabin in the Hualapais, he knew the full amount was present. He also knew if Moore had not been shot during the robbery, the gang would have split the money the first day, gone their separate ways and Moore would have taken a lion's share and Miranda.

He could not imagine what horrors would have been visited upon his lovely cousin.

Thank heavens Duncan had killed Moore and the whole gang, as well as the train robbers, otherwise, this trip to Prescott would be about mourning and saving his political career. Though retrospectively, Brodie was a military man and was not sure he liked civilian service with its patronage and whining citizens. His troops did not whine. At least not to him. He was a strong, resolute man. His favorite times had been the Nez Perce and Apache Wars which had preceded the ill-prepared Spanish American War. Unlike his friend Teddy Roosevelt, he knew how a war should be run from experience. Roosevelt knew, but from perception borne of a very high intellect instead of having previously experienced it.

Brodie often reflected on the war in Cuba. The Army had provided the wrong guns, wrong uniforms for a tropical war, incorrect training, bad food and water, non-existent shelter, spotty transportation, little or no appropriate medical support—especially against disease. America had good on-the-battleground leadership by people like Roosevelt, O'Neill, Rynning, Pershing, and yes, himself. Otherwise their victory would have been reported in history books as a disaster. He finished writing the drafts for the telegrams to the banker and the state Attorney General, and his wife, Mary Louise, and headed back to the hotel where he had several rooms set aside for the group.

He wanted to sit in on Rynning's debrief of Duncan and to get a play-by-play report from his cousin and to study her to determine what really happened to her. He suspected if she had been assaulted, she might not admit it and it would take his experience as both an officer and a negotiator to get to the full story.

***

The doctor ushered his patient and the group into his building and past the waiting area to an examination room. Angus Duncan was still retrieving the horses.

"You ladies, wait out here. Captain, since he's your man, I don't mind if you want to come in while I conduct my examination," he said.

"I beg your pardon, Doctor. I have been taking care of James for a week and have been covered with his blood. He means quite a lot to me, and I will not give him up to you or anyone else."

Miranda said this with such a fierce determination it actually took the small man aback. The six-gun she wore conspicuously at her waist certainly punctuated all she said. Rynning grinned. Ann Duncan nodded and added, "Goes for me, too. I bore him, raised him and have a very vested interest in his condition. I'm coming in too."

The doctor looked to Duncan, who just shrugged and tried to hide the grimace from the pain the shrug caused.

On the examination table, the first thing off was the gun belt, which was handed to Rynning who hung it on a nearby chair. The doctor cut off the shirt and put warm water on the part cemented to Duncan's chest by his blood.

Ann gasped as she saw the small black hole, bruised around its circumference.

Miranda walked around the table and checked the back wound. The doctor's mouth started forming "Do you mind?" but, seeing her expression, swallowed the words before they became audible. Rynning, still observing the interaction between the doctor and the very possessive young woman, grinned again. Ann Duncan saw him, nodded, and smiled back sweetly.

It struck Rynning the fastest gun he had ever seen has met his match with these two women. Duncan sure has his work cut out for him, the ranger captain thought.

Rynning was new to this lawman life, but he was an

experienced soldier who had seen more than his share of bullet wounds. This one did not look bad, either by size or how it had been treated. Duncan's fights before this bullet wound had healed, and the loss of blood they caused seemed to him to be the primary cause for problems now.

Talking as he examined the wounds, the doctor said as much. He cleaned and stitched the entry and exit wounds, complimented Miranda on the care she had given, bandaged the shoulder, and applied a sling once again.

"You, young man, should take it slow and easy for a couple of weeks. Try to avoid fist, knife and gun fights, breaking wild horses and chopping firewood. You, young lady and you, Mama, please enforce these things. It is my opinion the ranger has leaked out about as much blood in the past week as he can afford for a month or so. He will need lots of broths, soups and water. Despite anything he says, it is not yet time for him to have a big steak, a bucket of fried chicken or the like. Give him liquid and go light with the solid foods for a week or so," the doctor ended.

Helped off the examination table, Duncan eyed his gun and belt on the chair. As is by mental telepathy, Miranda picked it up and in recognition of the sling on his right arm, buckled it from the back. The butt of the deadly Colt faced forward on his left, carefully adjusting its position and lifting and settling the gun lightly in its holster as she had seen him do. She had seen his left-hand draw and its lethality. They draped his long coat over his shirtless torso.

This time, the two women took charge of steadying Duncan. Rynning stayed behind for a moment to pay the doctor for caring for wounds sustained in the line of duty. He stretched his long legs and caught up with them on the short walk to the hotel.

"The governor got rooms for everybody," he said.

"After a dinner with all—excepting you, Sergeant, who needs bed rest—the governor and I want to question Miss Miranda about what happened from the bank robbery until the train pulled in to Prescott today. Tomorrow, James, after you are rested, you will get your turn at giving your official report. I will send a combined report, signed by you both, along to the attorney general. In your report"—turning to Duncan—"I want the locations of the robber camp and the cabin where you killed Moore. I will have my lieutenant, if he's back in time, lead a small posse of rangers and Yavapai deputies to recover bodies and gear to try to determine who they are. The several rangers who came with me are already on the trail delivering the recovered money bank to the bank. I will give you your signed evidence receipt at our meeting tomorrow. Other than the inconvenience to Miss Miranda and you stepping too close to a Mauser pistol, this operation will go down in history. A beautiful kidnap victim and a ranger shot but still killing seven outlaws, will make it all the more exciting to folks."

"Boss, that's the longest speech I ever heard you make," Duncan said. Rynning looked back, one dark, bushy eyebrow lowered, and said nothing.

Porters from the railroad depot had already brought their gear to the hotel. Angus Duncan met them there with the two rifles and told them the horses were being fed, watered, hooves checked, and then curried.

"Pa, is Ace okay, in your opinion?" Duncan asked

"Aye. He said you abused him terrible on this trip and he'll throw you on yer butt next time ya mount up, Lad. But I think he was just kiddin'." Father and son smiled at each other as they had for twenty-five years. Miranda watched, taking it in, learning. Ann watched Miranda every bit as intently, a smile on her face.

"Why don't you all go to the dinner with the governor?" Ann Duncan asked. "I will stay here and look after my boy." Miranda began to form words and Ann preempted her, saying, "You are the primary witness in this meeting, Miranda. I know the governor and the captain want to hear every detail you can share. I can look after James for now. You spell me tonight after the dinner."

Duncan also started to speak, to protest he was not an invalid, but the part about Miranda looking after him tonight had more than a little appeal, so he held his words. He knew the mother who wanted him married was working a plan. A plan he would help along any way he could. "What a mother," he thought to himself as he smiled proudly at the lovely blonde woman in her late forties.

The Duncans had one room for the three, Miranda, the captain and governor each had a single room. Miranda went to hers for the first time since arriving and found her newly acquired possessions waiting for her. There was a fireplace and it had a swing arm with a coffee pot on it. She checked. It was full of water. She swung it over the coals and put some more coals on the fire from the iron hod next to the fireplace. Soon, she had hot water to put in the pitcher and bowl on the scarred dresser so she could wash. There was one wash cloth and one larger towel. The latter would not qualify for a bath towel anywhere north of Lilliput. She hoped the hot water would somewhat sterilize the towels, which did not have the freshness borne of being hung to dry in the bright Arizona sun.

Within half an hour, Miranda was as ready as she could be. She wore the plaid shirt, the long riding skirt over boots and, for the pure devilment of it, the Colt's single action with which she had killed two men. She liked the feel and the lack of recoil of the .32-20. It allowed her to shoot multiple shots quickly. As she had done on the train. She had every confidence she could keep the revolver. She checked the cylinder. She had reloaded it like Duncan had taught her. It was hard to think of him having a called-by name. The hammer rested on an empty chamber. Load one, skip one, load four, fully cock the hammer and ease it down on the empty chamber.

The corridors were cold. It had begun to snow again. It had been an odd winter, with now in areas not known for it. She returned to her room and got her coat to wear to dinner. Hopefully, the cafe would be warmer.

Miranda tapped on the door of the adjacent room. Angus Duncan opened it, looked down at the open coat at the revolver and smiled. He nodded in approval and stepped aside to allow her to enter.

Duncan was sitting up in a chair holding a mug of thin soup and sipping it. His mother was hovering nearby.

"How are you feeling, James?" she asked.

"I could have used the two of you in Cuba. My gunshot was not a puncture wound, but the environment made the likelihood of infection high," he said.

"So, you mean the gash on your upper arm?" Miranda asked. He nodded yes.

"Dear, I wish I had a blouse to give you for dinner. But Angus and I thought we'd be taking the buckboard back to the ranch tonight with you and James riding along. We still want you to come and stay before returning to your students. I straightened up James' room for you. He can sleep in the small bunkhouse we built but never seemed to have money for hired hands to use," Ann said.

"I would like to do that, Missus Duncan. I would love to see a real Wild West ranch. There is a backup teacher for my school. She will be happy, because she could use the money. I am in no big rush to return."

Duncan caught her eyes with his over the mug of soup.

She instantly read he wanted and expected her to stay. She never had this extrasensory perception communication with her former husband. Or, maybe she did and just did not recognize it through his usual drunken stupor and characteristic anger.

"And, honey, it's Ann," Mrs. Duncan said. Miranda nodded in assent. "And, Angus, lass," to which she nodded again.

"How good are you with your revolver, Miranda?" the senior Duncan asked.

"I have only shot it a couple of times, but it seems right for me," she responded.

"Pa, she shot a train robber coming into our car, gun out. He fell where he stood and didn't get up. There was a big bruiser on top of me choking the life out of me. He did not seem affected by the .45 slug I had put in him. Before I passed out, I felt movement, heard Miranda say something, and saw her kill the man who was killing me."

"What did you say?" asked the mother.

Red-faced, the younger woman said, "I don't remember. It was something in the heat of the moment. But whatever it was, I know I meant it to the depths of my heart."

Ann Duncan tilted her head and thought. She was sure the young woman remembered exactly what she said and just did not want to share it. And, the mother had no problem with that. Some things were personal and better not shared.

"If you'd do me the honor of letting me escort you to the dining room, we should be leaving," Angus said to Miranda. She loved the burr in his speech. She detected a faint burr in Duncan's and had heard a more pronounced roll of R's while he was speaking feverishly.

Ann walked over and lightly kissed her Scot on his

cheek and hugged the beautiful brunette she hoped would become her daughter-in-law.

Turning her back to the two, Miranda looked at their son and pursed her lips soundlessly. He beamed and nodded, in full view of his parents. He was not yet comfortable throwing a kiss.

Having counted coup like an Indian warrior on her lawman, Miranda put her arm in his father's and walked out the door.

Finally alone with her son, Ann prompted him.

"Tell me what's going on with this young woman. Clearly, you two have deep feelings for each other after such a short period of knowing one another."

"I guess," he responded, "we do care about each other a lot. We have not really spoken in detail about what to do about it. She has a teaching job in Wickenburg. I 'spect the Captain will want me based out of Prescott. Of course, you and Pa are here..."

"Well James, aren't the two towns only sixty or so miles apart? I don't see a major problem there. As long as you are in this area and a place with a post office and telegraph, why would it matter to Captain Rynning which town?" she said

"I guess it wouldn't," Duncan said, pensively.

"Life is short. You have seen in the past few days how very short it was for some people. I do not think you should put off happiness, Son. Tell the girl how you feel and see where it goes. Your Pa and I like her, from what we know. I gather from Governor Brodie she had a bad marriage to a drunk and abuser. And, it's over. Then, she put her life in order with the help of a very influential relative—and a good man we are lucky to have as governor, I might add—only to be kidnapped. She deserves a lot of happiness. So do you. You have been a good son and a faithful peace officer. No reason you can't continue to be those things and be a happy husband, too."

"No, Ma'am," Duncan said, "no reason at all."

"Then, I'd say you should speak with her sooner than later. Time and people slip away," Ann said. She knew she had gotten through to her son and was confident enough he would follow her advice, so she did not expect an answer. And, did not get one. He just looked at her and smiled.

Angus Duncan returned from dinner first. He said the governor and tanger wanted to "question Miranda about events from the bank robbery to her captivity and escape with you, then to the train robbery".

"It's pretty much to be expected, Pa. They'll ask me about most of the same, plus details about where they can find the bodies I left scattered around. Though they'll be frozen stiff, I expect the critters will have had at them in this amount of time," Duncan told his parents.

"They ought to be pretty happy Miranda is back safe and was not harmed by Moore, the money was all recovered, Moore got the death the court sentenced him to, and the bank and train robberies were solved. All of which ought to make the rangers and the governor look good. Unless the gazettes take an angle like 'the ranger was too violent and should have captured everybody. Then magically brought them back a hundred miles through a blizzard to jail, all tied together'. Nothing would surprise me," Duncan said.

"Aye, son. The press reports according to the political party it's trying to hurt or help. It's always been that way. It's shite on paper," Angus said, his brogue increasing with his passion. Ann frowned at the vulgarity but agreed too much with her husband's line of thought to say anything about his word choice.

"This Miranda is a braw, bonnie lass, Son. I like her. She handled herself well with the captain and the governor both. She was funny, charmin', and took no guff from her cousin. She's a strong woman, like yer Ma. If she needs an endorsement—and I ken she doesn't—she sure has mine," Angus said.

"I appreciate your opinion, Pa. You know I always have and always will. But, this time, she doesn't need an endorsement. I'm sold. I just hope she's as sold on me."

"It doesn't take more than to see the way she looks at you, James, to confirm. Do you love her?" Ann Duncan asked.

"Aye, I do, Ma."

"Have you told her?"

"Maybe. I remember trying to say it, then things went blank," he said.

"Well, just maybe you should ride the same trail again before it gets too cold, son," his father suggested.

"I will, Pa. Tonight if possible."

"About anything is possible, James, if you make it so," his mother suggested.

***

After the dinner, the two government officials took notes as Miranda recounted the bank robbery, the escape, the captivity, the gunfight where Duncan killed the gang, the gunfight at the cabin, care of the ranger, and the train robbery. Her story was poignant and detailed.

After, the Governor told Rynning he would like a few moments to talk future and family matters with his cousin. The lawman excused himself and went to Duncan's room to check on his protégé before retiring for the night.

"Miranda, you have been through a lot in your young

life. I've been holding this," Alexander Brodie said as he handed her the purse she had dropped on the floor during the bank robbery.

"I took the check out and deposited it in your account, since it's why I figured you had it with you. Your divorce decree, signed by a judge in Richmond, is still in it. Congratulations for severing with the rotten scoundrel and his worse father. Money does not breed class or good behavior. These people prove it," he said.

"Captain Rynning said the gang leader, Frank Moore had been sentenced to death in Phoenix for murder and rape. He escaped and killed several more people. Young Ranger Duncan did you and society a favor sending him to hell. I have to ask you, cousin, did he harm you in any way? You know what I'm asking," Brodie said.

"I kept the derringer you gave me hidden on my person. They never searched me, so they never found it. I never undressed until I had the opportunity to wash after he was dead. If he had made any move to assault me, Cousin, I would have used it. And, he would have tried. I'm sure. He told me so repeatedly. Luckily too, he was in dire pain from the bullet near his groin, so I think his manly abilities were negligible. Thank God, James Duncan prevented me from ever knowing. I owe my life to him." Brodie nodded.

"Miranda, you killed two men. Both deserved it and it was self-defense and defense of another in danger of imminent bodily harm or death. What the law calls a justifiable use of deadly force. But, how do you feel about taking two lives? Do you need to talk to a minister about it?"

"No, sir. James and I spoke about killing outlaws as opposed to murder. What I did was right and justified. I will not fret over either. Killing the first one saved my life, killing the second saved my dear James'," she said with conviction and finality.

"You two seem connected, for lack of a better description. You have only known each other a couple of weeks," Brodie began.

"Cousin, it has been an intensive two weeks. I could not have fallen into a relationship with more of a gentleman than Ranger Duncan. His bravery and deportment were exemplary. I pray our relationship will move forward. I cannot imagine my life without him in it," she said.

"Just don't rush. You are both young and there's plenty of time."

"I saw firsthand how quickly 'plenty of time' can end. I think with losing my father, being married to one animal and getting out in time to be kidnapped by another, I deserve happiness and a good man, don't you think?" she said.

"You do, dear Cousin. And, I admit this: I have known this young man for nigh on to six years. As a Rough Rider sergeant, and an Arizona lawman. He has impressed me at every turn. My only fear is the long lonely and deadly trails he has to ride. How can he be there for you?"

"I don't know...I only want to try working it out. But we have not even had that talk yet. But I feel it's coming soon."

"You," the Governor said, "know you have my support in all things. You are more like a niece, no, a daughter to us."

She leaned over and kissed her cousin on top of the head and giggled as he turned red.

"I feel about you and Mary Louise the same way and am blessed to have you. The Duncans have asked me to spend a few days with them before returning to Wickenburg, and I'd like to do that." The governor nodded affirmatively, and she smiled.

She asked Brodie about James Duncan's history as a Rough Rider and a lawman. The Territorial Governor gave a first-hand account of the former and a knowledgeable account of the latter. He tirelessly filled in all the blanks she had about Duncan. He truly was a legend, she realized. She also realized he had no clue about how many people knew and respected his exploits.

"Now, I have to go check on my patient. Thank you for filling me in on James' history, Cousin." He stood as she arose and escorted her back to the Duncan's room, where he bade her goodnight.

She tapped lightly on the door, carrying a cardboard box with a hot dinner and cup of hot tea from the restaurant for Ann. Ann was up and accepted the tray with a smile. Both men were asleep.

"Guess I won't get to visit with our ranger tonight," she whispered to Ann.

Duncan's eyes popped open. He rose on one arm and looked at her.

"How about if I walk you back to your room and we can talk quietly with the door to the hall open?" he asked.

Miranda knew from the grimace as he moved who would walk whom back to the room. She also knew to play the cards she was dealt.

"You got your pants on, Ranger? I'm waiting for you to make good on an offer of some sort," she said.

Ann rolled her eyes at this forward humor but liked the way young 1900's women were coming out as people instead of just wives and mothers.

Duncan got up without help and stuck the small .38 in the pocket of his dungarees after pulling his braces up. He did not bother with the sling. He looked at his boots in the corner, shook his head and padded to her in sock feet.

He held out his arm and she took it. Her grasp was far stronger and more guiding than what he would have expected of a Virginia belle. But then, he knew nothing of the tough, strong steel magnolias who settled the early colonies of the South and held their ground alone during a terrible war in the 1860s. They went to the room two doors down and entered, leaving the door open in the interest of Miranda's reputation and family harmony.

Miranda pointed to the bed and he sat on it. She took off her new boots and gun belt and sat on the only chair in the room. She built up the fire again. Then, she moved the chair close to the bed so they could speak in hushed tones with the door open.

"How did the part about what happened go after you ate?" Duncan asked.

"It was fine," she said, beginning to tell her version from the start to coincide with his story in the morning.

"My portion will mirror yours exactly, though we've nothing to hide about what happened," he said.

"Does your cousin agree with you staying with us for at least the rest of the week?" he asked.

"Yes, he's fine with it."

"Good. I am really looking forward to it, Miranda. I wish I was in better shape to take you riding and out for a snowy picnic, but we can talk. Talk about things obscure and things important."

"Like us?" she asked.

"Especially," Duncan said.

She sat there smiling at him, saying nothing. He thought for a while before speaking. This was an area he was not sure he had broached before and he wanted to get it right but was not exactly sure how to do it.

"I dreamed I said 'I love you.' Did I?" he asked.

"If you did, do you want to retract it?"

"No. I just want to make sure you know it. That's all," he said.

"I guess you could tell me again..."

He motioned for her to lean closer. It was late and they could hear snores from the thin-walled rooms.

As her face got within inches of his, he whispered, "Miranda Hancock, I love you. I want us to be together always."

"I love you too, James. And, I want us to spend our lives together, too."

"It may be a bit inconvenient for a while until we work the kinks out. Like with me relocating to Wickenburg. I have not seen the cottage the school provides. Does it have a corral and stalls?" he asked.

"No, it is about the size of the cabin we were in for a week, but without a corral or even lean-to for the horses. It's a short walk from town. It is on the main road and has no privacy at all. Not bad for me but may not be good for us. Presuming we would be living together," Miranda said.

"Us living together will be an absolute fact. I will ask you all the proper things when a couple errands are complete. Are you fully divorced from your husband? We never spoke about your situation with him."

She opened her purse and took out the derringer, some money, the deposit receipt and a divorce decree, placing the latter in his hands. He read it and looked up with a smile.

"So, I won't have to kill him?" he asked.

"Not worth the cost of a bullet," she replied. "And, I have a final settlement of ten thousand dollars in the Farmers & Merchants Bank of Wickenburg."

"Hmmm. Beautiful, smart and rich."

"No, I was rich. And, miserable. Now, I have a nest

egg for us and am getting happier by the minute," she said.

"I have a little nest egg too," Duncan ventured. "The only thing I ever spent money on was food, a little equipment like blankets, axe and cookware, and a new rifle. I saved the rest. I have five thousand four hundred and twenty-eight dollars in a couple of Mason jars buried under the bunkhouse at the ranch."

"What would most of all of this money added together get us?" she asked.

"I'm not sure without looking around, which the two of us ought to do. It would be ideal to find a small ranch near Wickenburg close enough for you to be able to get to school in any weather. Are you aware of any for sale?" Duncan asked.

"No, but this is not something I have given any thought to before a week or so ago. There is a lawyer in Wickenburg who Cousin Brodie knows and recommended if I ever needed one. He also does real estate and deed work. He might be a good place to start," she said.

"You know," Duncan said, thinking aloud, "Walter Stone at the bank there might be a good resource too. He'd know of anyone wanting to sell out in the area. Plus, he must be pretty pleased with you and me now, what with getting all his money back for him."

"Well, we seem to have a plan. What's next?" she asked Duncan.

"There is something I have to do, then something I have to ask." He looked at the wedding band, now on her right hand, signifying nothing but wearing a gold ring.

"I'd like to borrow this," he said, not asking.

"Why? It means nothing," Miranda responded.

"It will tell me what I need to know."

She knew exactly what but was not going to make this

too easy for him.

"I wear this as a reminder to never again marry the wrong man."

"As well you should. But, as long as I live and breathe, you won't," Duncan said.

"Won't what?"

"Won't marry the wrong man. You will marry the right one. And, no other," he said.

"How can I be sure?"

"You are already sure, Miranda Hancock."

She padded to the door barefooted. No lurkers. She went back and kissed the man sitting on the bed. No peck on the cheek. A hot, deep, long kiss took as long to break away as it lasted. He looked at her and moved his lips but no sound came out.

Uncannily reading him as she had from the very beginning, she whispered, "Just get your preparations done and ask your damn question. A day or so does not matter and...well, it will be well worth your wait, dear James."

He stood shakily. She straightened his clothes and walked him to the door. He walked down the hall and tapped on the door and identified himself before walking in on the former US Army scout and outlaw to the Crown of Victoria. Angus Duncan did not carry a revolver but was so fast and deadly with the carbine always close to his hand, he did not need one. The father acknowledged quietly, and Duncan eased in and laid on the portable bed, dressed except for the boots he had left there before going to Miranda's room. He thought and planned for a long time before falling asleep.

11

ARIZONA TERRITORY
1904

The next morning, a much improved and fully-armed and badged ranger sergeant joined the Governor of the Territory and the head of the Arizona Rangers for breakfast. They sat in a corner and kept their conversation to themselves. Rynning wrote in the hand of a craftsman as Duncan related his trip to Phoenix, to Wickenburg and the snowy trail after the outlaws. He spoke of being bushwhacked, taking on the gang as they slept, the location of both firefights. He told how Moore had chosen his money and Miranda over his boots to escape the camp, though wounded a second time in the gunfight. How he had shot at Moore but killed his horse. And, how Moore had gotten on Miranda's horse and ridden off. Duncan told how he had fallen from his wounds and laid in the snow for some time. How long, he did not know. How he had taken food, blanket and another horse to be a packhorse for the trip back after he had gotten Moore and freed Miranda. And, of the final gunfight in the cabin and his fever and the care by the woman he admitted had grown so special to him.

Finally, Duncan related the story of the train robbery. Of killing four and of Miranda killing two, saving him. And, saving him once again by stanching the blood from his reopened wounds before arriving in Prescott. Duncan accounted for selling the spare horse for railroad tickets. He also returned the personal money he had "borrowed" from the dead outlaws for the long trip back. Captain Rynning noted the locations of the ambush on Duncan, the camp with the dead outlaws, and the cabin with Moore's corpse. Rynning would add his already-prepared notes on the train robbery and the full return of the bank robbery money to the end of both Miranda's and Duncan's oral reports. There was a secretary at the Sheriff's Office where Duncan had worked before and after the war. She had an Oliver Visible model typewriter and would transcribe his written reports to Phoenix on it, complete with onion skin copies. He gave Duncan an evidence receipt for the returned bank monies and money confiscated from the outlaws.

Duncan, tired from the long verbal report asked the two men if he might take a few more minutes of their time on another matter.

"Gentlemen, Missus Hancock and I have become quite attached to one another. My first request is to the Governor. Sir, I would like to have Miranda's hand in marriage. We have spoken and I am sure it is what she wants also," Duncan said.

"Well, young man. Though sudden, this is not unexpected. It is pretty obvious you two are smitten with each other. I have known you for six years. In person during the War, where I watched you and promoted you gladly at the direct order of one of the men you saved. The man is of course, the President of these United States. Another man you saved sits at the table with us. Captain Rynning, an old friend from the Indian Wars and the Spanish American Wars wired me after the bank robbery he was sending me the deadliest gunfighter and man-tracker in Arizona, if not the whole West, to bring back my cousin. I knew who he was sending before even reading your name and was mightily relieved when my eyes verified what I had surmised."

"My answer is, yes, you may marry my cousin. I appreciate your courtesy but have to note the strong willed young woman is fully emancipated and can decide on her own. However, as your boss up the ladder, I ask you let me give her away since her father is dead." The governor ended and shifted the conversation back to Duncan.

"Thank you, sir. I think it appropriate and an honor for you to grace our wedding and give her away. I hope your lovely wife, who I met briefly before riding on from Phoenix, can assist her with a simple wedding."

"I am not strong enough a man to even think about denying her the opportunity to help plan the wedding, Sergeant," the governor said smiling.

"Now, you, sir," Duncan said, turning to Rynning.

"I know you wanted me stationed here in Prescott which does make sense. But Wickenburg is only sixty miles away and has wire, mail and some telephone capability. Since Miranda teaches there and I will be riding all over this part of Arizona, I would like to ask if I can work out of there instead of here?"

"Well, James, Prescott would be better long term. Why don't you settle briefly in Wickenburg and spend six months or a year looking for both a place here and a teaching position for Miss Miranda. Prescott is going to have more opportunities for her and perhaps for you," Rynning said.

"For me, Captain?" asked Duncan, a bit confused. The two older men looked at one another, quite pleased with what secret information they possessed.

"Down the road, you might have a couple young ones. Those long trails might get longer and tougher. You are already a sergeant. I only have a slot for one lieutenant which I don't see changing. I could see you being Sheriff of Yavapai County in the not-so-distant future. You are respected all over the Territory and beyond. But you are a solid known quantity here. Local boy made good sort of thing. Talk to your wife-to-be. I bet she likes the sounds of such a plan."

Duncan saw the Territorial Governor shaking his head up and down in support. Did these two already know something? The idea did have some appeal. And, the job paid a lot more than any job at the rangers, probably even Rynning's.

"Captain, I would like to discuss it with Miranda, but I have to say, as proud as I am to wear the ranger badge, it does hold some appeal to me. It was Buckey's job, of course."

Rynning nodded and turned to Brodie.

"You weren't on the particular part of the line when Buckey was shot, Alex. Buckey O'Neill was a close friend of us both and a hero to young Duncan. I ran to the spot and saw Buckey was dead. Duncan was prone in the firing position beside the body and pouring thirty caliber rounds down range into the Spanish. His rifle barrel was so hot you couldn't touch it. Buckey's men were shooting as fast as they could work their bolts, their faces tearstained. This is the kind of respect and love every good leader strives for and most of us never achieve. I think of Buckey O'Neill every day, and our talks about Greek literature and European politics and art. Our conversations ran the full gamut. I have a feeling Duncan remembers his friend every day too," Rynning finished.

"Yes, sir, Captain. It was Sheriff O'Neill riding into the street we are on right now with prisoners in tow and a bullet hole in his hat. He was holding up his arm and waving at the folks. They loved their sheriff. And, at ten years old, I wanted to be just like Buckey O'Neill," Duncan said.

Brodie began to speak.

"Other than your family and Miranda, all of whom should be told to keep your plans to themselves for now, don't talk about the things we have discussed here, Duncan. Governors and heads of police agencies have a way of making things happen. Just remember and bide your time. Make yourself as indispensable as you can to the folks of Yavapai County. And, stay on the best terms possible with the Sheriff's Office including and especially Acting Sheriff Roberts. Be their partner, not a competitor. Sheriffs are already getting contentious about the success of the rangers and some of the hard-handed methods they feel like you rangers employ. Don't play into those kinds of opinions. Be their friend. It will serve you well. I suspect you know if an Arizona Territory Acting Sheriff was to decide to step down or move on, it is the Territorial Governor who names his replacement," Brodie advised, and winked broadly.

The two leaders stood, signaling the end of the meeting. It had been an interesting one for Duncan. Very interesting. He would discuss it tonight at the ranch with the three people he cared about most in the world.

***

While the two women helped the still-weak Duncan with their gear, Angus retrieved their two horses and his horse and buckboard. The gear, except Duncan's and Miranda's rifles, was loaded onto the buckboard.

The newspapers on all sides of the political spectrum released issues about the freeing of the beautiful kidnap victim school teacher, the brave ranger who had killed eleven men in two weeks, enabling the return of all the bank robbery money, and the prevention of mail, a payroll, and everything else from being stolen from the train by a different set of robbers. Frank Moore and his death by a quick draw Arizona Ranger rated a separate sidebar in each paper.

Rynning, the Territorial Governor and Duncan held an impromptu news conference on Main Street. At the end, Duncan said, "The Yavapai Sheriff's Office will be taking over the case now. They will be riding with a small number of rangers to collect and identify the dead outlaws at three sites near Hualapai. As always, the rangers appreciate the fine efforts of the lawmen of the great sheriff's office. I was proud to serve with Yavapai County until becoming a ranger several years ago." He saw Sheriff Roberts in the crowd, nodding and smiling. Ev Masters was beside him.

He tipped his Stetson at Roberts and Masters.

When the Duncans and Miranda arrived at the ranch, the ranger slid off Ace and steadied himself against his mount.

Once sure of himself, he spoke to the rest.

"I have some very confidential information from Governor Brodie and Captain Rynning. I have been formulating it in my mind during the ride here and need a little more time to organize what I feel about it all. I'd like to discuss it with you all at dinner, okay?"

With quizzical looks, each nodded and Miranda stepped forward to help him unload Ace, before going to the buckboard to help Angus with the rest of the gear. Ann entered the ranch house, started a fire and coffee, then joined Miranda and Angus bringing items into the ranch house and taking Duncan's kit into the bunkhouse.

In the bunkhouse, Duncan quickly started a fire. The split logs were seasoned well, and he had a hot, roaring fire going quickly with his newly acquired Austrian ferrocerium rod and the spine of his folding knife's blade. Why waste a match, he thought with the frugality of a Scot?

He sat in one of the several ladderback chairs, warming his hands in front of the fire and thinking. Duncan knew his conditioning and constitution would have him back to patrol status quickly. The life decisions posed by his two direct superiors—he had not met the furloughed lieutenant yet so did not include him—were not as readily absorbed.

He had given some thought to having to leave a new young wife who had just been kidnapped even before the broad hints he received last night. What the Governor seemed to have in mind would solve a number of worrisome issues. The Sheriff of Yavapai in 1904 picked and chose what trails he wanted to ride. He did not patrol like his deputies. He generally went home to his wife and slept in his own bed at night. Though Duncan liked the adventure of being a deputy and a ranger, the prospect of being sheriff had a great deal of appeal to him, all of a sudden.

Duncan knew the main thing he needed to do in the next few days was to get a ring and propose. Until he did those two things, the rest would not fall into place. He determined to practice his shooting skills with his "weak" or left hand more while at the ranch. Maybe he and Miranda should practice together, he thought.

Miranda came into the bunkhouse and brushed his shoulder with her hand as she proceeded over to the fireplace and stretched her hands forward to warm them.

Her touch sent cold chills through him and it was not the temperature of her hands.

Following the lead of her future mother-in-law, she took the coffee pot out to the pump and filled it with water, then returned and measured coffee into it. She swung the iron arm out, placed the bail of the coffee pot on it and repositioned it over the flames to brew. Miranda pulled a chair over next to Duncan's and sat down. She took his big hands and buried hers in them to finish warming.

"You haven't forgotten the question you have been wrestling with yet, have you?" she asked coquettishly.

"I have not. I was just sitting here pondering it."

She arose and poured them both a cup of coffee into chipped mugs sitting on a shelf.

"So, what is it you will speak to us about at dinner tonight?" Miranda asked.

"Well," he began, "it's about the possibility of changes your cousin and my captain think are in the wind. Changes with a positive effect for you and me. Of course, it all depends on how you answer my question."

"James, why don't you just ask me the damn question? I know what it is, and I am ready to answer right now."

"I just want it to be right. It's for a long time and I want you to be able to look back and think it was a special moment," he said.

"Honey, I know you want to include your folks in this discussion. But we will have to make decisions by talking things out for a lot of years to come. Let's start right and start now, okay? Please tell me what the Territory's leaders told you this morning. And, why it prompted you to give a very nice political speech on the sidewalk. You are a little young to be the next Territorial Governor, so what is going on, for the Lord's sake?" Miranda asked.

"First off, I asked the governor for your hand in marriage," he said. She gulped, not having expected to hear this first.

"He said 'yes', only if he could give you away. And, the First Lady will help plan...well, you know."

"Yes, I know. What else?" she asked.

"I asked the captain if I could relocate the ranger office from Prescott to Wickenburg. He said 'no'."

"Why, James?"

"He said start off there to be with you, but for both of us to spend maybe six months looking for a teaching job for you in Prescott and a ranch for us near the school in Prescott. It was agreed there is and will always be more opportunities here than in Wickenburg. Which all makes sense, Miranda." He paused to collect his thoughts.

"So, James, you will be the Sergeant in charge of this portion of Arizona Territory...what's next? Will we always be here? Or on to Phoenix? Or Washington, DC?" she asked, knowing her cousin and a bit of what he thought of James Duncan.

"Assuming you agree, I have no reason to want to leave this area. But, there's something else. Remember my words this morning about the Yavapai Sheriff's Office? And, what great people they are? First off, I happen to believe them to be. Second, the two senior leaders today suggested I work closer than ever with them as a partner. Keep the relationship strong, not only with the deputies and chief deputy, but with acting sheriff Jim Roberts himself. They hinted he did not want the job full-time, so he will be moving on sooner than later.

"The Governor hinted he would appoint me sheriff. A four-year term would start with my swearing in. So, I wouldn't have to face an election for a while. Both men said we might want to start a family and you would appreciate having a husband home most nights instead of riding long trails days at a time. Plus, a ranch, even a small one, takes some work. I couldn't do you or it justice if I was gone five or six days a week.

"For you and Ma and Pa, this has to be kept secret. Particularly the part about Sheriff Roberts." Duncan ended.

Miranda let a long breath out, sounding like an unintentional "Whew".

"It's a lot, James. Should I get used to calling you 'Sheriff'," she asked.

"Call me anything you want, just stay by my side. That's all I want," he replied.

Continuing, Miranda said, "It's a lot to think about. But, at first blush, it all sounds good, logical, and workable. Having my husband at home most nights has a lot of appeal. Did you know I can actually cook?"

"I know the bean soup in the cabin was the best thing I ever had," he responded.

"Under the circumstances, you would have probably thought dishwater was good. But I can do better. I cooked for my parents for years. My former husband and his family were wealthy, so cooks and servants did those chores in Richmond."

"Well, Miranda, as Rabby Burns said, "May auld acquaintances be forgot and ne'er brought to mind," Duncan said.

"Rabby? You mean Robert?"

"Rabby to us Scots. It's like Bobby," he said.

"Oh. Guess I may have to learn some Scot," to which Duncan just smiled and shrugged as if it were of no consequence.

Ann Duncan called out of the front door of the ranch house to say dinner was ready. Both arose immediately and went over to the house.

The bread was freshly baked and smelled wonderful. Vegetables had been canned and stored in Mason jars just after being picked from the Duncan garden. The meat was venison, shot by Angus and aged in a lean-to against the back of the house.

After dinner, all turned to the younger Duncan.

He repeated what he had told Miranda in the bunk-house. The parents were pleased with him ultimately staying near them. They were already happy with the prospect of the woman sitting next to him becoming part of the family. They knew being sheriff of the county would lessen him riding the long and dangerous trails. All in all, it seemed a good plan to them.

"Son, when are you going to ask this young woman, who we both have grown very fond of in a short time, to join Clan Duncan?" his father asked.

"Very soon, Pa. I have to take care of one thing first. An easy thing. I already asked for her hand from the Governor and he approved as long as he could give her away and his wife could help plan the wedding."

"And, Miss Miranda, what are your feelings in all of this?" Angus asked.

"My feelings...hmm. I cannot give away an answer to a question as yet unasked. But I would like to spend the rest of my days with your son. As to the locations, his potential job...well, it all sounds just about perfect to me."

"As perfect as your response, my dear," Ann noted.

The men rose and as appropriate for the times, the women began to clear the table. The rest of the evening was spent with talk and a game of checkers. Angus smoked a bowl of Virginia leaf in his briar. Several hours later, Duncan stood and excused himself to go to bed in the bunkhouse. Mindful of appearances, Miranda joined him and watched him practice drawing his unloaded Colt left-handed from reversed holster on his left hip. He would have to rely on his weak hand until this right was not encumbered by the sling. The doctor had ordered him to wear it for several more weeks.

Miranda, who had seen him draw and fire left-handed and drop his attacker, still marveled at the speed. Soon, she stood on tip toes and gave him a kiss. He walked her back to the ranch house and bade her goodnight, whispering how much he missed her at night after their week at Hualapai. She whispered, "Soon," and smiled before disappearing inside.

Duncan returned to the bunkhouse and moved the cylinder retaining pin and slipped the cylinder out of his Colt's .45 revolver. He ran an oiled swab through each chamber in the cylinder and the barrel of the 5 ½" Artillery Model. He reassembled it and wiped a slightly oily cloth over the exterior and reloaded. He hung the holster with the gun in it on the left side of his bed and hoped this dramatic change in position would not prove his undoing in a nighttime emergency.

He went to sleep immediately, restless because of his wound. His revolver was not necessary during the night.

***

Early the next morning, Angus insisted on saddling Ace for his son, mindful of the pull against the wound lifting the saddle over the back of the large blue roan would cause.

Duncan put his lighter .30-30 in the scabbard and ammunition, iron nippers to hold any prisoner who presented himself for arrest, and sandwiches provided by Ann Duncan. He kissed Miranda goodbye and rode towards Prescott.

The air was sharp and cold, the day clear. Duncan could smell the woods and, as he got closer to Prescott, the hardwood smoke from chimneys.

He rode into town and stopped at the Sheriff's Office. The Chief Deputy, who always seemed to be there, greeted him.

"Hiya, Chief. Anything new in this part of the Territory?" he asked.

"Quiet for now, Duncan. People are cold. I 'spect somebody who's laid up in a cabin will drink too much and stab his bunkmate before long. But it hasn't happened yet. At least as far as I know."

"You're probably right. Listen, if you were looking for an engagement ring or wedding ring or something, where would you look?"

"Ha. Something I kinda wondered about when I saw that fine-looking young woman holding onto you like she had already burned a brand into your ass-end. Congratulations, son. I guess I'd look at Palmer's Pawn Shop, here on Gurley Street. Folks are always hard up for money, and jewelry they brought from back East is first thing they pawn to buy food or seeds."

"Thanks. I'll try there. Was afraid I might have to go to Phoenix to find a jeweler, Ev," he said.

"Well, ole man Palmer was a jeweler in New Jersey. He may be as good as anybody you'd find in Phoenix. Hell, I'd take Prescott over Phoenix for anything anytime. I just don't like Phoenix."

"I'm kind of partial to here, too," Duncan responded.

"Ev, I am about a week—maybe less—away from being able to hit the trail again," Duncan began. "Anything y'all have going on I can help with?"

"Nope. Not right now. How's your left-hand draw?"

Duncan looked around and made sure no one was in

the vicinity, slowly drew and unloaded his .45, then holstered it, butt forward on the left.

Facing away from the Chief Deputy with his left side visible, Duncan drew, his hand a blur.

"Holy Lord in heaven, boy. Your left has to be as fast as your right hand," Ev Masters said incredulously.

"No, Ev. Not really. But I hope good enough to get me safely back in the saddle again. I'm going to go over to Palmer's and buy a ring for Miranda. I'll see you later on."

Duncan reloaded, re-holstered and left.

Looking at the big clock above where he stood, he realized two things. He had an hour to kill before any retail establishment in Prescott opened and he was famished.

He walked over to his favorite of the cafes in town and sat down. Duncan really did not have to look at the chalk menu board on the wall. He told the proprietor, "Full breakfast and a coffee...black," and selected a table.

He sat with his back to the wall and his left arm unencumbered for a draw, if need be. He thought and scanned the area unconsciously until the coffee came. It was rich and strong Ariosa, just like had been used on cattle trails for years until the railroads took cattle to market. Each bag had a peppermint stick in it and the chuck wagon cooks would break it up and give pieces to the young cow herders. Most were in their mid-to-late teens and still boys at heart.

An hour, breakfast and three cups of coffee later, Duncan paid and walked down to the pawn shop.

Palmer looked up as he walked in, focused on the badge first, then the sling and said nothing.

"Mister Palmer, I'm James Duncan. I need a ring to give to my intended. I have one of her rings as a guide to the size of her finger. Do you have some wedding ring sets I could look at?"

Still not saying anything, the old man nodded to the counter perpendicular to where he had been standing.

Duncan met the man on opposite sides of one as Palmer opened a drawer in the back of the counter. He withdrew a box with a number of ring boxes inside. He flipped open the lids on all.

The ranger looked at all, comparing Miranda's ring he had bought for size. One box had yellow gold rings with a medium diamond and, when he compared with the ring, it seemed like a perfect fit. The owner confirmed the sizes were the same with a metal measure.

Speaking for the first time, Palmer asked, "What finger does she wear this ring on?"

Duncan replied, "It was sized for her left-hand ring finger. How much is this?" His knowledge of jewelry in general and diamonds in specific was so lacking he had no idea of costs. Palmer took out an inventory book and compared the number on a tag in the box with his inventory.

"Hunnert fifty," he said.

"Hmmm....would you take one hundred thirty cash right now?" Duncan asked.

"Make it one thirty-five and you're done."

Duncan took some cash out and counted off one hundred thirty-five dollars from a small roll, the rest of what he feared he might need was secreted in another pocket.

He laid the money on the counter while Palmer counted it. The pawnbroker wrote out a Cash Paid receipt and handed the box and receipt to the ranger in a small paper sack. Duncan folded the sack and put it in his button-down vest pocket opposite the one where he kept his backup gun.

He stuck out his hand to the older man, they shook, and he turned and walked out the door. Duncan held back the broad grin until his back was turned.

At the Sheriff's Office, he untied Ace from the hitching post, mounted and rode back to the ranch, whistling loudly, but a bit off-key.

***

He got back to the ranch in time for lunch. After, he joined his father in a pipeful of burley, lighting his own pipe for his monthly bowl.

"Wish me luck, Pa. Today's the big day for the question," he said quietly, knowing a low voice did not carry as far as a whisper. They could hear the two women talking across the room.

"I dinna think you'll be needing much luck, Son. The luck will come from recovering from the punch she'll give you for waitin' so damn long."

"Doesn't seem so long to me," he responded.

"You'll ken what I'm talking about, and it won't take you forever to learn," his father said philosophically as he puffed his pipe, nodding to himself.

"Son, I need to split some wood. You shouldna be doing work yet, but perhaps you could pick up and stack the pieces with yer good hand?" Angus asked.

The two men, so much alike in height, but differing with red versus sandy blond hair, arose and tapped the dottle from their pipes gently into the large ash tray by Angus' chair before walking outside.

Angus took off his heavy coat. At forty-eight, he was tall like his son, but more heavily muscled than James Duncan's lean rider physique. He picked up the Hudson's Bay pattern axe and began to yield it with practiced efficiency, the ranger picking up and stacking the firewood left-handed. Duncan used a leather glove on his working hand to protect it from splinters.

It was the sign of a man who lived by the gun. Each protected his gun hand from injury to the greatest extent possible from cuts, splinters, burns or anything that might slow his draw or impair the accuracy of a shot which might be the difference between life and death. Protecting the gun hand and using the "weak" hand made many gunmen somewhat ambidextrous, hence Duncan's dexterity with his revolver left-handed.

Wood stacked, lunch eaten, Miranda and Duncan donned their heavy coats and walked out by the corral to check on Ace and Miranda's commandeered horse, which she named Traveler. Her father had ridden for Marse Robert and she used Robert E. Lee's horse's name in her father's memory.

Duncan took her hands by the corral and again professed his undying feelings towards her. She moved to him and rested her cheek on the lapel of his coat. She could hear his heart beating.

"Miranda Hancock, will you marry me?" he asked.

Caught off-guard, she hesitated, then shook her head up and down and said, "Yes, I will marry you. I would be honored to be Missus James Duncan."

They kissed and she said, "What in heaven's name has taken you so long to ask? You knew what the answer would be. We've already started to plan a life together." Careful to not hurt his wounded right shoulder, she punched him on his left one. The blow was spirited but softened by the heavy jacket as she knew it would be. As always, Angus Duncan was right.

"This is why I waited," he said as he slipped the diamond ring on her left ring finger. He did not know it at the time, but the wedding band he used for sizing was all her wealthy first husband had given her. She turned the ring and it caught the late morning sun. She seemed mesmerized by the sparkle, then turned and kissed him again. "I love my ring. I love you. I will wear this ring every remaining day I have on this earth."

They walked back to the ranch house to make their announcement. Later in the day, Miranda and Duncan rode into Prescott to send a telegram to Mary Brodie in Phoenix about helping Miranda and Ann Duncan with a simple wedding.

***

The next day, shoulder healing, but arm still in a sling outside his heavy coat, Duncan rode into Prescott to check in at the Western Union Office. He had a telegram from Captain Rynning and it was disconcerting on several personal fronts.

Rynning said Aaron Piyahgonte of the Yavape band of Yavapai had left his assigned area with a small war party. Duncan was ordered to apprehend him before an Army patrol, now being assembled, got to him and a bloodbath followed. The captain was unaware Aaron had been Duncan's closest friend for the past decade. Duncan decided to keep it that way.

Quickly back at the ranch, Angus put a sawbuck packsaddle on a strong, dependable sorrel named Bub. Bub had proven his ability as both a riding horse, a buggy horse, and a packhorse.

Duncan was in the ranch house, shirtless, as Miranda and Ann tightly wrapped his shoulder wound to protect it somewhat without the encumbrance of a sling.

Just after leaving the telegraph office, Duncan had gone by the gunsmith and picked up a left-handed revolver holster. Once his shoulder was wrapped and his shirt back on, he threaded it on his Mills belt, having a rare two-gun rig. He had already chosen the second gun from the ones he collected at the outlaw camp after the gunfight. The five and a half-inch barrel Colt's .45 had walnut grips and closely matched his own revolver, except without the tuning by Chris Madsen.

Duncan always kept basic cookware, food, ammunition, and a bedroll ready to put on Ace. Only heavier long-term camping gear went onto a packhorse.

The two women prepared biscuits and beef stew for the trip and set out a side of bacon, bag of pinto beans, coffee beans, and a Mason jar of honey protected in a canvas bag, rolled and tied with twine.

Duncan was going to try something new this ride. He had bought two new German vacuum flasks made by a company called Thermos GmbH. Whether they would stand up to a hard ride remained to be seen, but Ann poured the beef stew in, hoping for the best. Thinking they might be too fragile for the trail, she also wrapped strips of an old blanket around them, tied with twine. Protection and additional insulation.

Duncan exchanged the larger .30-40 rounds on his belt for the .30-30 cartridges that went with the light, fast Winchester '94. Two guns on, Bowie beside he pinned the silver star on the outside of his canvas and wool-lined long coat. Miranda wrapped a long woolen scarf around his neck and whispered, "Come home to me at all costs, ya hear?" He heard and had every reason in the world to do just that.

He kissed her and his mother and hugged his father.

Mounting Ace and taking the lead for Bub, Duncan rode off. He did not look back. He knew he would return. He just had to.

12

ARIZONA TERRITORY
1904

Duncan rode through light falling snow to the primary winter encampment chosen by the government for the Yavape band. Much of the tribe had been moved north to the Apache reservation.

He wanted to talk with Noah Piyahgonte about where his son, Duncan's longtime friend, may have gone. And, the blue death riding after them.

He arrived late in the day. The camp, characterized by domed hogans made from ocotillo branches, clearly showed distress. He found his father's old friend Noah Piyahgonte, who exhibited signs of having been beaten.

"My father's friend, and mine. What has happened?" Duncan asked, trying to emulate the formal way his father and the Indian leader spoke to one another.

"Young Duncan. It is bad. Aaron rode off with some braves without permission. A patrol of soldiers rode in. I would not tell where my son had gone. They beat me and took my nephew, Thomas Agave, with them. I did not resist. If I had, they would have killed me, then started on the band. I believe they will torture and kill the boy to find out where Aaron is. The chief of the soldiers said if we follow, they will kill all of us and bring more soldiers to destroy this village. He is an evil man and has no honor. But I believe his words."

"I will go after Thomas first. They better not try to kill me. I am known to President Roosevelt in Washington. If they kill me, the survivors will feel Roosevelt's wrath. I promise you, Father," Duncan said, using the term of respect to the leader. The man, only slightly older than Angus Duncan, nodded.

"Which way did they go and how long ago?"

Noah Piyahgonte painfully raised a powerful right arm and pointed northeast.

"They left with Thomas a short time ago," he said.

"Father, I need to ride fast. Will you ask a brave to unload and watch my packhorse until I return? I came prepared for a long trail, and still believe it will be such," Duncan said.

Noah motioned for a brave to take the lead to Bub. Duncan spun Ace and galloped off in the direction the soldiers had gone.

Ace was fresh and Duncan pushed him harder than usual. He had a bad feeling about this Indian teen.

It was hard country to track in. But, then, so was most of Arizona. Duncan did not know the difference, having only tracked in Arizona Territory. Periodically, he would dismount and look at displaced stones, hoofprints, drag marks, and broken branches. The US Army did not think about hiding its trail. They were the Army; who would deign follow them?

Duncan scowled. "Ask Missus Custer how underestimating the Indians worked out for her late husband," he said to himself.

Despite a great deal of respect for Rynning, Brodie and Roosevelt, nothing he had seen about the Army in general in the recent war had impressed him. Quite the contrary.

Duncan blew the air out of his nose and, raising his face upwards, sniffed in a lungful of air. He smelled horse and wood smoke. His smell was not as refined as his father's nor as any Indian's. But he knew there must be a camp close. He could smell horses suggested to him it was more than several. So, either a cavalry patrol or gang of outlaws, one as deadly and unpredictable as the other.

He circled off the trail and soon spotted the camp. Horses were hobbled but still saddled. Krag carbines were still in their scabbards. While coffee was brewing on a campfire, the primary focus of attention was on what was happening to the young man tied to a tree. A big trooper was punching him in the face or stomach each time the officer asked a question, without regard to the answer.

Their operational security was so lax Duncan quietly rode in without anyone turning. He slid off his horse, badge shining in the Arizona sun and coat open.

A soldier saw him and ran for the rifle on his horse as the others turned towards him.

Duncan drew both guns with almost identical speed.

"Arizona Ranger. Anybody pulls and ten of you will die before I go down. I give you my word on it."

The lieutenant motioned for the men to stand down and approached Duncan.

"I don't care who you are. This is Army business. You interfere and you will be tied to the other tree or dead, you understand me?"

"You are holding one Thomas Agave. I have a warrant for his arrest from the Attorney General of this Territory. So, under federal territorial law, he has been mine since the warrant was signed several days ago," Duncan lied.

"Where is this damned warrant?" the officer asked curtly.

"In Prescott. They contacted me to arrest him by telegraph. And, I will take him into custody. Right damned now. You are beating my prisoner and I will not stand for it."

With an intentional flourish, Duncan twirled both six-guns and slid them into the greased holsters.

"Maybe you want to pull your girly little .38 Colt on me and be the first one here to see hell, soldier boy? I might go down, but I'll take a bunch of soldiers with me after you and survivors will be court-martialed and you will be buried in dishonor. I'm game, you ass. Make your move."

After almost a minute, the lieutenant turned to his men. "If he's got a warrant signed by the Attorney General of a federal territory, we have to release the prisoner to him. Cut him down."

He turned to Duncan.

"I am First Lieutenant Nicholas Smoot. Remember my name, because you are on my list now, boy. I will be looking for ways to screw you over. Got it?" the officer growled at Duncan, trying to save face in front of his men.

Duncan walked close to the officer and spoke in measured tones audible only to the man in blue.

"My name is James Duncan, Sergeant of the Arizona Rangers. You better keep ten or so troopers close to you for a long time. And, they better be good with those silly little guns in the awkward holsters. Because I will remember you. And, I suspect I will be coming for you for what you did to this kid. And, when you get out of federal prison, you won't have any fancy-ass bars on your shoulders. If you make it to prison. And, if you make it out of prison. Don't mess with me, Smoot. You are way out of your league. Now, give me my damn prisoner. One of your men goes for a rifle or revolver and I will promise you this: I will kill you first, him second and the next eight as fast as I can cock and fire."

Thomas Agave could not mount his pony. Duncan dropped his hands by his revolvers and nodded to the nearest trooper who frowned and helped him up.

Duncan did not trust the soldiers in the least, especially the officer who had been embarrassed and likely soiled himself.

He bade Thomas ride slowly in front. Ace backed smartly along the trail, enough sideways that Duncan could see the camp and pull and fire if necessary. It was not, but he would take no chances until the boy was safe.

"Thomas, I am Aaron's friend. My name is James. What did they do to you?"

Duncan, in looking at the Yavape, in his late teens, could see a variety of wounds but not determine cause except for the fist-battered face.

"For a long time, they tied my feet and dragged me behind my pony. Then, they questioned and beat me. Nothing more," he said.

"Dragging and beating's more than enough. I am not going to take you to camp. I am going to take you to Prescott and get you some medical help. Then, I am going to try to do something about the damn officer. Can you ride for another five hours today?" Duncan asked.

"If it gets me away from the soldiers, I will ride as long as it takes."

Knowing the patrol had no scouts, only uniformed troopers and a sergeant and the lieutenant, Duncan did not fear they would be tracked...only ridden down fast. So, he and Thomas veered off the main trail and picked their way through rocky terrain which was slower but had a number of draws and canyons they could use for cover and even high ground. He did not want to ambush the patrol and kill American soldiers, but he knew if they rode fast onto them, it would not be for friendly reasons.

The boy was suffering, though in silence. Duncan had him drink water from his extra canteen every fifteen minutes by his best reckoning. They made it to Prescott by night. The first stop was at the doctor who had so recently tended Duncan. He took the boy in and promised to watch him overnight.

Duncan woke up the telegraph operator and sent a telegram to Captain Rynning. He detailed what had happened and said he thought he had temporarily taken the Army off Noah Piyahgonte's trail. He detailed the actions of Lt. Nicholas Smoot and requested Army Judge Advocate General or Department of Justice, initiate appropriate action against him. He knew it was a long shot, but if Teddy Roosevelt got involved, it might happen.

Rynning was an old Indian fighter, as was Brodie. But both were fair and humane men. The Territorial Governor sent a telegram early the next morning to his friend in the White House.

Secretary of War Elihu Root and his judge advocate general were summoned to the Oval Office.

Root was one of the most respected administrators in government then or since and had much to do with the remaining US Territories. Notwithstanding the historic view of the Army towards the Indians, he correctly read the not-too-subtle wishes of the president. Before the coffee was cold, Articles of Court-Martial and an arrest warrant were drawn for Lt. Smoot. A major from the JAG Corps was detailed to go to Prescott by train and, with a Deputy US Marshal and Sergeant James Duncan, to execute the warrant against Smoot and bring him in to be held in the brig until tried.

When he heard by wire later in the day, Duncan was pleased but skeptical. The Army had killed far too many Indian men, women and children to make such a big deal about roughing up a teen and later releasing him to a lawman. Smoot, Duncan reckoned, had chosen the wrong man to mess with in the form of the president.

If he resisted arrest, so be it. He would not lose a moment of sleep about bringing a bad man in power down, even permanently.

Duncan knew the Army would still feel compelled to go after Aaron. He knew, too, he would do all he could to make sure would not prove a successful venture. Time was the critical factor. Would another patrol be mounted while he was bringing in Smoot? Would he lose precious time in catching up with his friend and helping him to escape to Canada, the best place out of reach of the Army? Duncan did not consider Mexico. He did not want President Porfirio Diaz to put Colonel Kosterlitzky on Aaron's trail.

He rode by the ranch for a quick breakfast with his family and fiancée before riding back to Noah's camp, recovering Bub and getting on Aaron's trail as quickly as he could.

Five hours hard riding later, he conferred with Noah, telling him he had recovered his nephew and the boy was under a doctor's care in Prescott. He advised the leader his father would bring Thomas back to him as soon as he was fit to ride.

The good news was Noah Piyahgonte had sent another brave on Aaron's trail to advise him of what happened and while watching his backtrail for soldiers, he should slow so Duncan could catch him and the two could decide where his final destination should be. Noah, knowing his son would pick the hardest to trail terrain for his ride, told the brave to drop subtle signs along the way the Army would likely miss, but Duncan would not. The ranger thanked his father's old friend. would ease his run to catch Aaron and his braves.

Duncan made camp with the Yavape for the night. The next morning, he was surprised to hear hoofbeats. His .30-30 at ready, he lowered it as Angus Duncan and Thomas Agave rode into camp. Noah, too, lowered his rifle. His nephew, looking much better than the day before, but still moving stiffly, stood before him. Both gazed at one another and the uncle nodded approval. The boy nodded and stepped back so Angus could speak.

"Thank you, my friend, for bringing my nephew back," Noah said to the Scot.

"Aye. It was my son who did the hard part. I have a message for him you are sure to like, Mastava."

Angus turned to his son.

"A Major Simpson from the Judge Advocate General's Corps arrives in Prescott tomorrow. You are to meet him and proceed to wherever the hell Smoot is and take him in custody. A deputy US marshal sent from Washington by the president himself will be in Prescott late tomorrow also, Lad. You are also authorized one experienced scout. He will tag along to see how well he taught ye o'er the years. I ken you know his name?" Angus said.

"Aye, Pa. Don't worry. You can cut the signs. I'll ride and learn. This is no time for a rookie mistake," the younger Duncan said, slipping back into Scot, as he often did with his parents.

The two Duncans turned to the Yavape leader. He gave an imperceptible nod. They knew this meant he was pleased with the plan from Washington. They had venison for breakfast and fry bread. Duncan had brought coffee and it was brewed and served. Father and son left after two hours, Bub in tow. Before leaving, it had been decided the brave who had located Aaron would return along his backtrail and advise the young man of developments. He would instruct him to find a safe hideaway and await the ranger's arrival after the Army officer was delivered to Prescott. Then, Duncan would go with the brave to Aaron's location and help him plan a getaway to Canada.

Away from the long reach of the Army until things settled down.

James and Angus Duncan arrived back at the ranch in time for dinner. Miranda did not withhold her emotions and rushed to the ranger's arms for a long embrace.

They spoke at dinner.

"Miranda, I will see you whenever we bring this officer back for court-martial. I hope I can leave testimony in the form of a deposition and can swing by here, see you and reload the packhorse and begin what could be a long trail. Hopefully, one of the last long trails. At least, this should not be a dangerous one," Duncan said.

"I will proceed with Mary Louise Brodie and your mother planning the wedding," she said, "with everything but setting a date. If you are gone over a week, I may have to return to Wickenburg and my students. My cottage is free to me as the teacher, so while I am there, I will see if the school committee will allow us to build a small corral and stable on the property. I can't see why they would object; it would add value to their land. And, it would be cheaper for us to build one and leave it when we go than to find a ranch to lease in Wickenburg. If we do that, we should have most of our nest egg intact for our real ranch near here."

"I hear the Hattons who own the half section part way between us and town are thinking of moving back East. Seems her mother in Arkansas died and left them a farm there. It's producing, unlike most around here. The three hundred twenty acres is part woods a few acres away from the house. The house is on mostly desert land like here. There is one canyon. The property has enough grass and water to sustain a few cattle or horses," Angus offered.

"What is the house like?" Miranda asked.

"Not much. They should have put the house near the woods instead of the scrubby land they built on. I'd build a new house near the canyon and scrape a road in there. Then, I'd burn the old house down. Otherwise, it would attract all sorts of vermin. Two-legged, four-legged and slide on the belly type, too."

She shivered at the last and asked, "Angus, how far a ride is it to the school in town?"

"It's on the same road as this...I 'spect it's about two, two and a half miles. 'Less there's an unusually big snow, it is not bad."

"If this county sheriff thing works out, we can ride in together and I'll swing by and pick you up on the way back from the Sheriff's Office," her fiancé added.

Continuing, Duncan thought aloud, "I wonder if any of the wood from the house would be salvageable for use in building a new house?"

"I wouldna fool with it. Last time I was there it looked half rotten, and I have a mind it's infested with some sort of bugs. A little coal oil and a match would be just the thing to fix it," Angus opined.

"The Army man and the deputy US marshal from Washington are due in on the five o'clock Santa Fe train. Pa, do you have time to ride over and talk to old man Hatton after breakfast?"

"Aye, son. I think it might be good to cement a deal. Prescott is growing and this is one of the closest ranches with any land close to the town. I'm pretty certain, it won't stick on the market long once word gets out," Angus said.

Ann spoke, having held her opinion too long. "It would be good if Miranda and I went, too. I take Missus Hatton some canned vegetables every now and then. It's been a while. Her husband has worked himself nigh to death trying to farm a cattle ranch. But, the land by the house is not fertile. They hardly get enough vegetables to live on. Thank heavens they have some chickens for meat and eggs and the old bony dairy cow."

"I am for going also, Ann. If I am going to live there, I'd like to see the lay of the land and visualize the ride to Prescott," Miranda said.

Angus nodded as he tamped tobacco into his pipe and scratched a match along the rough edge of his boot to light it.

"Maybe after," Duncan began, "we can have lunch at the cafe—on me—and Pa can bring y'all back. I need to spend some time at the Sheriff's Office and check the telegraph for messages from the captain. By the time all's done, I'll meet the two Washington men at the Santa Fe station and walk them over to the hotel. Then, I'll come back here for the night. Pa, I figure, we'll let them get an early breakfast and we'll all hit the trail, don't you think?"

"Aye, son. That's exactly what I think."

13

The Santa Fe train arrived. Duncan stood back and observed. Of the small crowd that disembarked, two men stood out. They were together. One was in an Army major's uniform, the other in a suit and tie. Both were handsome men, of average height and fit builds. Their ages were similar. Probably early forties. Their medium brown handlebar mustaches were virtually identical.

Duncan, his coat open to show the ranger badge despite the evening's cold temperature, stepped forward. He extended his hand to Major Simpson first.

"Evening, gents," he said. "Sergeant James Duncan, Arizona Rangers."

"Hello. Henry Simpson, JAG Corps," the uniformed man said as he shook Duncan's hand. Duncan looked closely at the man, realizing he had seen him before.

"Were you in Cuba?" Duncan asked.

"I was. I was a lieutenant and just behind you on the way up Kettle Hill. Saw you draw and save Rynning and then the president twice," the major said.

"Just lucky shots," Duncan said. The Army man just shook his head.

"Deputy US Marshal Bud Roth. Assigned to the White House for special duties. Like this," the man in the suit said. He opened his coat to show a silver crescent-topped star.

"Glad to meet y'all and we appreciate you coming way out here to help correct a wrong. I believe what happened to the young Yavapai Indian boy was wrong as hell. Nobody deserves to be dragged miles by a horse then beaten senseless."

"Well, Sergeant, we'll bring him in and give him a fair court-martial and see," Simpson said.

"First off, did you gentlemen eat on the train?" Duncan asked.

"We did. And, it wasn't half bad. We've been fed well all the way out from Washington," Roth said.

Duncan nodded and turned to Simpson. "Better than we had from Tampa to Cuba and all the way back to New York State, I bet," he said. The major grinned. "Helluva lot better." Duncan nodded in agreement.

"Since y'all ate, let's walk over and get you settled in your hotel. If you'd eat early, we'd like to hit the trail around seven tomorrow morning. We will have the Sheriff of Yavapai County and one of the top former scouts during the first part of the Arizona Indian Wars helping me cut sign and find this patrol. I understand they left before word to hold in place at the fort arrived. The party led by Aaron Piyahgonte has a pretty good lead on them and I know where they will be going, so the trailing to catch up with Lieutenant Smoot won't be too hard. He's not trying to hide his trail. I'm an okay tracker, but the man who taught me is better. And, he is our scout. Angus Duncan."

"Kin?" Bud Roth asked.

"Yep. My Pa."

They arrived at the hotel and Duncan left as soon as they checked in. He noted neither man had bedrolls or much in the way of camping gear. He and Pa would take care of at dawn from gear both had. The Duncan ranch had sufficient horses and saddles to cover needs. They agreed one pack horse would suffice. It would be a short trail to get the lieutenant into custody. They had spoken on the way to the hotel and the JAG major said he would take command and they would head back to Prescott to the fort, dismiss the patrol and place Smoot in the brig to await the military trial.

During dinner, the family speculated about how a branch of the service so determined to exterminate a population of people would opine in the case of one officer who had abused but not killed one Indian. After all, Crook was considered a hero in the Army. Yet, Angus said, what he and others had done was planned genocide, pure and simple.

It was his son's feeling, or perhaps hope, the very human president's influence might impact the trial enough for justice to be served. His father feared not. The proof, Angus noted, would be in the pudding.

The next morning, two women watched their men leave on what may be a dangerous trail. The older one had experienced the feelings before, but not for a while. To the younger woman, it was different. She was more used to being with her man in the face of danger. Of having his back. She did not like him leaving her behind. She was his partner. Soon to be officially.

They rode off, Duncan leading two saddled quarter horses, Angus leading Bub with his pack of food, tarps, cooking gear and bedrolls.

The two Washington men were waiting outside the hotel. Roth had a Savage 99 and a pair of valises for saddlebag items. Major Simpson had a valise, but his pistol belt was obvious on his uniform this morning. It did not take long to transfer valise items to the empty saddlebags on the two quarter horses and mount up. Duncan noticed the major wore a .45 Colt's Army not unlike his own, instead of the issue .38 double action. Rank has its privilege, he thought.

Angus introduced himself and Duncan introduced Sheriff Jim Roberts, already a greatly respected but atypical gunfighter. Roberts, a taciturn man, had first been appointed deputy by Buckey O'Neill. He was noted for not wearing a holster. He carried his Frontier Model Colt in his pants pocket. He was famous, too, for raising but never riding, fine horses. On patrol, he preferred the mule tied to the hitching post outside the hotel. Simpson noted but, kept his smile to himself, knowing General Crook always rode mules, too. A habit quite unbecoming a general officer. Or, any officer, Simpson thought.

Duncan, his father, and Roberts greeted each other warmly in what was one of the few times Roberts spoke for the next several days. He was quiet, but an efficient lawman, perhaps more comfortable as a deputy on his own than the acting administrator in charge of a sheriff's department. Which, Duncan realized, may have been why Brodie was so convinced he was going to soon have to appoint a new Sheriff of Yavapai County. Roberts was known as a deadly shot with the scarred nickel Colt's revolver. From what was showing out of his jeans pocket, it looked as worn and unkempt as Chris Madsen's...clear evidence appearances can be very deceiving.

Roberts' actions in the fifteen-year Pleasant Valley range war before beginning the peace officer part of his life would play a role in a book by Zane Gray. The war resulted in the deaths of as many as fifty men and an unknown but significant number were at Roberts' hand.

Duncan had studied Roberts from his first own appointment into law enforcement in 1892 by Buckey O'Neill. Roberts' approach was different than the one Duncan had evolved. Duncan drew fast and fired fast, using Bill Tilghman's efficient stance. His aim was unerring. As was Roberts'. But Roberts took his time, avoiding the first shot fired by his adversary and carefully preempting a second shot by shooting the gunman in the head with his .44. It was, Duncan decided, an example of the interplay between cold nerves, accuracy, faith in the other man's inherent lack of shooting ability. And pure-ass luck. He also took solace in the fact he and Roberts, the two most deadly lawmen in Arizona, worked together on the same side.

The five-man posse rode to the fort and began their trail from there. The commanding officer was not pleased. One of his officer's name was on a warrant, but he held his opinion from the senior legal officer with the warrant.

Angus Duncan, in a man-tracking mode his son had never seen, rode with his well-used 1873 Winchester .38-40 carbine in hand, frequently bending down from his paint, Beau, to "cut sign", or dismounting to study tracks for dust blown in to help estimate how fresh the track was. It was rough country, with rocky ground, canyons and scrub trees which did not lend to easy tracking. But, as in the case when Duncan first rode out, the Army was not trying to hide its trail. The men threw cigarette butts and bits of wrappers along the way. Their horses left prints where the ground would indent, but moreover left droppings. They were easy for the Duncans to age by hardness and odor. A number of times, both scout and lawman dismounted and examined evidence of passage, the older explaining the reasoning behind his estimate of age and the younger one either agreeing or asking for further details. Roberts watched and approved, saying nothing, as usual. The deputy US marshal watched also. He had been a manhunter back East, but not a man-tracker. His observations were with interest more than contributory experience.

Smoot picked the easiest path, so Angus did too. James Duncan watched his father put his teachings to work. He did not learn much he did not already know but took pride in seeing the master tracker work for real instead of teaching a boy.

By the end of the day, Angus told the rest he thought they were less than half a day behind. The patrol, he said, seemed to be in no hurry and did not have a trained scout.

The ranger shared, knowing the direction Aaron Piyahgonte was heading, the patrol was offcourse by large measure.

The posse stopped for the night. As usual for the high desert country with its red and orange hues, no rain was in sight. Angus and Duncan quickly pulled the tarps off Bub and erected several shelters then spread bedrolls out. Roberts unrolled his own from the mule and placed it under a pinon a few feet away from the rest.

Duncan built a fire and set up the iron tripod for coffee and the grill supported by several large flat stones for cooking. He fell back on his usual trail fare of beans, bacon, coffee and biscuits. Nobody complained, the Easterners more interested in resting sore muscles not used in Washington.

"Pa, do you think we need a sentry?" Duncan asked.

"Only against rustlers...no hostile Indians around here. The patrol is ahead and likely bedded down for the night.

Maybe you and I will take turns keeping a wee bit of a watch."

Duncan nodded and agreed to take the first half. He leaned against a rock outcropping and wrapped his blanket around himself and his carbine. A cacophony of snores soon joined the night sounds. Duncan lay awake, listening and watching. And, thinking about Miranda.

***

The following day, the posse continued to the northwest, heading to increasingly higher ground towards the seventy-five-hundred-foot Mohon peak. Angus noted to his son and Roberts the horse droppings were fresher and the tracks, when seen, had less dust blown in. He figured they were an hour or two behind the Army patrol by lunch. The men drank water from their canteens and munched biscuits and jerky as they rode through lunch. It would buy them the hour or so the patrol would spend stopping to eat.

By three in the afternoon, the posse caught the patrol. The three lawmen made sure their badges were prominently displayed and Major Simpson moved to the head of the group, hailing the patrol in a command voice the posse had not yet heard.

"Patrol. This is Major Henry Simpson, from Headquarters Army in Washington. You will halt forthwith."

They did, and a confused and agitated Lieutenant Nicholas Smoot turned his horse and rode back towards them frowning. He moved to adjust his revolver and Duncan drew in a blur and said, "Don't touch your gun, Smoot, or by God in heaven you will die on your horse right now."

"I would take the ranger's advice, Lieutenant," Simpson said. Raising his voice, he called, "Sergeant, dismount your men and stand at ease by your horses while we transact official business here."

"Lieutenant, I have brought a warrant for your arrest, signed by the Judge Advocate General of the Army in Washington, DC. You are charged with exacting cruel and excessive punishment on a person you illegally took prisoner. His name is Thomas Agave and he sustained serious injuries and torture at your hand. You acted against US Army regulations and in a way unbecoming to an officer."

Continuing, the major said, "This is Deputy US Marshal Bud Roth. Marshal Roth will serve the warrant now. Dismount, Lieutenant."

Smoot slid off his horse, as did Roth, Duncan and Roberts. Smoot looked at Duncan. If looks could kill, Duncan would be dead from that look. The three lawmen, federal, state and county, approached him. Roth unfolded the warrant and showed it to Smoot as Roberts slipped the Colt's .38 revolver out of the officer's butt-forward flap holster. Duncan took Smoot's wrists and clamped the iron nippers on. The man seemed to be in a trance, so shocked he was at the turn of events.

Finally, he managed to blurt out, "He was a damn Indian. This is wrong."

The major looked at him and said, slowly enunciating, "He is a boy. What you did, Smoot, was wrong. And, the President of these United States, in reviewing this matter, would argue with you on the point of who the boy is. He called him a human being, not an Indian. The president was appalled at your actions, as am I. I would advise you to hold your tongue for your own good. Anything you say from this moment on is going to be read into the transcript of the court-martial."

Smoot started to open his mouth, and Simpson held up a hand, saying, "Shut the hell up, Smoot. And, I am not requesting. It's a direct damned order."

Roberts, wordless but careful, patted around Smoot's waist and his boot tops, where he extracted a small dagger. Under the eyes of the stunned patrol, he flipped it a couple times in his right hand and then threw it at a tree twenty feet away. The knife stuck perfectly in the tree and quivered for a second as Duncan walked over to retrieve in, grinning at Roberts. He handed the knife back to Roberts, hilt first.

Simpson walked over to the patrol to address the sergeant. The federal lawman walked with him, backing his move.

"Sergeant, this is a serious matter. Should I have any concern any of you will try to intercede on Smoot's behalf?" he said.

The sergeant spoke, "No, sir. We follow orders. But it don't mean we like or respect everybody giving them. We had orders to bring them Indians in because they jumped the rez. But, it's all they did. The lieutenant, he was gonna have us kill them all and say they shot first. Some of us were in action like before and it don't sit well with us. We ain't gonna give you no trouble. We will ride protective escort back with you, if it's okay, Major."

"It's quite okay, Sergeant. Let's mount up and get some riding towards the fort at Prescott done before dark. Then, we will make it in by tomorrow night and your men will sleep in a barracks instead of on the cold ground."

The sergeant snapped to attention. "Yes, sir."

"Dismissed sergeant. Have your men mount up and wheel their horses about. We will be underway shortly." Simpson walked back to the lawmen and scout. He nodded and mounted his horse, liking the Western saddle more every day than the hornless McClellan military saddle.

Roberts and Duncan went through Smoot's tack and made sure there were no weapons hidden in the saddle, bags, or the binocular case. They removed his carbine and put it on Bub with their other gear.

They rode until dusk and stopped for the night. The sergeant had his men set up camp. Simpson had him detail an armed guard to watch Smoot all night, spelled by another around two in the morning. The Duncans and Roberts watched the watchers from their adjacent bed-rolls. All three were confident the most the Army would do was give Smoot a slap on the wrist. None of the three would have lamented it if he tried to break away.

The trip had been largely through desert, punctuated by saguaro cacti, sand and tumbleweed. The trees were few and far between much of the way. There were, however, thickly growing short junipers and the occasional creosote, or greasewood plants.

They had not seen the usual rabbits, rattlers, or lizards due to the winter weather.

The best campground Angus located, scouting ahead of the column was barren at best. While the soldiers gathered enough fuel for a rudimentary fire, the arresting party pitched camp. Duncan ranged out and, taking his hatchet, hacked down several four-foot junipers and two creosotes. Back at camp, the former was reduced to a pile of branches and a smaller pile of kindling. Creosote branches were added to the latter pile. Using his trowel, Duncan carefully scraped away the frozen surface and dug one two-foot diameter hole and one a half a foot wide, and a foot and a half away. He connected the two with a trench several inches deep. He improvised, covering the trench with flat stones, as the sand was not solid enough for a tunnel. Building a pyramid of creosote and juniper kindling he dragged his ferrocerium rod along the top of his knife, showering sparks onto a bit of charcloth from a tin he carried. Once he had a glowing coal, he transferred it to underneath the kindling until a flame arose. He blew out the glow on the charcloth and returned it to his air-proof sealed tin. Duncan fanned and blew on the fire until it flamed sufficiently to accept the larger junipers. The main fire grew hotter yet with limited smoke as the heat of the fire drew superheated air in through the small pit and improvised tunnel.

Angus laid a large canteen and the cooking kit from Bud, on the ground beside the larger hole. His son placed the grill from the kit on the hole, filled a coffee pot with five handfuls of coffee and a whole pot of water and set it on the grill to brew. He split the remaining biscuits and arranged them on the grill to toast. There was no meat left, so Duncan set out a container of honey.

The wind on the desert picked up. The five posse men crouched around the fire and wrapped cold hands around hot metal coffee mugs and ate biscuits and wild honey for dinner.

One of the troopers played a harmonica until he was drowned out by coyote songs. All were asleep before the moon was at full height, except for the sentry and at least one of the lawmen.

It was a long cold night on the trail, the faint scent of the junipers riding on the wind, with the occasional sound of a hunting owl. Even the coyotes ceased their calls after a while.

The next day was a repeat of the earlier one, except

the riders encountered more grass and trees. They still pressed on to make the fort by dark. Once arrived, Simpson claimed rooms in the officer's quarters for himself and Roth. Smoot was locked in the brig.

***

The Duncans started home to the ranch. Roberts rode his mule back towards Prescott after a nod to the Duncans. "A good man, but a loner with a badge, not a leader," Angus observed. His son nodded silently.

During the ride to the fort, Simpson had said he would organize the court-martial and it would be held at Prescott. He would bring in officers of major and above grade from several other Arizona Territory bases to serve on the tribunal. He would act as judge, representing his supervisor, the Judge Advocate General of the Army.

The Army would still go after the Piyahgonte band and bring them in, albeit hopefully without the violence that Smoot planned. The fact they had left their assigned area was still punishable. Both Duncan men took this information with stone faces, giving away nothing.

The ranger mentioned to Simpson he had a major case and wondered if his testimony could be in sworn transcript form instead of testifying. Simpson told him to come to the fort the following day to be deposed. Duncan agreed.

As the three rode back towards Prescott from the fort, they spoke privately.

"Pa and sheriff, I am going to ride after Aaron and his band and guide them away from this part of the world. I'm thinking they need to go to Canada, out of the Army's reach. What do you think?"

"I think you are right, son. They will get brig, if not

prison time. The overall feeling of the Army towards In-dians is still pretty negative. When your ancestor charged the damn English, he yelled 'Freedom.' It's been our cry ever since. These boys deserve freedom like any other human. If you want to quietly guarantee they get it, I will support you all the way."

Roberts nodded his head up and down once.

"I will come into town tomorrow after the deposition and spend some time at the Carnegie Library. I don't know much about Canada or its Indians, but I will before I hit the trail," Duncan said.

14

ARIZONA TERRITORY
WESTERN STATES AND CANADA
1904

Duncan rode into the fort and tied Ace outside the head-quarters building. He went in and a corporal showed him to the room Major Simpson was using. There was a scribe present. Much like a law enforcement interview, Simpson set the tone with some preemptive inquiries and got Duncan talking. The scribe wrote quickly, interrupting several times to ask for clarification. Simpson did also, to make sure the items he wanted in the deposition stood out.

At the end of his comments, Duncan was asked to raise his hand and if he "swore the testimony he had given was the truth, the whole truth, and nothing but the truth, so help him God." He said "yes", lowered his aching right arm and signed the deposition. Major Simpson had a lieutenant witness it and Duncan shook hands with him and departed.

Half an hour later, he was seated at the Carnegie Library in Prescott. He had been lucky, finding a tome on the indigenous tribes of Canada. He wanted to take the party by way of California due to the enhanced rail service offered there compared to riding straight up through New Mexico or Nevada into Idaho. While there were more people along the California to Oregon to Washington route, the trip would be much faster. He already planned on using some of his Mason jar grubstake to get the braves haircuts, jeans and shirts and coats and train tickets.

Angus had a horse he did not like. Duncan would ride him with an old saddle and, with Aaron and his braves, sell the horses at the stepping off point in California. They would get more horses in Canada.

Duncan's research pinpointed the Nlaka'pamux people. As he read about the land around the Nicola River and its confluence with the Thompson, he began to settle on a probable destination. The Cook's Ferry Band seemed to be right. Demographically, they had more women than men, and no light horsemen to enforce tribal law. Aaron's party could fill those needs. Or, so Duncan hoped fervently.

He headed back to the ranch, told his fiancée and parents if they did not know where he was going, they would not have to lie about it if the Army came. Duncan and Miranda walked out to the corral and he unsaddled and brushed Ace, talking to him and telling him to behave and he would return as soon as possible. Miranda watched, a wry smile on her lips as he spoke to the horse. Then, Ace shook his head and whinnied loudly in acknowledgment. Miranda's smile faded into a look of disbelief.

"Honey, I don't know how long this trail will be, but I do not expect it to be particularly dangerous. I have had to withdraw some of our money, but it's for a longtime friend who needs it badly. I have a plan to get him away safely and return with nobody the wiser. I have sent a bogus wire to Captain Rynning saying who I was after. He will know from the name it's a dodge and I am on the assignment he gave me. I expect you will have to return to Wickenburg to resume teaching before I get back. So, I will come directly back there to you," he said.

"How long do you think you'll be gone?" she asked.

"No more'n a month. I cannot send you telegrams or letters along the way, because any good Army investigator can track me by the postmarks. So, just know I am okay and thinking about you every minute."

She nodded and stood close to him, coat to coat. "Hopefully, spring will have sprung by the time a month has passed. We'll be able to walk and take rides and have picnics," Miranda whispered.

He nodded and lowered his lips to the level of hers and kept them there for a long time. They walked back in the house and he picked up a cold camp food bag. Lots of biscuits, jerky, coffee and some flour, salt and pepper. Both canteens were full. He had four boxes of cartridges for his carbine and sufficient rounds for his revolver. Angus had saddled the black gelding, Charlie, for his son to ride and sell. The ranger turned and rode due west into the rolling scrub hills. He stopped at Noah's camp and told him he would advise of Aaron's whereabouts when he got back, thinking of the treatment Smoot had dealt out trying to obtain Aaron's location before. Noah gave Duncan a medicine bag to give to his son. He knew it was not likely he would ever see him again, but the warrior did not show the emotion Duncan knew he was experiencing.

Duncan nodded and rode north along the trail the other brave had directed him. He made one camp and rode into Aaron's hidden camp at twilight the following night, whistling a familiar signal first.

Around a fire, Duncan shared his plan and Aaron looked up their destination in the library book Duncan had checked out. The next morning, they set out at dawn. Los Angeles and the train were roughly three hundred fifty miles due west. There, they would sell their horses and buy cowman clothes and Stetson hats to cover newly short cut hair. Aaron and his small band would portray Indian cowmen looking for more work. Then, they would get on a northbound train to San Francisco, Eugene, Portland and Seattle. At Seattle, they would buy horses and saddles and ride into Canada. They would offer their services to the chief at Cook's Ferry. Given success at placing Aaron and his men with the band, Duncan would retrace his trip, with the new horse in a stock car. He would get off the train at Los Angeles and ride to Wickenburg. And, Miranda.

***

Horses sold and Aaron's party looking more like cowmen than a marauding war party, they got on the train at Lost Angeles and began their journey of several days to Seattle. The two friends worked with the braves on their English and on how to live in both the white man's world and Indian country at the same time. Duncan shared the Cook's Ferry Band, according to the book in his hand, grew maize, beans and squash and fished for salmon, primarily in the rapids of the Thompson River.

Once the train had moved out of Los Angeles, Duncan had the Yavape split up and sit in available seats in different cars to be less remembered as a group. He was not sure it made any difference but was doing everything he could think of to reduce the image of one white man escorting a group of Indians up the West Coast, should the Army send an investigator. It had been sufficiently long, he knew, since California had experienced Indian raids. The prejudices were less than in Arizona, where every adult remembered experiencing the terror or hearing about it from family and friends.

The dining car food was new to the braves as were the plates and utensils. Duncan went to the diner first and ordered a luncheon plate and returned to his seat. Moving the braves to the far end of the sparsely crowded car, he demonstrated how to use the knife and fork and eat off a plate. The braves laughed at him spearing pieces of meat and potatoes instead of more easily be picking them up in one's fingers. He agreed but told them it was good information for them to have in the future. Aaron tried to seriously corroborate his friend's words, but had some difficulty keeping a straight face. The most difficult barrier facing Duncan was to have the braves place their rifles in a corner, rather than holding them, sheathed with fringed, beaded buckskin scabbards, on their laps all the time. The carbines were a combination of 1866 Winchester "Yellow Boy" .44 rimfires and 1873s in various calibers. All had brass beads decorating buttstocks and fore ends.

Duncan understood they felt as odd as he did when he changed trains in New York City, coming home from the war, but he did not want any hint of wildness or threat to be remembered. Not only was his concern for his friends, but also for himself for aiding and abetting fugitives from the US government.

The young men had made good progress in their eating and interactive skills during the several days preceding their arrival in Seattle, Washington.

Seattle marked the spending of the remainder of their

grubstake. They had five hundred dollars Duncan had withdrawn from his Mason jar bank. The money from the sale of the horses in California had purchased the rail transportation, including food, and clothes. Duncan kept the saddle he rode in on and the money from his father's horse separate.

They added heavy canvas flannel-lined chore coats to their newly acquired clothing and bought horses and a variety of used saddles and tack. Duncan put his saddle on a strong-looking quarter horse. It was a brown and white paint. He knew Angus would like the horse in exchange for the one he had ridden to San Diego. The small party avoided the ferry and rode into Canada surreptitiously by a more eastern route, doubling back towards the Thompson River Canyon and the confluence of the Thompson and Nicola Rivers.

Late in the day, Aaron Piyahgonte rode alone into the village to ask for sanctuary. He met with Chief Tetlenitsa and described his situation and his men. He offered for all to work hard hunting, farming or as light horsemen, policing the area for the Band. They smoked and spoke, and the chief considered. He told Aaron to go to his men and the white "Mountie" and he would look at them in the morning and give his decision.

As Aaron rode back towards the woods, he saw a tall, very beautiful young woman watching him. She had a most comely form. He turned to her and doffed his new Stetson. The waning sun reflected off her long black hair. She reddened, but smiled beautifully, her teeth white and perfect. "How did Duncan know this?" he wondered as the rode back to where his friends waited.

"Duncan, did you somehow arrange for a beautiful woman to hide behind a tree and smile at me in the village?" Aaron asked, a look of mock seriousness on his face.

"Me? Nope. Must have been your good looks and charm. I had nothing to do with it."

Which Aaron knew, logically, to be true. But it still was close to the description of the beautiful women his friend had promised. Just in case, Aaron determined he would look into the situation on this one. What if she was the only one like her? He determined to be first in line. The rest of his life was a long time, and a tall beauty with long, glossy black hair and a beautiful smile would be a good way to spend it.

He continued with his friends. "I spoke with the chief. He said to come in after sunrise and he will look us over and decide." They made a hasty camp and ate prepared foods brought from Seattle. They slept, Aaron thinking about the tall young woman and Duncan thinking of Miranda. As soon as the chief agreed to taking the party in, Duncan planned to bid farewell to his friend and reverse his trip to California, then ride to Wickenburg and start building a temporary corral and shelter barn on the school-owned property.

The next morning, after coffee and a simple breakfast of fry bread with honey, they rode into the Cook's Ferry Band's village. Everyone was up and, and apparently, awaiting them.

Aaron led the horsemen in and dismounted at the chief's cabin.

He greeted the chief and introduced his friend Duncan first.

Duncan did not extend his hand, rather he nodded solemnly and stood tall as the chief appraised him.

"You are like a Mountie?" Chief Tetlenitsa asked.

"Yes, Grandfather, I am a policeman for the State of Arizona, many rides south of here. Aaron has been my closest friend for over ten years."

"Are these men your prisoners?" the chief asked. "I understand your Army is in search of them."

"No, they are not anyone's prisoners. They are my friends. As you have noticed, they have their rifles. Prisoners would not be armed. Yes, the Army wants to speak with them because they left their reservation—or, reserve, as I believe you call it in Canada—without permission. I was asked by my chief to assist them to find sanctuary in a place the Army could not come," Duncan said.

"Will your Army send a paper to the Mounties and then they will come here?" the chief asked.

"It is possible, Grandfather, but I do not think it will happen. I think once Aaron's party is out of Arizona, they will fall out of the Army's mind and be forgotten. At least I hope so."

The chief turned to Aaron. "What does your presence offer my band, young one?"

"We offer strong bodies and willingness to hunt, fish and farm and help protect you from whatever or whoever would seek to harm anyone in your band. We just want to live free in the forest and be left alone by outsiders... much as I suspect you do," Aaron said to the chief and to the gathered band. He noticed the girl from last evening was not hiding behind a tree. Rather, she was near Chief Tetlenitsa and was watching him intently, something the ranger also noticed.

The chief nodded gravely and walked down the line the Yavape braves had formed, appraising and stopping to ask questions of each.

The chief returned to Aaron and said, "We should smoke on this. After, I will give you my decision."

As the band watched, he bade the visitors sit in a circle around a smoldering fire pit. He took a leather bag from his belt. It had cigarette tobacco in it. He took a pinch and offered it symbolically to each of the four points of the compass, uttering words in the Nlaka'pamux dialect, one foreign to the Yavape.

The old man then sat cross-legged like the young visitors and, though both Aaron and Duncan expected a pipe to appear, he poured the tobacco into a paper and rolled a cigarette. He lit it with a glowing twig from the fire and took a long draw.

Tetlenitsa then exhaled a stream of off-white smoke into the air and passed the cigarette to Aaron. Hoping he should follow the same protocol as the Yavape had, he took a shorter drag and passed it to Duncan. Each man did the same in turn, until the chief finished the butt and flicked it into the fire.

He sat there, eyes closed for several minutes, clearly considering.

When he opened his eyes, he looked at Aaron and nodded.

"We will do this thing," he said. "We will try it until the season is hot like a fire and we do not need to use our sweathouses. If then, I believe it is best for my people for you to stay, you will. If not, you will leave the day of my decision. Do you accept this?"

Aaron looked at each of his men in turn. He said to the chief ,"Yes, Grandfather, we will gladly accept your kind offer."

"You will need to have places to live. For now, they can be hogans. If you stay, you will need to make cabins before the cold weather and snow. Do you have tools to cut wood and knives to make string to use to tie the wood together to make a Hogan?"

The men turned to Aaron, but Duncan interceded. "I have a bit of money left. Where can we buy tools and what do you recommend?" he said.

"The men have good knives I see, as I look closely. They should each have several blankets, cooking gear and a good axe."

"Where can we buy these things?" Duncan asked.

"We have a small store here with such items. Anything more, you would have to ride to Kamloops." Duncan nodded his appreciation.

"I will show you our village, then we will eat and then you should begin building your hogans," Chief Tetlenitsa said.

They rose and he took them to the garden, which had mounds with vegetables growing on top.

"These are the Three Sisters. They are maize, climbing beans and squash. We fertilize the mounds with rotting fish. Once the maize gets to the chest on a man, we transplant the beans and add a stick for them to climb. Then, we plant the squash. There are two mounds for every family here. Each has to tend to its own.

"The men and women go to the river and net salmon and some trout with large dip nets. The river is swift, and we have lost men in it. The ones who go to the farthest rocks to get to deeper water are tied to the rocks so they will not fall in. We have few hunters to kill deer or bears. We do not have rifles of enough power to kill a moose or the big brown bears."

Aaron looked at Duncan, wondering what a moose was and how powerful a rifle was required to kill such a thing. Duncan looked back without any knowledge to help either.

Chief Tetlenitsa walked the men outside the village and into the woods. As luck would have it, they spied a creature having traits in common with a deer but was larger than any horse ever born.

"There is a moose," the chief said with a smile, his

arm outstretched and an arthritic forefinger pointing. "It would feed our band for a while, if we could kill one."

It was a bull, with a rack many feet across. Duncan wondered if it would laugh at his .30-30. He knew Aaron's .44 rimfire, basically a weak revolver cartridge, would just enrage the animal, and could only take a small deer at close range. He thought a buffalo gun of .45-70 or even larger would be required for the moose. Hell, he wondered, given the size of moose, how large were the bears? He knew he would be leaving his friend Aaron seriously under-gunned for Canada-sized big game and an idea was forming on what to do about it.

***

Tetlenitsa assigned a brave who had senior ranking in the band's hierarchy to instruct the men in the building of hogans. They were to build four, with Aaron having one and the others partnering. The man, a tall brave, was named Walkem. Aaron soon found via water being brought to Walkem and himself, the Indian was the father of the beautiful young woman who had occupied so many of Aaron's thoughts since seeing her on the way outside of camp at dusk.

Her name was Wenonah, which meant "first born daughter".

Walkem laid out the dimensions of the hogans with a stick driven into the dirt for each corner. While the Yavape went into the woods to cut trees and bundle saplings and evergreen boughs, Duncan took the trowel from his saddlebags and scraped and leveled the ground for the floors. When he encountered roots, he cut them with his hatchet and dug them out with the trowel. By the time the men returned with the materials to make the hogans, all four had smooth floors, swept with a spruce bough.

The hogans were all completed before dark. Duncan noticed his friend had built a wider than usual frame for his sapling and spruce bough bed. He felt compelled to look approvingly at the bed and mouth the word, "Wenonah?" Aaron looked at him sheepishly and shrugged. Nonetheless, Aaron pointed to the other side of the hogan and said, "Why don't you throw your bedroll here for the night? It is too late to start the long trip back to Arizona." Duncan heartily agreed. The two were asleep before it was totally dark.

Early the next morning, Duncan got directions to Kamloops. He rode to the town and found a general store with a rack of used rifles in the back corner. The shop-keep came over and asked what he was looking for. Duncan told him something big, in the range of a .45-70. The man removed a heavy Remington carbine.

"This should fill the bill, mister. It's a rolling block single shot carbine in .50-70. Only one round, but it loads quickly and packs a helluva punch."

"Would it be good for moose or grizzly hunting?" Duncan asked.

"Yes. If you get him hard the first shot. If either is charging, you would not have time to reload," the man said.

"Anything else this powerful?" Duncan asked.

"No, most of our sales are to fellas who want to shoot deer or keep wolves away from their livestock. This is about it. I got a .45-75 surplus Northwest Mounted Police lever gun, but it's in poor shape. The barrel and action are good, but the stock is awful," the shop-keep said.

He removed the Winchester and Duncan operated the familiar action to look inside. The action was tight, though it made the 1876's famous "clank-clank" when levered. The gun was unusual to him because it had a full-length wooden musket-style stock covering the bottom half of the barrel almost to the end. He saw the stock was cracked near the top tang and in the middle. Both could be repaired, he knew, the old buffalo hunter way: wrapped in wet buckskin and tacked when dry.

Duncan saw a price tag of twelve dollars on it.

"Do you have any cartridges for it?" Duncan asked.

"Let me look. Yes, I have three boxes."

"Can you order more, if needed?" he asked.

"Yeah, these are pretty popular around here. It's said your Teddy Roosevelt favored this gun for hunting big bears."

"Tell you what," Duncan began, "I'll give you the full price if you throw in the three boxes of shells and a leather or canvas sling."

"I can do the deal," the man said, glad to get rid of a piece of inventory which had gathered dust too long.

Duncan stopped at a café and ate and purchased food to carry on the ride to the ferry to Seattle and the first part of the train trip home.

He got back to Cook's Ferry by late afternoon, realizing he would have to spend another night there and leave in the morning. He presented the Winchester and ammunition to Aaron who was both surprised and grateful. Now, he could contribute moose meat to his adopted band.

Aaron knew what the sling was but questioned it because he had never used one. Duncan showed him how the Army had taught him to twist it around his left arm to help steady his hold for an offhand shot at a distance. He noted most of Aaron's hunting would be with his tried and true '66 Yellow Boy carbine but having a powerful backup would be good in case a big bear or a moose presented a shot of opportunity...or attacked. His friend agreed heartily.

The two worked wrapping the wrist of the stock with fine wire from the small store and using wet buckskin and fancy head brass tacks to secure the repairs and decorate the stock. When the buckskin dried, it would tightly squeeze the crack in the stock and secure it for many years to come.

By the time they were finished, the rifle was sound and ready to hunt or fight. Duncan moved the adjustable sight to its lowest position, knowing Aaron would use it on big, dangerous game at reasonable distances. He knew the rifle would hold true for a hundred yards, probably the longest shot necessary in the thick woods.

Once night had fallen, there was a feast of smoked salmon, and corn, squash and beans cooked in a big pot. It was held in commemoration of the completion of the newcomer's hogans. Some of the younger men and women—including Wenonah—presented an oral history of the Nlacka'pamux people. Aaron lamented to Duncan he had not been able to finish writing for his Yavape. Duncan promised he would work on a pardon so Aaron, hopefully with a new wife, could return to see his father and mother and complete it. Seeing the beautiful forests and rivers in Southwest Canada, Duncan suspected his friend would return here after his visit instead of staying in Arizona.

At dawn the next morning, Duncan paid his respects to Chief Tetlenitsa and embraced his close friend. He doffed his Stetson at Wenonah on the way out of the village and rode to the ferry to Seattle. He knew he had to board his horse on a stock car all the way to Los Angeles, then ride to Wickenburg. It would, as the trip up had, take him the rest of the week. Then, Miranda.

15

Miranda finished her class, giving the older kids reading homework and telling the younger ones to practice their arithmetic. The texts were old and tattered and had to suffice for several grade levels. She knew there was a paucity of both school funding and text selections, and she had to make do with what she had.

She walked across to her cottage and picked up a wrap. Though spring was in the air, it had not totally sprung yet. On a previous trip with Duncan, he had supplemented her derringer, which he said was borderline worthless, with a Harrington & Richardson .38 breakopen. It differed from his S&W primarily by having a shroud that covered its hammer, making it virtually snag free. She made sure it was in the dress pocket she had sewn in and covered with an apron.

The walk into the center of town was about half a mile and she strode briskly. There were a couple of things she needed at the town's general merchandise.

She bought the items and the shop-keep's wife put them in a paper sack while they discussed her son's progress at school.

As she walked out of the shop, she heard the train arriving in the nine-year old Wickenburg depot. As it squealed to a halt, steel on steel, there was a loud hiss of steam escaped the Class 759 locomotive. She walked past the bank, missing her friend killed in the robbery.

Miranda headed down the dusty street towards the school. Behind it was the cottage that came with her job. It had been a place to live, nothing more. Now, once Duncan got back, it would be home. Like her parents' house had been. Like the Duncan ranch is. It would be their home until a more permanent ranch and job for both was available for both in Prescott. She walked on, smiling in the cool afternoon.

***

Miranda had left a new pot of beef stew simmering over the coals while she was teaching. At each break, she had slipped over to the cottage and stirred it. By the time she went into town for a few items, it was done and the arm upon which the pot hung was pushed over to the side, where it would be kept warm yet not burn. She was used to an oven for bread and pies at her parents' home in Petersburg. There was no stove here and she had not yet tried to make fry bread in the fireplace with her large cast iron skillet, or biscuits in a Dutch oven. It was something she needed to perfect before she became a housewife. After eating a bowl of stew with biscuits from the diner, she wrote a quick letter to Ann Dunlap asking for her recipe for bread and biscuits made without a full oven.

She remembered Ann had an oven but did not doubt she could make both in the fireplace, or, a campfire. After all, they had lived as outlaws in a cave in the Highlands of Scotland. No ovens for baking there, she knew.

She put her jacket on and walked around the cottage. There was room, she thought, in back for a shed for two horses to have stalls and to store saddles, other tack, and feed. A small corral could be built out from it. Miranda was not sure whether Ace, the big blue roan would require more space than was available or economical to build. James would have to make that decision. He and his horse knew each other so well. They were like partners. They were partners.

She went in and prepared her lesson for tomorrow for each of the four levels she currently taught. She would only have to add a new lower level as younger children entered the school. She was not aware of any waiting to turn six years old and begin schooling for the coming term. As to the rest, she would supplement their knowledge with more advanced material with each year.

An hour later, she finished and began to heat water in a large pot to put in the bathing tub, which she dragged over from a corner. Four buckets of cold water—damn cold she thought—from the pump outside were added while the pot heated over the fire. The result would be about three inches of water to sit in and bathe. Water up to her chest would be a luxury she would not enjoy tonight. It would require far too many trips with buckets to fill the tub and an equal number to empty it. Finally, all was ready, and she stripped and stepped in with a washcloth and bar of store-bought soap that had a sweet smell. It was one luxury she allowed herself on her meager salary. How nice it would be, she thought as she made suds on the cloth and bathed, to have her big strong soon-to-be husband prepare a deep, hot bath and scrub her back. She wished she could lay back in hot water and think about that, but the layer of water she put in barely reached her bottom, so it was a dream for another time. Hopefully, a time not so far off. Miranda stood in the tub and dumped the remaining still-warm water from the pot over her shoulders and let it run down her body, both warming her and washing off the sudsy water from washing. She reached for a towel and dried before stepping out and drying her feet.

Putting on a cotton nightgown, she scooped the water from the tub, bucket by bucket until she was able to tilt it and pour the last bit into the bucket. She moved it back to the corner and locked the front door. She knew few folks in Arizona Territory locked their doors. But, few of them had been kidnapped by outlaws. So, she took the precaution. She had sufficient split, seasoned wood for the fireplace, so she stoked the fire for the night and climbed into the cold bed. Her body warmed the space under the covers and soon she was asleep to night sounds. These were somewhat muted compared to when she and Duncan were in the cabin in the Hualapais.

***

The morning dawned over the Territory as any other morning. Nothing was amiss. Further west, in Seattle, Duncan boarded a southbound train, his horse in a live-stock car, and ordered coffee from the diner once the train began to roll.

He knew Aaron would fit in well with the Nlaka'pamux Cook's Ferry band. Duncan instinctively liked the chief. And, he observed, the people. There was a disproportion-ate ratio of women to men. The young Yavape men would prove both welcome and useful to the band. With Aaron's new rifle, they would be able to provide moose and large bears to the food supply...and increase the safety of the people from these noble, but inherently dangerous beasts.

Duncan agreed with the beliefs of Indian people, about both stewardship of the land and about honoring and absorbing the spirit of an animal killed and fully utilized. And, to never kill for sport, only for sustenance or self-defense. Other beliefs, he thought, paralleled the Ten Commandments, if not in exact words, certainly in concept.

With the replacement horse and saddle safely in the livestock car, Duncan had placed his saddlebags on the shelf above the seats and his sheathed Winchester between his seat and the side of the car. He settled in for a long ride to the City of Angels, and the horseback ride east to Wickenburg. There was a significant break in the weather, so he would likely not encounter snow and cold as he had on the trip over with Aaron.

***

Miranda, still smelling clean and sweet from her bath, dressed and walked over to the schoolhouse. She built a fire in the large heating stove and set out the primers on each desk. She put four lessons to discuss on the chalk board and smiled as she knew several of the older boys would not listen. They would be too busy staring at her moon-eyed. It came with the territory and she chuckled to herself. Word had already spread in the small town her fiancé was Duncan, the famous gunfighter and lawman. She doubted it would deter her twelve-year-old suitors, but it should any older ones.

An hour later, she was teaching.

Miranda taught and worked to make the cottage look

more like a home for her future husband. She knew until the day of their marriage, propriety would cause him to reside elsewhere, but she had modest pride and wanted Duncan to like the cottage, no matter how temporary it may be.

The ranger sergeant rode trains for several days, then claimed and saddled his horse at the rail terminal in Los Angeles.

He picked up some provisions on the way out of town, filled his two canteens and headed east. He would have to camp seven times before arriving in Wickenburg.

Duncan thought again about how much he had liked the green woods of the Pacific Northwest and Canada. His ride across to Wickenburg would be through desert and mountains like he was used to. It had its own beauty, but he knew it was less hospitable than the beautifully forested country he had just left. There would be stretches where he would have to search for water, for wood for a fire and for trees to use to stretch a tarp shelter from. Where sidewinders would far outnumber rabbits or squirrels as a dinner source.

He had bought enough prepared food in Los Angeles to take him most of the way home without having to soak beans and make fry bread on the campfire. Duncan had found the Thermos bottles worked surprisingly well to keep food hot for a day, then at least warm for a few days. He filled them with soups in the city and had a supply of rolls and biscuits to eat with them. For luxury, he had added a few cans of peaches in a sugar syrup to his stores.

The paint was not as exceptional a horse as Ace, but he admitted he might be a wee bit prejudiced regarding his beloved blue roan. He knew Angus would be pleased with the trade and may even adopt the paint as his primary riding horse. The man that sold it to Duncan said the horse, called Chief, was trained to work cattle and was not particularly gun shy, something his father would appreciate.

Duncan pinned his ranger badge inside his vest, using the lining for the pin to prevent it from showing on the front. He could meet anyone on this trail and preferred to show his law officer identity when he was ready, not just to any rider who happened by.

As it was, he rode the whole way without encountering a single soul. He saw what he guessed might be a prospector leading a mule once, but the man was too far away to be positive.

Duncan finally hit some mountain country. It made it harder on the horse, but provided more cover, forage and a better place to pitch camp at night.

A week later, he rode into Wickenburg around dusk. He knew approximately where the schoolhouse and adjacent cabin were from Miranda. But he had to go into town first and send a wire to Captain Rynning to tell him he would be back in Prescott in several days and had a successful time afield. He stopped by the livery and curried, watered and put a feedbag on Chief. He resaddled Chief an hour later, turned west, and rode to his Miranda.

***

Duncan rode out the road towards the schoolhouse, scanning for ambush points Miranda should watch for. He saw virtually none as the mile trip was open, with a couple cottages along the way. The dirt road was wide and visibility in every direction was excellent.

He spotted the small schoolhouse on his right. It was dark, but the cottage adjacent had smoke coming from the chimney and a yellow light, probably from an oil lamp or two, showed through the drawn curtains.

Duncan dismounted Chief and walked him towards the door. He called out, "Miranda. It's Duncan, I'm home."

Within a moment, the door cracked and the lamps backlit a familiar face, apprehensive and not yet smiling. Once she saw him, the apprehension immediately changed to a smile and she leaned a long-barreled scattergun against the door frame and ran out to greet him, arms outstretched.

Miranda jumped into his arms and he lifted her in a bear hug, her feet several feet off the ground. Lips found lips and the kiss began and ended from on high.

"You are all I have been thinking about, honey." he exclaimed. Head buried in his chest, she mumbled something gleefully, but he was unable to discern it. Duncan leaned until her feet touched the ground and she walked with him towards the door, holding his hand.

Before reaching the door, she said, "James, what are we going to do with this horse? Are you staying here tonight? What if you are seen? The old ladies on the school board will have a conniption. They will probably tattoo a scarlet letter on my breast."

"Anybody, man or woman, who touches those breasts will be meeting Mister Bowie or Colonel Colt pretty fast," he said. "I will walk over to the schoolhouse and tie Chief here up to the hitching rail the kids use. The next thing I will do, is to pitch camp, clearly away from the house. I will hobble the horse close to camp. Once we have a camp, I will come in and visit."

"An idea I quite like," she said.

After tying the horse temporarily, they both gathered a bit of split firewood the county delivered for her and moved it to a clear spot about fifty yards from the cottage. Duncan had spotted it when he rode in. It had a clearing and several trees from which to suspend his lariat and hang the larger tarp over to make a lean-to. Miranda helped him do and watched as he dug the Dakota fire pit, something she had seen him do before, but still marveled at how such a simple idea worked so well. The tunnel between the large and small holes proved difficult in the soil, so Duncan dug a trench and covered it with flat rocks, as he had done after arresting Smoot, and many other times. Miranda got a galvanized bucket and brought water out for Chief for when he was hobbled.

Duncan laid his bedroll inside the lean-to without unrolling it and brought Chief over and hobbled him. The horse had some water from the bucket and investigated a stand of grass, more out of curiosity than hunger.

The lawman and teacher walked to the house, hand-in-hand.

"Be it ever so humble..." Miranda said. "I have tried to make it homey, but it's small and temporary."

Duncan eyed the single barrel shotgun she had moved to a corner.

"I figured I may need something more...influential... than the revolvers. It gives me a feeling of security," she said.

"You know, people say the Winchester '73 like Pa has was the 'gun that won the West', but it wasn't. The shotgun in the corner or over the fireplace was the real one. And, a lot of times, it was wielded by the woman of the house while the man was herding cattle or working fields or whatever. I'm glad you bought it. It was a good idea."

She put coffee on, and they sat, her on the bed and him in a rocker he pulled up closely. He reached out and took both her hands and held them.

"I missed you, James. Did you get your friend and his

band settled?"

He chuckled. "I did. We built hogans for the guys to live in, to be replaced at their leisure with cabins before real cold weather sets in."

"What's so funny about building hogans?" she asked.

"Oh, nothing. I was laughing about the fact my Yavape friend already has a tall, glossy-haired Indian maiden making eyes at him. He's thinking ahead. He made a double bed instead of a single one," Duncan said.

"How do you know?" she asked.

"I helped him."

"What does she look like?"

"Tall as he is. Long black hair. It shines a lot. Good shape. Smart. I spoke with her a bit while we were building his hogan. She seemed to have an interest in how his was built."

"You seem to have noticed a lot," she suggested, showing jealousy he had not seen before.

"Aaron is the closest thing I will ever have as a brother. I have a vested interest in his welfare. I just escorted him illegally to another country on my—our—own money. So, you better believe I would check out this woman he was planning to spend the rest of his life with before he had even spoken one word to her."

"Men. I just don't understand you all."

"But you love us just the same," he suggested.

"No, just you."

"I'm all you need to love. Unless some little Duncan comes along. You'll have to love him too."

"What if he's a she?"

"A beautiful little daughter would be just fine with me."

"Well then, we have a project. After the ceremony, of course," she said.

"Of course."

"How about if I camp out with you. Anybody passing by will think I am in the house."

"Sounds like a good plan. Kind of like our old days," he said.

"Oh, you mean the old days a month ago?" she asked.

"Exactly. Those old days."

"Guess I better get something warm to sleep in," she said.

"Haven't I always kept you warm?" Duncan asked.

"Yes, but of course I had something on."

"Miranda?"

"Yes?"

"I was not always unconscious like you thought I was."

She turned red, then said, "Guess there's no need for warm sleeping clothes then."

"There never was," he said softly.

He put some wood on the fire and she wrapped the shawl around her nightgown again and they went out to the lean-to. Duncan banked the fire and they retired for the night, planning to arise before anyone rode by on the road during dawn's first lights.

***

Duncan disarmed and undressed down to his long Johns. Miranda slipped the shawl off and climbed into the bed-roll. They just held each other, looking into one another's eyes in the firelight for a long time, holding tightly. A time for love. She fell asleep in his arms. He laid awake for another several hours thinking. Savoring the moment. Then, he fell asleep. It seemed like no time before he heard the clip-clop of a buggy going by seventy-five yards away. He looked at the sky and guessed it would be light in half an hour. His movement made Miranda stir. She nestled back into his shoulder and went to sleep again. He gave her five more minutes and awakened her with a kiss and a caress. She took his hand and placed it back on her.

"I wish, honey. But we have to get up. You have kids to teach and I have a temporary corral to see to. It's going to be a busy day." No one was on the road. She arose and wrapped the shawl around her and went to the cottage. Soon, he smelled coffee and bacon. He knew there would be more items, but those two smells satisfied him without the "more".

He saddled Chief and rode into town to inquire about a lumber mill where he might purchase some split rails for the corral fence. And, some boards for the shed. He found out and ordered both plus some tarpaper to put on the roof to keep everything dry. Duncan arranged delivery, then returned to town to buy a hammer, saw, nails, and a shovel.

He stopped by the post office for Miranda. She had a letter. It was in a very familiar handwriting. His mother's.

He returned to the school's house and gave her the letter. She opened and read it, smiling.

"Your mother wants me to meet her in Prescott and plan the wedding over the long Easter week, 'cause there's no school. Cousin Mary cannot come this week, but we can get some basics out of the way. Since my commandeered horse is at your folks' ranch, can I ride in to Wickenburg double with you and we can hire a horse at the livery? Then, I can go with you when you ride to Prescott," she said.

He happily agreed and they rode into town and rented a horse and tackle for her. They sent a wire to his mother.

The delivery came shortly after their return. He began his measurements. Having learned from Walkem at the

Cook's Ferry Band, he staked out the dimensions of the shed and the corral before the supplies had ever come. When they did, he was ready. He started and was finished the shed by lunch. He pushed hard and had completed the corral by the end of school on the third day. Digging postholes with a shovel in the hard earth was neither easy nor fun. He protected his gun hands with heavy leather gloves.

The construction was not a great feat of engineering. But it would certainly suffice for the next several months or so. He was pleased. He had never built anything until one hogan a week ago. And, this endeavor had cost far more sweat than equity.

The next morning was Saturday, so Duncan saddled the horses while Miranda packed clothes and some food for the sixty-mile trip.

They arrived late and went to the ranch first. Angus was very pleased with Chief and immediately led him into the stable to care for him. He would take his test ride the following morning. Beau was getting old and Angus would keep him in shape with rides into town and use Chief for longer hunts or longer cattle trips.

He had not heard anything about the court-martial that occurred during his son's absence. Duncan would ask Roberts the next day. It is likely the local sheriff had been apprised of either progress, or, by this time, outcome. Duncan planned to spend time at the Sheriff's Office tomorrow anyway.

Ann Duncan made her son turn over his trail clothes to wash. He hauled buckets of scalding water to the tub behind the ranch house. He arose pink but as clean as his newly washed clothes.

After breakfast, Duncan dressed in a new pair of pants, clean boots, a light-colored flannel shirt and a dark tie.

After all, Rynning said his rangers should be more formal in town. His right arm and shoulder had become supple enough to position his Colt's .45 in its usual position. He buttoned his vest, donned his long coat and Stetson and rode south to Prescott. He passed the ranch he had visited with his family and Miranda with an eye to buying.

Duncan rode on, less carefree than when he had left.

He tied Ace to the hitching rail at the Sheriff's Office and went in. Chief Deputy Ev Masters greeted him.

"Where ya been? Haven't seen you for nigh onto a month, Duncan."

"I was on a long trail but had to stop along the way, miles from here, to recuperate a bit. The shoulder wound was acting up. But, it's fine now. I am ready to bring in some criminals."

He hated to lie to his friend and former boss. But what he had done, though with the approval of Rynning and knowledge of Roberts, who would not mention it, was illegal.

"Ev," he began, "What do y'all have going on? Anything I can help you with?"

"No, Duncan. It has been real quiet lately."

"Chief, Dad and I have been looking at the Hatton place to buy for expansion. What do you think of it?" asked Duncan .

Chief Deputy said, "The Hatton place is not the farm he tried to turn it into. It's ranch land and it's all it'll ever be. So, for your purposes, it should be fine if the price is right. But it will never be a farm. You can't put a wig on a pig and call her a dancing girl."

Duncan had to chuckle at his friend's turn of a phrase

"Know where the sheriff is?" he asked Masters.

"Probably over to the café drinking coffee. He don't like mine for some reason."

Duncan, having sampled Masters' coffee many times, could definitely relate. And, Masters drank a couple pots a day of the stuff. His gut must have been made of cast iron.

"I might saunter over and see if he knows the status of Smoot's court-martial," Duncan said. Ev Masters just shook his head and shrugged suggesting he had nothing to add on subject.

Duncan knew which café the sheriff favored. It was the same one he did. He had to play his conversation just right. Too many questions and Roberts would just clam up.

The ranger saw him at a window table, sitting so he could see outside and the door at the same time. The same way Duncan always sat. Roberts was dressed like he would for church, if he ever showed up there. He dressed the same for court or the trail, also. He wore tweed pants, tie-up black shoes and a white shirt. He had a black derby hat pushed back on his head. Duncan could see the badge pinned to his shirt and the black butt of the nickel-plated .44 stuck out of his front pocket.

Duncan knew the .44 had a lot of credits. Nobody but Roberts knew how many. But, most in the know said it was more than John Wesley Hardin had. And, Hardin was the only man Hickok feared.

Hardin had been shot, some say murdered, by Constable John Selman nine years earlier, in 1895. He had shot Hardin the same way Jack McCall had killed Hickok. A shot in the back of the head while the former gunfighter was gambling. Then, several shots into his body as he laid on the floor to make sure. A year later, US Marshal George Scarborough had outdrawn his old acquaintance Selman following an argument.

Duncan got a mug of black coffee and walked over to

the acting sheriff, his spurs clanking on the wooden floor.

"Sheriff, might I bother you for one minute?" he asked.

Roberts just nodded towards the empty chair across from him. He would have to sit back to the door but trusted the older lawman to cover his back. He would watch Roberts closely, too, and if his eyes changed as he looked over Duncan's shoulder, the ranger would spin and draw instinctively.

"I wanted to let you know those folks we talked about are out of the country. For good, unless a pardon is granted later on. I had to lie to Ev. It hurt me grievous. But it was the only thing to do," Duncan said.

Roberts nodded. He could tell from that the sheriff was pleased the matter had been resolved. He was a deadly man but had reputedly never killed anyone who did not need killing. Those young Yavapai Indians did not.

"Anything on the court-martial while I was gone?" he asked

Roberts took a sip of coffee to wet his throat. He had probably not yet uttered twenty words today.

In a low voice he said, "They stripped Smoot of his rank and gave him the boot. Dishonorable Discharge. No more than that. No prison time. No fine. Just out on his butt."

It was Duncan's turn to nod. He knew this meant he would likely have to meet Smoot in the street one day and kill him.

The sheriff knew the same thing.

"Thanks, Boss. I will keep in touch with Ev to see if there's anything I can help your office with. Have yourself a real good day." He doffed his hat at his former boss and turned and left, leaving the empty mug and two bits on the counter.

Duncan rode back to the ranch. Angus had hooked the

buggy up to Bub for the women to drive into town. He pulled back the canvas covering the back storage bed and nodded to the gun in a scabbard hidden there.

The ranger reached in and took it out. It was an 1897 Winchester pump shotgun. He had heard about them, but this is the first he had seen. It had a short throw pump forearm and Angus had shortened the barrel to the point it was the same length overall as his old lever action carbine. Duncan nodded appreciatively as he turned the gun over in his hands. It was 16 gauge. He knew it was as light as a 20 gauge but hit near as hard as a 12. It felt good in his hands. He put it back away and recovered the bed of the buggy.

"Kinda new-fangled for you, Pa," he observed.

"Son, I buy good things and make them last. Due to my Scottish nature and yours, too. My old Winchester has been fired thousands of times. It's never let me down. The action keeps getting slicker and better over time. John Browning designed yours over twenty years later. It will be like new and be all you need at age eighty. But, our old ten-gauge single barrel was cheap to begin with. And, it kicked like a mule. So, I traded it on a new lifetime gun for around the house and on the roads. I like it and your Ma calls it her own. She shoots it like a house on fire. Wait 'til you see. It just tickles ole Satan out of me. It's worth a wee tease or two when you see the opportunity."

They shared a conspiratorial grin as they had done since the son was a tyke barely able to stand.

The family mounted up. Angus was going to ride Chief on his first long trail. He was going to ride fifteen miles north to Chino Valley then a similar distance beyond to buy a few head of cattle from a rancher he knew and herd them back. It would be an overnight trip. The other three were going into town, then split up and go about their businesses.

16

ARIZONA TERRITORY
1904

Duncan went to the telegraph office first. There was a wire waiting for him from Rynning. It had been sent early today.

It advised Duncan forty head of cattle had been rustled from the Bar 7 Ranch, just southeast of Winslow, up on Clear Creek. He was ordered to go there with all possible haste and search for a trail and follow.

He looked for the ladies and found them at a dry goods store. Duncan told them he had to hit the trail on a rustling matter for a few days and would be back as soon as he could.

Leaving them, he bought a bag of corn pones at the café and some cheese, beans and coffee. He knew he had sufficient ammunition, salt, sugar and flour in his saddlebags for this impromptu, but short duration trip.

As he rode up Gurley Street, he heard the Santa Fe train let out steam after it had stopped at the station. He looked at the station.

Several people got off the train. One was a drummer. He sold printing press parts. Since it was late in the day, he walked on to the hotel, carrying his small suitcase and towing the parts in a large case with wheels and a tow strap attached. The redness of his face suggested hypertension or too much liquor in his life. Or, both. He would call on the editor of the Daily Courier in the morning. Now, several drinks and a bed were calling to him after a long trip from New York City.

Two other passengers disembarking from the Santa Fe train were an older husband and wife. Though it would be almost a quarter of a century before Grant Wood would paint American Gothic using his sister and the local dentist as models, the two travelers could have modeled instead, and the resultant painting would have looked much the same. They hurried on to the livery stable nearest the train depot to reclaim their buckboard and particularly pernicious mule, Abe.

The final passenger for Prescott was a man whose dress more than suggested he was from elsewhere. He was six-feet tall and about thirty-five years old. His brown hair was slicked back with too much pomade, not a Western affectation. It was parted in the middle. His matching mustache was a handlebar. He had on a derby, a striped shirt with a celluloid collar, and a tan suit under a dark long dark coat with a fur collar. A handsome man, he came across as a bit of a dandy. Until you looked into his eyes. There were dark brown and cold. His lips smiled under the mustache, but the eyes overruled.

He carried a carpet bag, yet almost forty years after the War Between the States, he would have taken great offense at being referred to as a "carpetbagger", and even more as a "scalawag". He was of the heritage who called others by those pejoratives.

Duncan saw him. Though he did not recognize the man, he did not like his looks and filed his description away for possible future use.

The man went to the new brick Hotel St. Michael and requested a room for several days. He told the clerk in no uncertain terms it was to be a single room and quiet. He was assigned one and given a key. Asking if the Palace Saloon next door served dinner too, the clerk replied with a nod of his head. The man stared at him coldly for a moment, then turned and walked up the stairs to room 210. He dropped off his topcoat and bag and washed his face with the pitcher and bowl and hand towel, after scrutinizing both to make sure they were fresh. He had heard about the lack of cleanliness in small town establishments. The man pinched both ends of his mustache between finger and thumb and, with a roll, made sure they were properly presented. He adjusted a shoulder holster. It sheathed a four inch-barreled Webley-Fosbery revolver in .455 British caliber. He shook his jacket out to drape over the awkwardly shaped gun to ensure it was not printing in the fabric.

He went downstairs, glowered at the clerk, and walked out of the door and forty feet down the sidewalk before pushing open the double doors of the saloon. Picking a table, he waited, smiling. His mien had changed from demanding to charming in a deliberate instance. A bar girl approached him, also smiling. He looked like a big tipper. He was. He ordered a steak and potatoes and a double bourbon.

The man finished his meal and his third double bourbon. His meal was ten dollars with the whiskey. He tipped the bar girl two dollars, the largest tip she had ever gotten. Her smile and eye contact were meaningful. He smiled, nodded at her and mentally scheduled her for a subsequent day. He had an agenda to follow which did not quite include her. Yet.

The man was there looking for somebody. He had three options: repatriate; ruin; or kill the person. He would have to give the choices more thought when he saw the person, and when she saw him.

His name was Riley Hancock II.

***

Miranda and Ann took bags of cloth for a wedding dress to the Hotel St. Michael dining room, where they planned to eat lunch. They were seated and put the bags in a chair at the unused end of the table, out of sight. They both ordered soup and split a sandwich. It was now getting warm enough for cold sweet tea to be back on the menu, so they both ordered it. She heard a customer speak to a server and turned around at the sound of the voice.

A tall man with a suit and Eastern hair was sitting across the room with his back to them. When she saw him, Miranda's blood ran cold, then drained from her face. Her eyes were wide circles and her mouth was open. Her hand immediately dropped to her lap and she pushed her hand into her bag, where she had placed the revolver today.

Ann Duncan stared at her.

"What's the matter, dear? You look like you've seen a ghost," she said.

"It's worse than a ghost, Ann. It is Riley Hancock, my ex-husband. What on earth is he doing here? He virtually never leaves Richmond. He hates traveling away from his club and his drunken friends. He has to be here for me. And, it's just you and me. James and Angus are gone for several days."

"Miranda, I am quite convinced we are enough for some tinhorn. But, what will you do? He has sat back turned to us since we walked in. We have not spoken loudly enough for him to recognize your voice. Should we leave? Or, do you want to confront him?" Ann asked.

"I don't know. I am frozen, Ann. I have never felt this way but once in my life...and it was the first time he raped me and beat me senseless. I want to walk over there and shoot him in the back of his head, but I can't just murder him."

The lovely Scottish blonde nodded her head thoughtfully and uttered under her voice, "At least not in public."

Unaware his quarry and the subject of his dilemma was forty feet behind him, Hancock continued to think about what he'd do when he saw her. Would he just throw it all to the wind and kill her? Would he beg her to come back, promising her anything? Or would he seek to feel the release he always thought after he had struck her? He knew the latter existed, though could not accurately describe it, since each time he had felt it, he had been seriously drunk. And, of course, perhaps the best revenge would be to ruin her reputation as a teacher and as a person. He was not sure how he could do it, but it was worthy of consideration, and he was sure he could come up with a way, given some time.

Always confident of his abilities, Riley Hancock knew when he saw her, her reaction would trigger him to do the best thing. Whatever it was. He continued to unconsciously pinch little pieces off the roll in his hand and drop them into a pile beside his plate. By the time his lunch came, the pile was a squirrel's delight, almost an inch-high crumbs of yeast rolls. He also unconsciously jerked his head in a small tic-like movement. Riley Hancock's mental condition was far more messed up than he or his cold, rich father could ever imagine. Perhaps only his ex-wife knew the real man behind the Richmond façade. He also had no idea how much she hated the man she knew.

Hancock picked at his pork chop and vegetable lunch, then motioned for the check. He left three dollars on the table and arose. He scanned the filled dining room quickly, not noticing anyone in particular and began the walk to the front. As he got within fifteen feet of the door, he saw two women sitting. One was a beautiful blonde woman who appeared to be in her mid-forties.

The other woman was Miranda Hancock.

They locked eyes in mutual horror, and both seemed to freeze. But part of Miranda was not frozen. It was her right hand below the tablecloth. It was in her bag and grasping the hard rubber butt of her revolver. She began to slide it out, finger on the trigger.

Hancock tried to mouth "Miranda," but no sound came out. His head ticked to the left three times in fast succession. He shook it vigorously to re-center. He turned slightly to the right and rushed out of the restaurant, knocking aside an older lady as she entered. She huffed "what a rude young man" and the owner quickly guided her to a vacant table.

Miranda stood, her purse dropped to the floor, the revolver in her hand, finger on the trigger. She realized people were looking at her, some in horror. She dropped her hand down beside her leg and buried the .38 into the folds of her skirt until she could replace it. But only after she was sure Riley was not coming back in, armed and dangerous.

Ann stood and motioned for their check. She bent and retrieved Miranda's purse and fitted it over the revolver in hand and quietly told Miranda to release the gun. She did and Ann felt the weight hit the purse. She drew the string on the top and presented the bag back to her. Miranda took it unconsciously.

The Carnegie Library ladies' group was leaving a small room to the side where they had had a meeting. Ann gently moved Miranda into the group of women to walk out in the middle of a crowd, something difficult to do in most cases in 1904 Prescott. Both women looked from side to side and neither spotted Hancock as they exited the restaurant and headed to the buckboard. Ann picked up the reins and reached under the seat and pulled the shotgun within reach between the seat and the side, yet still out of public view. She released the brake on the rear wheel and clicked her tongue as she lightly touched the reins against Bub's back, and they started home to the ranch.

"Keep your eyes peeled and your revolver at hand, okay?" Ann said to Miranda, who was already doing both of those things.

They knew it was of no use to go to the Sheriff's Office. Domestic matters were handled or not handled within families and not by law enforcement officers. There were rumors in some places certain secret men's organizations sometimes visited abusers and warned them, but it had not happened in Prescott yet as far as Ann knew.

Riley Hancock II watched them go by from behind the curtain at room 210. Maybe tonight. He figured the pretty blonde woman would have a man. Some of these Western men could be dangerous, he knew. Damn near all of them had a gun on or close at hand. He walked down to the front desk in his shirt sleeves, something he would never have done in a Richmond or Baltimore hotel.

"I swear I just saw an old friend from Richmond go by in a wagon with a pretty blonde woman. Do you know where she is staying? I'd like to ask the whole family to be my guests at dinner while I am in town," he said, his tic catching the attention of the clerk.

"Which way were they riding on the main drag here?" the clerk asked.

Hancock had no idea about direction, so he turned to the street, extended his hand and pointed.

"Hmm..." the clerk intoned. "The blonde woman could be Missus Duncan. They have a ranch about four miles out. You can see the house from the road. I hear her son's fiancée, a school marm from Wickenburg is visiting. She's a pretty brunette. She stayed here when she was recovered after being taken hostage in a bank robbery over there in Wickenburg."

"Yes. Sounds like my friend. She is a teacher in Wickenburg. Is there a good restaurant in Wickenburg to take them to when I pay a visit?" Hancock asked, not even thinking about the fact only Miranda lived there and not the Duncans.

Receiving a dismissive shrug from the clerk, he turned and went to room 210 to retrieve his jacket and shoulder holster.

Having gotten his jacket and gun, he walked in the opposite direction from that Miranda had gone. He had seen a livery stable from the train depot.

He reached the livery in good time and went in. The owner was brushing a horse.

"Hello. I'm in town a few days and would like to hire a horse," he said.

The livery stable owner looked at the Eastern dude standing there and asked, "Do you ride?"

Hancock's expression flashed from benign to aggressive in less than a second.

"Why the hell else would I want to hire a horse? To walk it down the street? I want a horse and it should be the best, most spirited one you've got. And, the saddle will be befitting of a man of my stature in my community."

The livery stable owner was also the town's blacksmith. He had arms the size of Hancock's thighs. He knew he could snap him like a twig. But money was tight, and this man looked like he had some. So, he faked a gratuitous smile and walked to the stalls out back.

Presently, he brought a black, saddled with his newest and well-shined saddle. He usually charged four dollars a day for him.

"This is Crook. How long will you be needing him?" he asked.

"Crook? Like an outlaw?" Hancock asked, his haute showing.

"No, like a famous general. How long did you say?"

"Two or three days, I expect," Hancock responded.

"Make it six dollars a day. Three days prepaid now. Make sure he has water and feed daily."

Hancock handed him eighteen dollars and mounted easily. He heeled the black and rode out of the wide and tall door onto the street. He trotted the horse to the Palace and tied him on the hitching rail.

"You got some of Van Winkle bourbon from Louisville?" he asked the barkeep.

"I do, but it's pretty dear."

"I'll take a bottle and a glass," Hancock said. A moment later, he was carrying the bottle and a glass to a table.

Seeing the particular whiskey choice and knowing its price, the bargirl walked over as seductively as she could manage and asked, "You want some peanuts or some pretzels to go with that fine brew, handsome? Or, maybe something else?"

"Some peanuts would be good. I have business tonight, but something else might come to mind late in the evening. You going to be around?" he asked.

She smiled and nodded and went off to get a bowl of peanuts. She reached in a big glass container and fished out five pretzels and added them to the bowl for delivery to the table.

By eight o'clock, a tipsy Riley Hancock had paid fifty dollars for his drink and snacks and the barkeep and his female server watched as he staggered out to the sidewalk. He mounted Crook less sprightly than before and headed out of town. They wondered where a tin horn would be going at this time.

***

The two women arrived back at the ranch soon after the meeting in town. They had talked about Riley and the Hancock patriarch all the way from Prescott. It appeared the ex-husband was in Arizona Territory alone. Ann knew he drank a lot and asked about whether he was a brawler.

"Oh, heavens no. He only drinks with his rich college friends from Richmond College. He generally goes to his club instead of saloons on Broad Street where he might get into a brawl. He is pretty good at beating up women. I doubt I was the first. But, like most bullies and abusers, he's a coward at heart. He'd soil his pants if confronted by Angus or James...unless he had a gun in hand and their backs were turned," Miranda said.

"Does he carry a gun or knife?" Ann asked.

"He has a funny English revolver and practices with it out at the family summer place in Goochland County. He has a dagger, but I have never seen him carry it. He thinks his family name is enough to protect him in Richmond."

"Can you think of any reason, Miranda, other than

you, why he might be in the Territory. It's all the way across the country from his home, so he didn't just accidentally show up here," Ann said.

"No, Ma'am. I really can't," Miranda responded.

"Well, he has no idea what he's facing with the two of us. He will rue the day he comes here or confronts us anywhere; our men present or not. So, let's get you down to your shift and I'll start measuring for the dress."

They did and one stood and the other measured and pinned for the better part of an hour. They cooked together and enjoyed some wild blueberry wine Ann had made.

After dinner, they sat, one in the outfit she had worn to town and the other in the thin shift she wore under her skirt and blouse.

Either Beau or Bub whinnied from the barn. Ann was not sure which. Angus had always said they did not need Guinea hens or a dog to alarm when someone came on the property, because his favorite two horses would make sufficient noise. The ranch house was set on a dirt path a quarter of a mile from the main road, with a gate and a sign with "Highlands Ranch. A. Duncan, Prop." on it. The only way someone would accidentally ride through the gate and down the lane was if they were illiterate. Both women knew Hancock was not, having graduated from a Baptist college founded some seventy-four years ago.

Someone rapped hard on the door, which Ann had locked, something she did not do usually.

Before Miranda could get to her purse with the revolver in it or the Colt in her valise, Ann motioned her behind the door.

She had the pump 16 gauge in hand when she said, "Who's there?"

Instead of an answer, the door was shouldered open and hit her as Hancock tumbled in. He jumped up before she could raise the shotgun from the floor and kicked her in the midriff. As Ann bent double on the floor, Hancock leaned down and punched her behind the head. The bun of plaited blonde hair caught most of the power of the blow, but, though cushioned, she received sufficient force to render her unconscious.

Barefooted and in her thin shift, Miranda leapt from behind the door and landed on his back, her bare legs wrapped around his waist and left arm around his throat. She immediately began to choke him as hard as she could. Gasping, he threw both of them against the door jamb and she took the full force of the hit and let go. In thrusting backwards, Hancock tripped over the unconscious Ann and fell unceremoniously on top of her. Miranda was stunned from the collision with the door jamb and staggered forward.

Hancock grabbed her as he stood up. He ripped the shift off her and pulled her nude body towards the bed he saw through an open door. She dug her fingernails into his arm and screamed at him, but he seemed oblivious to both. Once through the door he threw her on the bed.

Miranda tried to get up, but he elbowed her on the side of the head, and she went down. He began to remove his trousers, then stood facing her in shirt and shoulder holster only.

Hancock moved around the side of the bed and heard a "clack-clack" from the doorway.

The sound of the Winchester pump shotgun's action was the last thing Riley Hancock II ever heard.

Buckshot from six feet only spreads a few inches. It blew a two-inch hole all the way through him, severing his spinal cord and everything in front and behind it. He crumpled dead on the floor.

Ann did not have to pump another shell into the chamber. The body on the floor with open staring eyes and a gory white shirt was all the proof she needed. A second shot would be wasting a perfectly good shotgun shell. Scots were never wasteful.

"Help me tie what's left of your shift around him to hold his innards in while we drag him outside," Ann ordered Miranda, who had already gotten off the bed and was standing staring at her ex-husband. She felt no sorrow. Only relief and hatred.

Miranda walked to the front door, closed it without latching it and picked up her ripped shift and brought it into the bedroom. James's room. Her room for the next few days.

Ann rolled Hancock's body onto his left side and placed an old flannel shirt against the exit wound. Miranda put half the shift under his side and Ann rolled him so Miranda could thread the rest of the shift through to the other side. She brought both halves together in front and tied it tightly in a square knot. Hancock's feet and hands were twitching slightly, but there was no need to search for a pulse.

Together, they dragged him out the bedroom door, across the main living area and out the front door. They continued around the house to the barn.

They stood there looking at him.

"So, what the hell do we do now? Get the sheriff?" Miranda asked.

"And, have to go through an inquiry...maybe a trial? Have your reputation dragged through the dirt by whatever sleazy lawyer his father sends out here? I'm thinking we need to make him disappear. And, keep the whole thing to ourselves. Forever. Do you think it makes sense,

Miranda?" Ann asked.

"I do. Can we get him up into the bed of the buckboard? Cover him up and take him somewhere and bury him where he'll never be found? And, get back before daylight?" she asked.

Ann thought for a minute.

"There is always the chance we will meet someone on the road, even in the dark. It would be easier to bury him here, but we don't want evidence on the ranch. I think we have to chance the buckboard and think about an alibi along the way. The first thing is you probably ought to put some clothes on. Help me get him in the bed of the buckboard and covered up first though," Ann said.

They did and walked into the house, one padding silently on bare feet.

They used mineral spirits and an old towel to clean up the blood on the wooden floor. Ann moved a scatter rug from the foot of the bed to the side where Hancock's body had lain.

Miranda dressed in riding pants, her flannel shirt, and strapped on the belt with cartridges and the Colt Single Action Army .32-20 in its holster. It should have been in her hand when the door opened, she thought.

Together, they rolled the buckboard in a circle and hitched Bub to it.

Ann lit a lantern and put it in the light holder on the side. They mounted, released the brake, and started out. Hancock's livery horse was tied behind with a lariat from the barn.

"A few miles up the road is a steep ravine. You can't see down it from the road. What if we took his gun, money, watch, wallet and made it look like a robbery gone wrong? We can free the livery horse. He will eventually make it back to the stable and a search will begin. They will probably think some tinhorn fell off. Either they will find him, or they won't. It won't matter to us. We never saw him, right?" Ann asked Miranda.

"Sounds good to me," came the response. "Miranda, are you sure you are all right with this?" Ann asked.

"I feel like a weight has been taken off me. Are you okay? You did the tough job. And, thank you for saving my life, Ann," Miranda added.

"As you have probably found, women have to be of tough mettle out here. A lot of people say the Wild West is no more. Just think about what you went through with the bank robbery, the gunfights and the train robbery. Angus is riding out alone on horseback to buy beeves and herd them back. James has been sent out to investigate rustlers and, if he catches them arrest or kill them. The only thing we do have is telephones spreading, some gas or electric lights. We have trains replacing stage-coaches. What we don't have is Indian attacks. Otherwise, it's not different here than it was most places in the west thirty years ago. It may be dead in Dallas and Denver and Kansas City. But I think we still live in the Wild West at its wildest, don't you?" Ann asked.

"I think we just proved it, Ann. So, will we ever tell the men?" Miranda asked.

"I think truthfulness is important in a marriage. Angus and I have always discussed everything. But, once we put a dead body in a buckboard and covered it and the death up, I think telling them is just making them accessories."

"But self-defense is not a crime," Miranda added.

"No, but not reporting a killing and altering a crime scene is," Ann answered.

"I understand . I guess seeing him and being treated a way I had tried so hard to forget has made me slow to think tonight. You are right. We don't have to bring them into it. We handled it. Especially you, taking the lead. I think we empty his pockets, keep the money, but take the wallet, watch, and gun and dispose of them totally apart from the body. If he is ever found, they will think it was just a highway robbery gone wrong. Just like you said," Miranda agreed.

They did not encounter any other late-night travelers on the road. It was a good thing, since they could not come up with an excuse about why the two of them would be traveling at one o'clock in the morning. There was nothing bigger than Prescott in front of them for miles. An excuse like "we were just going up to Paulden to sit with a sick friend" would be too easy to debunk. Going to Prescott could be logical, except for the fact there was no good place to hide a body in the several miles between the ranch and the town.

At a curve in the road with a steep ravine on the left, Ann pulled the buckboard over. They listened for hoof-beats ahead and behind and heard none. Throwing the canvas tarp on the bed back, they removed Hancock's pocket watch, revolver, and wallet. Miranda, now fully invested in the job at hand, removed her ex-husband's money, which she insisted Ann take. She then located anything on him which could serve to identify him, including the receipt from the livery stable and his hotel key. They would dispose of those separate from the watch, wallet and gun.

The moon was out and cast an eerie light on the activities at the curve in the road between Prescott, Chino Valley, Paulden and on up to Williams. Both women peered apprehensively over the edge of the deep ravine. It was steep enough for the body to roll all the way to the bottom. There did not seem to be any outcroppings for it to hang up on.

Ensuring once again no one was coming, they got Hancock's body and dragged it to the edge.

Ann said, "Should we say a prayer or some sort of funeral words first?"

Miranda gave the body a hard push, saying, "Burn in hell, you rotten bastard." They could hear rocks rolling and "thumps" as the body hit larger rocks on the way down the ravine. Then, silence. They could not see where the body landed in the dark, even standing on the edge.

Ann gave a slightly uncomfortable chuckle which grew into rolling laughter. Then, Miranda started. They laughed hard but nervously as they crossed the road and climbed up on the buckboard. They untied the livery horse. He walked to the side and began to munch on some grass. They left him, knowing soon he would begin his automatic trip back to the livery stable for his next meal.

As they rode, Miranda balled up the livery receipt and threw is off the road into the deep ravine. Same for the room key.

Ann had a location in mind for disposing of the wallet, watch and gun. It was a deserted homesteader's well at a shack along the road. It took one minute to make those items disappear, probably for their lifetimes, if not forever.

Back at the ranch, they took the bloody material they had used for cleanup and put them in the fifty-five-gallon drum used as a burning barrel. The mineral spirits flashed as the match hit them and within minutes the contents were immolated, and only gray ashes remained.

Ann and Miranda sat at the table, exhausted. They finished the bottle of blueberry wine and sat looking at one another silently for a while. Finally, Ann got up and walked over and kissed Miranda on top of the head. "We need some rest, girl. It's been a helluva day. But we got through it. I think..."

They retired to their beds. Miranda feared she could not sleep in the bed she had so closely come to be ravished in. But she took solace in the fact it was the bed James had grown up in. The stress of the evening won over and she slept soundly.

Ann Duncan gave a lot of thought and prayers to the fact she killed someone. Then, she approached the issue logically and dealt with it. She saved her soon-to-be daughter-in-law from rape and probably murder. After which, she would have probably been murdered. What choice did she have? None. She tossed and turned, but she slept until after sunup. She was awakened by the smell of the coffee Miranda had brewing.

***

Duncan rode into Winslow and made a few inquiries. He headed south out of town and followed a road roughly paralleling Clear Creek until he got to the entrance for the Bar 7 Ranch. He rode in and followed the entry road almost two miles before coming to a settlement of ranch house, bunkhouse, two barns and multiple corrals. He stopped at the house and knocked on the door.

The ranch owner was George Henry Jones. Mrs. Jones, a plain but pleasant woman of about sixty answered the door. She said her husband and the foreman were at the larger barn and were waiting for him.

He rode down and dropped Ace's reins. Duncan walked in. Unusual for working around the ranch, both men were wearing pistols. The older man was short and stocky. He was probably in his late sixties. The other man was pushing fifty and had the lean build and leather sun-tanned face of a longtime rider. Duncan walked up to the older man and stuck out his hand.

"Mister Jones? I'm Sergeant James Duncan with the Rangers."

"How do you do?" Jones asked in response. "This here is my foreman, Buck Lavier. You alone?"

"Yessir. I'm checking the lay of the land, so to speak. Have you contacted the Navajo County sheriff?" Duncan asked.

"Yep. He's away. Talked to some deputy who didn't have anybody to send for a while. Sheriff a friend of yours?" Jones asked.

"Nope. Never met him," Duncan said.

"Well, he ain't not Commodore Perry Owens," Smith said, referring to the first sheriff of the county, a gunfighter who had taken on four men in a gunfight and walked away leaving four bodies.

"Heard you equaled Owen's four man record on a train and beat it overall, having killed a bunch of outlaws the week before," Jones commented.

"Where'd you hear that, Mister Jones?" Duncan asked.

"Read it in the newspaper. For coupla days. Is it true?" Jones asked.

"Pretty much."

"Read the girl with you killed two more. What happened with her?" Jones continued his query.

"Gonna marry her as soon as I see to your cattle rustlers, sir."

"Well then, we better be getting to it. Trail's a couple days old now. How do you want to start?"

"Rangers haven't heard of any gangs operating through here, though could be some guys passing through. Any chance of an inside job?" Duncan asked.

Jones and Lavier looked at each other meaningfully.

Duncan noticed it and waited.

"Could be, Ranger," Lavier said.

"Go on."

"We had a fella we had to let go last week. Name of Red Hyatt. These beeves were all in one pasture about four miles up from here. He had been one of the cow men who watched them. He wasn't any too happy when we let him go. Stormed off," Lavier said.

"Anybody else go with him when he left?" Duncan asked.

"No."

"Was he close with any other of your employees?"

"Not really. Which is why we let Red go. He had a bad humor and got into arguments and even fist fights. George and I figured if we didn't get him out of here, we'd eventually have shots fired," Lavier said.

"How long before you get a group of your riders back so we can talk with them?"

Jones looked up at the sun and thought for a moment. "'Bout an hour, I expect, we should have five in here what bunked with him."

"Assuming we get some leads, could one or both of you and a few men become a posse to go with me to try and get those beeves back?"

"Yep," Jones began, "we was going to pull together a posse, but knew there'd be gunplay or a hanging involved. So, we figured it would be better to wire the law to make it all official-like."

"Probably a good move, Mister Jones. How many? One or both of you and three others, maybe?"

Jones looked at Lavier. "Can we spare three if both of us are riding?" he asked.

Lavier said, "Not really, but I figure you, me and two of the boys could bring the herd back okay. I doubt they got more than three or four rustlers, including Red.

Would be five of us, including the ranger against four of them. Should be fine. 'Specially with the ranger wheeling his six shooter."

"I agree. I'd go after three or four alone. I grew up on small cattle spread, but I'm not sure I want to try to drive forty cows back alone over unfamiliar ground," Duncan said.

"You ain't worried about the shooting part, then?" Jones asked.

"It's what I do."

The men retired to the ranch house and Mrs. Jones served a meal of steak, potatoes and apple pie. Duncan thought it seriously beat the trail meals he would have this week. He was right.

Once the men returned, Duncan asked if he could talk with them alone. Jones did not want him to, but Duncan insisted, stating sometimes employees talk more openly if their boss, or in this case, bosses were not listening.

He met with them in the bunkhouse.

"Men, I am Sergeant James Duncan of the Arizona Rangers." He could see some recognized his name. "I have been called in to investigate the rustling of forty cows from this spread. It appears the suspect may be your former associate Red Hyatt. I have asked Mister Jones and Lavier to speak with you without them present. I want you to speak openly. We need to get these cattle back to the Bar seven as soon as possible."

He paused and looked at the five men.

"Did Red Hyatt ever express anger with this outfit? Desire to have his own spread? Getting even?" he asked.

Silence.

He waited a full minute.

"Come on now, men. He was a troublemaker. One way or the other, two of you are going to be part of a posse to capture him and drive the beeves back to the ranch. I need your input here."

One man spoke up.

"Red was a hard case. I didn't like him and fought with him once. Most of us did. We had some money missing a couple of times and couldn't pin it on anyone. But, we sure as hell didn't think it was one of us sitting here now. So he was left."

"So, you think he was a thief to begin with?" Duncan prompted the man to continue.

He looked around at his fellow riders. They all nodded. "Yeah, I think he was. And, it shore is suspicious. The cattle disappeared a day after he left," he finished.

"Did he have any friends off the ranch or any local relatives who might help him?" Duncan asked.

Another rider spoke up.

"Red had a couple of worthless bums he drank with when we went into Winslow. I expect if he looked for help, they'd be the first place he'd look. He would know not to ask any of us. We been with Mister Jones for ages and he's been righteous with us," he said.

"Do y'all have any ideas about where he would drive a small herd?" Duncan asked.

"Well, he'd want to get it off this spread. And, this is a big one," the first man said.

"A couple of places along Clear Creek are off the road and have grass and water both," he continued.

"How obvious are these places to people traveling by?" Duncan asked.

"Not very."

Duncan thought to himself. If these places were off the busy, traveled road, it would be easy to pick up the tracks of forty cows and three or four horsemen once they left the road.

"How far off the road are each of these places?" he asked.

"First one is about a mile next one is longer. Maybe four miles to the creek. I'd check the first, but figure it would be the second, if I was tracking," the man said.

"Are there other similar places with grass, water and privacy y'all can think of?" Duncan prompted.

"Not real close by," a rider who had not spoken yet chimed in. "There are some way off to the west in some rough country twenty miles or so further down, but I don't think he'd want to drive stolen cattle so far on a public road. Red is an ass, but he ain't a stupid ass."

"Last question, for now at least," Duncan said. "How far are these places? Can we ride to them today, or start at dawn?"

The last man who spoke did so again.

"The first is twenty miles, the second another five miles on. We could make it today but would have to camp too near where they might be. We'd be better to leave early, ride hard, and check the first. If they ain't there, go to the second and take them down. If Fred here was right about the place way off the path west of the road, it's going to be a long trail."

"Okay. Sounds like a good approach. I will go talk with your bosses. They will come back and either ask for two volunteers for the posse, or just put you on the posse. Either way, we will set out first light with guns, and camp gear and grub for maybe three days. Thank y'all."

Duncan turned and walked out of the bunkhouse door and towards the ranch house. He wanted to get some rest for tomorrow. He knew the riders would want to talk half the night, so he would pitch his normal camp off somewhere away from the houses once he spoke with Jones and Lavier. He checked with the riders and found where to feed and water Ace and put him for the night.

***

Duncan talked with Jones and Lavier. They selected two men to ride with them and Duncan as the posse-men. Lavier said both had handguns and the ranch would provide Winchester rifles, saddle scabbards and ammunition. Mrs. Jones insisted Duncan join them for dinner and bunk in a spare bedroom in the main house. He accepted. Eschewing the china pitcher and bowl, he grabbed a hand towel and went out to the pump and washed his face and hands with very cold water. Unintentionally invigorated, he went in for an excellent dinner with some good coffee and followed by some good whiskey from Tennessee. The men plied him with questions about trailing the bank robbers and then the shoot-out on the train. He answered, trying to play down his role as much as possible. They were more impressed with his gun toting fiancée than even his exemplary performance. Quite frankly, he was too. Jones said to be up an hour before daylight for breakfast and be ready to ride south an hour later.

The men were full of black coffee, steak, eggs and fried potatoes when they mounted up. The sky was beginning to lighten. Mrs. Jones had put two bags of victuals out and one of the riders tied a short line between the bags and slung it over his saddle, a bag hanging on each side. He was the usual cook for roundups.

The other posse man, Randy Giles, was the man who had told Duncan about where he would hide the stolen herd south of the ranch.

It took the posse the better part of the day to reach the first area to check. Along the way, Duncan rode off the road and located consistent cattle tracks. But, he knew, this was a busy road and it was not unlikely others may have driven a small herd along it.

At the first cutoff into the first meadow, Duncan asked the posse to stay on the road and let Giles and him ride quietly into the area to see if it was being used by Hyatt to hide the stolen cattle. The posse-men knew to come riding in fast if they heard shots. But, in the first several hundred yards, Duncan could not cut sign. No cattle had been driven this way. They returned and suggested it would be a good place to set up camp, having water and forage, since they did not want to ride blind into the second alternative location, only an hour or so ride away.

"Giles, can you recognize the cutoff to the second place in the dark?" Duncan asked while the men were sitting around Duncan's signature fire pit.

"Yeah, shouldn't be too hard. Once we go out to the road, it would be around five miles south from here and then almost four miles in. We could do like today. You and me ride ahead looking for sign. Iffen we find some early on, the others can follow us a few hundred yards or so back, so they can come up fast shooting." Duncan agreed with the plan and the men all smoked and talked a while then rolled up in their blankets. There did not seem to be a need for a sentry. Besides, Duncan had Ace hobbled in the remuda. Ace would whistle if anybody or anything came around.

***

The cook put coffee on at four in the morning and the men were on the trail heading south by four-thirty. Before five, Giles had found the cutoff and Duncan rode along it slowly with the rider as the others followed out of sight behind them.

Duncan immediately found several day-old tracks for a large number of cattle for such a small path. It was still dark, and he found them by dismounting and holding a lit wooden match over the path and the grass beside it. He sent Giles back to apprise the posse and remind all to take caution to be as quiet as possible. Duncan rode on ahead, rifle held across his pommel and dismounting to look for sign periodically. After several miles, he dismounted and led Ace. Once he could hear cattle in the distance in the gray dawn, he tied Ace to a tree and awaited the other four.

Duncan greeted the men with his '94 Winchester held high. He pointed to it with the other hand, signifying the men should draw their own long guns. Going into his saddlebag, he removed two boxes of twenty cartridges each and put them in his coat pockets.

"When we get within a hundred yards of their camp, I want two men to move out and flank them on either side. Don't get across from each other, I don't want any of our men shot in a crossfire. When I see or at least figure y'all are in place, I will fire a shot over their heads and call out for them to surrender. Don't be the first to shoot. I'd rather take them prisoner and let the Territory handle them. Everybody ready to move out?" The men nodded, somewhat nervously. Experienced riders, these were still men who were not used to people shooting back.

Duncan saw the two sets of flankers move into trees on either side of the meadow. He knew Clear Creek lay directly ahead. Once they disappeared from his view in the dawn, he gave them four minutes to get set.

He fired the .30-30 at a 30-degree angle over the camp, just high enough to go over the horses and cattle between the camp and the creek. The sound was loud in air heavy with moisture before the sun rose to burn it off. The crack of the Winchester reverberated in the trees on either side as the twenty-three hundred foot per second round blasted over their heads.

After a few seconds, Duncan called out, "Arizona Rangers. You are surrounded. Throw your hands up and surrender. Now."

Three drowsy men struggled to their feet and raised their hands.

"Posse move in, rifles at ready," Duncan ordered.

They lined the men up and Lavier stoked the campfire back to life for some light.

It did not take Allan J. Pinkerton to see which one the ringleader, Red Hyatt was. The other two were confirmed to be the gadabouts he used to drink with. Maybe now, he would have the opportunity to share a cell with them, Duncan thought.

He showed the posse-men how to pat down the suspects for weapons. All they found was two pocketknives. The revolver belts were rolled up by each man. There were no rifles in camp.

Lavier walked back by the remuda. He located three horses with Bar 7 brands on their flanks. He suspected there would be a lot more. Walking back, he said, "I guess you can add horse theft to the charges, Duncan."

"Will do. Mister Lavier. Could you or one of the boys get me a final count on the number of beeves stolen for my report and testimony? And, if all the cattle are branded Bar 7, too." Lavier nodded to the cook who went through camp to where the herd was grazing.

He came back with a head count which coincided within a cow to what Jones and Lavier had estimated being stolen.

All had the Bar 7 brand, except for a few unbranded calves.

"Mister Jones, as the victimized party, it would be good if you went with me to Holbrook where I put the prisoners in the county sheriff's jail to be held until tried for cattle and horse rustling. Maybe we can take the prisoners back to your ranch ahead of Lavier and the two riders driving the cattle back. Then, you decide whether you want to take them to Holbrook on the stolen horses and bring the horses back or put them in a wagon and drive the wagon back. Whatever's best for you. But I need you to leave a signed statement they were recovered with your property and I arrested them for rustling after we caught them red-handed."

"Duncan, I think I'd rather go to the ranch, transfer them to a wagon and take their sorry butts to Holbrook that way," Jones replied.

"We won't be able to get them all the way to Holbrook today. Do you have a place we can lock them up overnight?" Duncan asked.

"How 'bout we tie them up to a tree and I will have my men take turns guarding them tonight at the ranch and we'll take them first light tomorrow?"

"Holding them here is fine, but the Territory only issued me one set of handcuffs. They are the good double-locking Tower model, so I can cuff two men together left hand to right hand. So, we'll have one we have to tie with rope. We can figure it out," Duncan said. He thought about the great deputy marshal Bass Reeves under Judge Parker in Ft. Smith. At least he left with warrants in his saddlebags and a driver with a wagon and chains following. Duncan did not have the same luxury a decade later.

The black deputy was also an ordained Baptist minister who preached to his prisoners nightly. The sermons, he felt, helped ready them for his boss, the famous Hanging Judge.

Jones and Duncan rode ahead, one prisoner handcuffed in the front, two tied in the front. Jones led the procession and Duncan followed the prisoners. Lavier and the two riders drove the cattle and quickly fell behind. The prisoners arrived at the ranch around dusk. Mrs. Jones had food for all.

Duncan left the men secured in front. They had to be that way to ride and now to eat and relieve themselves. Otherwise, Duncan felt more comfortable when prisoners were secured with their hands in back. He got three lariats and tied each of the men around the waist with one lariat and the free end around a tree. All were tied to the same tree and had ten feet of movement. They remained under guard throughout the night.

The next morning, they were fed and put in the back of a buckboard driven by Jones. Duncan followed and they went north, then east to Holbrook.

Midday, Jones pulled the wagon up in front of the sheriff's office. He watched the prisoners, as a large number of town people looked on, and Duncan went in. He returned shortly.

"The sheriff is in and he and a deputy are rearranging some prisoners in cells to make room for these. The Circuit Court Judge is riding his circuit. He won't be back here for ten days. The sheriff is getting a justice of the peace to come over and formally charge the prisoners and sign for them to be held without bail until the trial when the judge gets back. Part of the process will be my arrest report and your statement about what happened and how you identified your cattle and horses in their possession yesterday. I will get a transfer paper from the sheriff saying I arrested three men and delivered them into his custody in good health with no injuries," Duncan told Jones.

"Seems like a helluva of lot of paper shenanigans

for three fellas who should have been hanged where we caught them," Jones said.

"The old way was simpler, but this is what we have to do now," Duncan replied as he was unloading the three from the bed of the buckboard. He took them in, and the deputy put them in three different cells. The cells already had other prisoners, so this broke up groups who knew each other. Strangers were less likely to plan escapes than friends.

Jones and Duncan sat at a table with pen and paper and Duncan walked the rancher through how to phrase his statement. He then filled out his arrest report in duplicate using carbonated paper for the justice's copy. Any mistakes either had to be crossed through and initialed or started over. He could not use an ink pen because the impression was too shallow, so he wrote in pencil. It was detailed enough for a report, but short enough the telegraph operator could readily convert it to a wire for Rynning.

The date of the trial was fixed, so he wired Miranda to give her his schedule. He was very conscious of having to work around the wedding. Duncan also knew the date for the trial was contingent upon the judge finishing trials along the circuit and getting to Holbrook when they thought he would. The justice of the peace reminded Duncan trial dates were not "cast in stone" until the judge was in town.

Duncan bade goodbye to the rancher and mounted Ace for the trip back to Wickenburg. It was about two hundred forty miles. He figured he might camp in the dense forest south of where they caught the rustlers, or maybe ride on to Payson and a real hotel. It depended on the progress he and Ace would make. Duncan contemplated and spoke to Ace as they rode on. It was nice to drop off prisoners instead of a trail of dead bodies for a change. The horse whinnied. Duncan took for agreement and patted him on the neck as they rode southwest.

Duncan spent the next two days transiting the Mogollon Rim, camping in areas with wood for fires and far more greenery than he often saw. Other than wanting to get back to Miranda, it was a good experience being east of Prescott. He had only seen the Grand Canyon once in the northwest of the Territory, bordering Utah and Nevada. But, having now travelled around, he marveled at the beauty and diversity of Arizona and enjoyed riding through it, with the possible exception of the high desert country, which made for difficult tracking and camping.

He passed through Prescott, sent a wire to Rynning saying where he was, and he was going to stay a few days there to reinforce the relationship between the Yavapai Sheriff's Office and the rangers. From there, he would patrol over to the Colorado River and back. His route would take him through Salome, a small town where he was well-known from his gunplay there.

Duncan got back to the ranch just before dinner. Miranda ran out and jumped into his arms. His parents came to the door and stood smiling. Coming home always gave the ranger a good feeling. Now it gave him an even happier feeling, as the time for him and Miranda being together came closer and closer.

After he had greeted his parents, Miranda helped him unpack Ace. She sorted his travel clothes and they put his equipment away and trailed behind him as he led the big blue roan to the barn for brushing, feeding and watering. After, when he turned the horse loose in the corral, it frolicked like a colt, causing the ranger and the woman holding his hand to smile and be every bit as happy as the horse.

***

Duncan spent the next day at the Yavapai Sheriff's Office, discussing what was going on in the county and how the two entities could work together to keep the peace. Ev Masters was helpful. Conversations with the monosyllabic Roberts were more difficult. He let Ev do the talking and nodded.

A rider at a small ranch near Tuzigoot had gone missing. Tuzigoot was a tall pueblo ruin known to the Yavapai people as Haktlakva. Angus had taken his teenaged son to see the large complex of rooms while on a wild horse hunting trip. Ev had sent a deputy up to investigate, but he had returned to Prescott with the suspicion an argument had broken out, the missing rider had been killed and his body roped up into one of the complex's hundred plus rooms to fade into eternity. Ev felt like it would be a perpetually open case. Other things going on in the county were misdemeanors and not felonies. Burglaries, shoplifting thefts, drunken brawls. Nothing really required Arizona Ranger involvement. But, as the sheriff, chief deputy and ranger knew, the situation could change in the time it took to cock a Colt. And, it probably would.

The following day was Friday. Duncan and Miranda saddled Ace and the livery horse and began the ride back to Wickenburg for the upcoming school week. Miranda knew , after a week off, she would have to re-tame the boys in her class but was confident she would do quickly.

It was almost dark when the two arrived at the schoolhouse. The road was virtually deserted on Friday night. While Miranda built a fire and began dinner with groceries brought with them from Prescott, Duncan turned the horses out into the corral and made sure there was sufficient grass and water available for them. He planned to return the livery horse in the morning and buy feed to keep in the shed for Ace. He would keep an eye out for a horse to buy for Miranda, knowing she had a strong preference for black horses.

Duncan put his tarp shelter up in the grass under a tree near the corral. Then built a fire pit and got a fire going.

Miranda walked out.

"You staying out here tonight?" she asked.

"Things are so quiet, I thought I'd put this up as a dodge," he replied.

"So, you were thinking of bundling with your fiancée?" she asked.

"I was thinking of a lot more, but just planning the bundling part," he said.

"You realize I am a formerly married woman and not a young maiden?" she asked rhetorically.

"Yep."

"We are within a few weeks of being married."

"Yep."

"It may not be too soon for us now," she said.

"Unless someone bushwhacks me and I leave a pregnant fiancée," he said seriously.

"Hmm...there is that. Of course, who's going to shoot you? A lot of people have tried. All are buried now."

"I could go up against a gang at one time, somebody could shoot me in the back...or, there's always going to be the one person who is faster."

"Doubt if he's been born yet," she commented.

"Hope not. But I suspect he has and he's out there somewhere. I figure a lawman has a certain number of wins. He won't ever know how many until the one after the last win. Then, it will be too late," Duncan said thoughtfully.

Miranda looked at her future husband silently for a long time before speaking.

"You are amazingly serious. Have you had a premonition or something?" she asked.

"Nope. Not at all. I'm just being realistic. Anybody can go against the wrong person. A farmer, shopkeeper, bartender. Anybody. But, a Western lawman in a wild territory has a hundred times more chance than those fellas. Maybe if this sheriff thing comes through, my job will get more administrative and the chances of gunplay may go down. Or maybe not. But, in the meantime, I have to keep my hand fast and have eyes in the back of my head. It's the nature of the beast, honey."

"So, we'll bundle. Maybe," she responded, then said, "Come on in and have some beef, beans and cornbread. I also fixed a pot of coffee. Nice and strong like you like it."

"That's my girl."

"You better believe it, honey."

The two walked hand-in-hand into the cottage. Duncan could smell dinner and coffee from fifty feet outside. For some reason, his mind went to his friend Aaron. Before he left, he asked him to check periodically for letters addressed to him at General Delivery, Kamloops, British Columbia. Duncan determined to write a letter to him this week.

They enjoyed dinner and spoke quietly about Miranda's teaching job and what they would do when she moved on to Prescott, assuming all their plans played out. Still hypothetically, they talked about the three hundred twenty-acre Hatton ranch between the Duncans and Prescott. After seeing it, they agreed with Angus burning the house down and building a new one would be the only viable choice. And, the new one would be near the woods towards the road frontage. Nobody could figure why old man Hatton had built in the most desert, scorpion-filled parcel on the place and then had tried to farm it.

They talked about the type and size houses they liked. Prairie style, Victorian, cabins were discussed. They agreed the best would be a one-story frame they could readily add to as the need arose. In other words, a Western ranch house. They would need a barn and corral right off. Maybe even before a permanent house was built.

The conversation continued in bed, her head on his shoulder until she went to sleep. Duncan thought for a long time. He was going to like married life, though it was something he had never given thought to until meeting this remarkable woman after the bank robbery. A lot had happened between winter and spring. He fell asleep, listening to the wind rattling the loose windows and night birds calling.

The next day, Duncan put some final touches on the shed serving as his temporary stable and tack room. He strapped on the Colt and rode towards Wickenburg. There was a rancher who raised horses on the other side of town from the schoolhouse. He introduced himself and the type horse for which he was looking. The man had it. He also had a good used saddle, bridle, saddlebags and a carbine scabbard.

With the horse saddled, Duncan rode her around the ranch. She was quick and seemed smart. She was quarter horse-sized and would be easier for Miranda to mount and dismount than a larger horse like Ace. Duncan rode back to the rancher and they reached a fair price and shook. Duncan headed back to the schoolhouse, leading the young black mare, Raven.

He tied Ace and Raven at the hitching post. He called out for Miranda to come outside. She was immediately on the horse and riding off happily at a trot then a full gallop.

17

ARIZONA TERRITORY 1904

Duncan stopped at the telegraph office as soon as he arrived in Wickenburg. There was no assignment from Rynning, so he sent a wire reiterating his patrol plan for the week. He also sent a letter he had written the night before to Aaron Piyahgonte updating him on happenings since he had been back in Arizona. He asked about Wenonah and how things were working out with them. At the general merchandise, he picked up a bag of jerky strips from the big jar on the counter, two pounds of pinto beans and a similar sized bag of Ariosa coffee. He also got a small bottle of French perfume for Miranda. He got a side of cured bacon at the butcher's shop and mounted Ace for the ride back.

When he got home, as he was beginning to think of the small school cottage, he gave Miranda the perfume and got a kiss in return. He knew he would have gotten the kiss with or without a gift.

They transferred a quarter of the beans and coffee into smaller cotton bags and tied them tightly with draw strings. While at the ranch, Miranda had learned from Ann how to make Indian fry bread in her black cast iron skillet. She had learned a lot from and about the Scottish woman. She also learned a lot she loved but would never share. The woman's secrets were as interesting as she herself was. Miranda wrapped a three-day supply of the fry bread and bacon in cheese cloth.

Duncan kissed Miranda again and mounted Ace. He turned the big horse due west and headed for Salome and the Colorado River beyond for his patrol. Duncan was not deterred from riding through and "showing the flag" as Rynning called it, though he knew he was not popular in Salome because of killing Tonopah Creel. Creel may have been a no-good killer, but he was Salome's no-good killer. And, he threw a lot of money around for drinks.

But, Rynning was serious about letting people know the rangers were out and about doing their job. And, in a manner where they might appear without notice anywhere. Rynning believed in a surprise element to enforcing the territorial laws and so did his sergeant.

Duncan rode high desert country with small mountains on each side until late afternoon. He did not see a soul. The lack of tall trees to block the wind made the high desert feel colder. He rode over dry sand. The only greenery was small junipers and the occasional pine. Duncan picked a spot with enough browse for Ace. He poured water from one of the three canteens he had put in his gear into his Stetson and set it down in front of Ace.

"Here ya go, boy. Drink up. We'll find some fresh water tomorrow in Salome," he said to the roan who seemed to understand every word.

He pulled the saddle and bridle off and hobbled Ace. Duncan laid out his saddlebags and bedroll. He took the trowel from the former and dug the two holes and adjoining tunnel for his fire pit. He collected a full night's supply of dead wood and cut it appropriately with his hatchet. Eschewing the big Bowie, Duncan took out his Barlow folding knife, and shaved a pine stick into a fuzz stick with enough sappy area to catch a spark. He struck the steel against his knife blade and the resin in the fuzz stick caught. He placed tinder on top of the stick. As it caught fire, he added larger and larger wood until he had a campfire going in the fire pit. He put his coffee pot with more canteen water on the grill and added some bacon to fry. He placed some of Miranda's fry bread to the side to warm it. Thirty minutes later, he had a trail dinner. He unrolled his tarps and blanket and slept under the stars, looking up at the Arizona sky for a long time before falling asleep.

The next day, Duncan rode into Salome. People turned away. The town had a feeling of criminality. The lawman sensed it every time he rode through. The reception solidified the feeling. He knew in most places he would have been a bit of a celebrity after the gunfight. But the man he killed apparently threw a lot of money around and was missed. He tied Ace up in front of the bar where it had occurred. It was the only place in town to eat.

The bartender should be more friendly after the lawman had let him keep the proceeds of Creel's belongings and horse once he covered the outlaw's funeral.

Duncan loosened his Colt's .45 in his holster and walked into the bar, spurs clinking on the wooden floor covered with sawdust.

The barkeep gave him a friendly look. A look not shared by his patrons.

"Howdy, Ranger. What brings you to our little slice of heaven this time? Warrants?"

"No, just passing through on patrol," he responded.

"How about a sandwich and a beer?" Duncan asked.

"I think I can arrange those. Ham okay? The beer ain't too cold, but it's wet at least."

"Wet is good after the ride over from Wickenburg. While you are fixing it, got a pump where I can fill my canteens?"

"Sure. The pump is in the back. Get your canteens and fill 'em up. By the time you finish, lunch will be on the bar here."

The bartender's word proved to be true. Duncan sat sideways at the bar, to be able to see anyone who came in the door or otherwise moved behind him.

"Anything of interest going on here?" Duncan asked.

"Not really. Things kinda settled down after you shot Creel. I've had to crack a few drunk skulls with my bat here," he held a short club up for Duncan to see, "but comes with being a barkeep in a town with no law presence. 'Cept for you riding by, of course," he said.

"Any mining going on? Seems to be spreading all around. Copper and all," Duncan asked.

"A little. Thank God. Half of these men are copper miners. They are the only ones around with enough jingle in their pockets to buy a beer. If I had to rely on the locals, I'd be out of business."

Duncan nodded, took the last swallow of his beer and rose.

"What do I owe you?" he asked.

"Two dollars ought to cover it," the barkeep said.

Duncan put two silver dollars on the scratched bar and nodded to the barkeep. He picked up the refreshed canteens with his left hand and kept his right hovering near the walnut grip of this .45 as he walked out of the door. He tied the canteens on with a latigo and untied Ace. Mounting, he continued his way west.

As he rode, he encountered more cottonwoods and greenery.

He camped along the Colorado River, its sounds lulling him to sleep, though with the Winchester in his bedroll beside his leg. This was rough country. He had not seen anyone on the ride over from Salome.

Though he still had two and a half canteens of water, he found water coming out of the rocks and running into the river. He tasted it. It was cold and pure. Better than he metallic tasting water from Salome. He emptied his canteens and refilled them with the mountain water and gave Ace a hatful.

On the way back, he stopped and spoke with several people riding west. One group was three miners heading for California to find work. Another was a pair of riders looking for cattle work. He ascertained they were unfamiliar with the territory and told them unless they were bound for California by way of the Mohave Desert, they had better head north to Kingman for work. They changed direction and rode off.

Duncan worried about anyone who was not more prepared for a journey. They would likely have ended up on the side of the trail with their bones bleaching in the sun.

On the second night, he rode into the school yard and whistled. It was not late and there was a light on in the cottage. Miranda, in a white nightgown, peered out, the old single barrel shotgun subtly in her hand.

She leaned it against the door jamb and came running out, silhouetted by the light behind her in the house. Duncan thought she was probably the most beautiful woman in the world.

He did not even pretend to pitch camp outside this night. He put Ace in the corral and climbed in the bed. They talked a while about the upcoming wedding. Miranda had coordinated a date two weeks hence by mail with

Ann and Mary Louise Brodie.

The next day, Duncan wrote his weekly report about the uneventful patrol from Wickenburg to the Colorado River and rode into town to post it. After he mailed the report, he checked for wires from Rynning at the telegraph office. There was nothing from Rynning. But there was a wire. It was from the governor summoning him to Phoenix at the earliest possible time. He rode back to the school and told Miranda.

Duncan hoped it was good news about the sheriff appointment but could not be sure. He knew he needed to represent himself well. He kissed Miranda and rode to Prescott. He left Ace with his father and they went to town in the buckboard.

Duncan bought a new black suit, a white shirt and tie, had his boots shined, and boarded the Santa Fe train for Phoenix.

Outside the station, he got on a Phoenix Street Railway car and rode to the capitol.

He went to the governor's office and presented himself. After a thirty-minute wait, the male secretary ushered him in. Alex Brodie stood and greeted him warmly.

"How is my cousin, James?" Brodie asked.

"Sir, she is as beautiful as ever and just as dangerous."

"Ha. Still packing the Colt's single action Army?" Brodie asked.

"Aye. Or the derringer you gave her. Or a .38 breako-pen. Or both. She is worried her former husband might try to do her harm. So, she's careful," Duncan said.

"Nothing about junior or his senior would surprise me. I hear I will be coming to Prescott for a wedding soon?"

"I hear the same, sir. I just got back from a patrol to the Colorado when I received your wire. But first, Miranda gave me the news about the wedding."

"Well, James. I have some more news. I suspect it might be beneficial for your marriage. Jim Roberts has decided he wants to go back to being a regional deputy near his ranch and raise fine horseflesh like he did before he had to step in as acting sheriff. He raises some of the best horses around yet continues to ride a damn mule. You may know I rode with Crook. He did the same thing. Rode a mule." Duncan nodded.

Continuing, the governor said, "I told you I had you in mind for his replacement. I have to appoint someone right away. Want it?"

Duncan did not pause.

"I have given it some thought and talked with Miranda since you and Captain Rynning brought it up. I would be honored to serve the office where our friend Buckey O'Neill was sheriff."

"Well, it's a done deal then." Brodie stood and the two men shook hands.

"I will prepare a news release. Since you are marrying my kin, I won't make it too suspicious by swearing you in here and sending you back to introduce yourself. Let it hit the news rags tomorrow and present yourself to the judge. He will be in Prescott tomorrow afternoon. I told him to get his butt there. He will swear you in," Brodie said.

"What does Jim Roberts think of all this?" Duncan asked.

"He was pleased with your selection. I understand he told the chief deputy, a fella named Masters, and he was really tickled. Masters said he taught you everything you know."

"He actually did. About being a lawman that is. My pa taught me the tracking and trail-craft and such. But, Ev taught me how to arrest folks, particularly if they are peeved about it," Duncan said.

"I take it most of them are peeved?" the governor asked.

"Pretty much," was the response. "Governor Brodie, what should I do about the Rangers? Keep the badge until I get sworn in as sheriff? Is Captain Rynning aware of this yet?"

"The answer is 'yes' to both. You will need to send a wire or letter to him resigning once you are sworn as sheriff. Keep the badge until the wedding. He and I will both be there," the governor said.

"Yes, sir. So, this is effective immediately?" Duncan asked.

"Effective immediately, but you actually start once you take your hand off the Bible. I would like you to be sworn as soon as possible. In the meantime, let's go down the street and get some early lunch so you can get back on the northbound Santa Fe train for Prescott. I'm thinking my cousin will be pretty pleased. Her husband will make several times more money, stay at home almost every night, and probably dress more like a banker than a rider every day," Brodie said.

"I know she will, sir."

Duncan found lunch with a politician was a matter of trying to get past people who wanted to talk or had pressing matters they wanted the governor to know.

Once seated, things calmed down a bit. They spoke about the president, Buckey O'Neill, now dead for six years, and Miranda. The governor outlined his vision for the territory, including taxation and voting for women. He said after his term, he would likely go back in the Army for the rest of his working life. He promised Duncan the normal Army life was not as messed up as Tampa and Cuba had been. Duncan politely nodded but did not buy it.

"Sir, before we part, there's something I'd like you to consider," Duncan began. Brodie nodded for him to continue.

"Those young Yavapai men who ran away from the reservation and prompted the court-martial of Smoot and all. They were not bad boys. Just a little wild like many their age white or red. Would it be possible for them to be pardoned, or the warrants out for them dissolved? It would be a good show of faith on behalf of the government to the Indians."

"I will consider it. On the surface, it sounds like the fair thing to do. There are some who will not like it, but it's time old prejudices are forgotten," Brodie said.

"Here is a list with their names on it," Duncan said.

"If I can't do something legal here in the Territory, I will contact Major Simpson in Washington. If he won't move, I will send a letter to Teddy."

"Thank you, sir, for anything you can do."

The governor stood and they shook hands. Duncan thanked him for the faith the governor had shown selecting him and promised to fulfil his duties to the best of his abilities. They parted and Duncan went to the train station and bought a return ticked. He sent a wire for delivery to the schoolhouse. He could not preempt the governor's formal announcement, so he coded it. "Things sped up Stop Swearing tomorrow Stop Get ready to move Prescott Stop."

The northbound train steamed in two hours later and he climbed aboard and took a seat in the middle, so he could control both doors to the car if need be.

The train sped through generally inhospitable country. Country he had ridden and had slept in many times. Sitting in an office did not have appeal to him. But, he reckoned, such was the price of being able to go home to a loving wife at night.

Duncan arrived back in Prescott before stores closed and purchased several more dress shirts and ties and two more dark suits. He added two vests to wear with the new outfits, finding neither had a pocket large enough for the .38.

All he needed was the gold badge of office and it would likely come tomorrow.

He stopped in at the sheriff's office. Ev Masters was still there and beamed at him. There were several other deputies in, and he chatted with each in his current capacity, as no one in town knew what was going on. Only Duncan, Roberts, Masters and the judge were aware at this point.

Duncan expected the announcement to hit the papers tomorrow. Ev Masters said there was court in the morning, so he better get with the judge first thing in the morning.

He walked to the ranch and surprised his folks. His mother had not had a chance to change the bed linens in his old room and the bed smelled sweetly of Miranda... and a lingering disinfectant smell just barely noticeable. He put his hat on one corner of the chair and hung his gun belt on the other.

His mother was just finishing setting the table when he walked in. Angus arrived from washing up at the pump outside at the same time.

"Well, son. You look like you are going to be the next territorial governor in that suit."

"Not quite, Pa," he began, "but, I have just met with him in Phoenix and had lunch with him. Tomorrow morning, I will meet with the circuit court judge before his cases start and be sworn in as sheriff of this county."

"The appointment moved a lot quicker than I imagined.

I figured it would be six months or a year. But, tomorrow. Congratulations, son."

"Yes, honey. Congratulations," his mother added.

"The judge said he and Captain Rynning would be here for the wedding. He said once I was sworn in tomorrow, I should send the captain a telegram resigning and give him my sergeant's badge when I see him at the wedding. The governor wants me to take over the office immediately," he said.

"Where is Roberts going?" Angus asked.

"The governor said Roberts approached him and said he was ready to go back to horse ranching and maybe being a part-time lawman," Duncan replied.

"So, it was Roberts' idea. I didn't figure he was being pushed out. He's not the friendliest man in the territory, but he is a fine lawman. Honest and feared some because of his skill with the beat-up old Colt he keeps in his pants pocket," Angus said.

Duncan chuckled. "Don't knock pants pockets, Pa. Remember, the Earps and Holliday used their pockets instead of holsters at the lot near the OK Corral. Only the cowboy gang had leather on."

"So, you will take over any investigations still open?" Ann asked.

"Yes, Ma'am. I reckon I will," Dunlap answered.

They began to eat, and the talk almost ceased, as was the Western way.

After dinner, father and son smoked their briars and talked about the Hatton place, what kind of house to build and whether to jump into ranching immediately. Duncan said he had given it some thought and felt it would be better to become sheriff first and rancher later. His father agreed.

"You know, son, the Hatton place butts up against

this ranch. Which means one day, your spread will be six hundred forty acres," Angus said.

Duncan laughed. "Or, your spread will be. I may be a better gunsel than rancher, Pa."

"I got faith in you son. I always have and always will."

"I know, Pa. I have the best parents anywhere. I will try to never let y'all down in any way."

"You disappointing us is not a concern your Pa or I ever had, James. And, you have proven it once again with your choice of a wife and with the faith the governor has in you," Ann said.

"I will get sworn in by the judge first thing, then go to the telegraph office and send my resignation to the rangers. I'll keep a low profile until the papers come out and announce my appointment. Then, I have this beautiful brunette over in Wickenburg to move here. It's going to be a busy few days," Duncan said, thinking aloud.

"Let us know what you need from us," Angus offered.

"I will, Pa. Thanks. My pipe seems to have smoked itself out. I think I will turn in. I want to be outside the courthouse before eight in the morning. I'd sure be honored if y'all would come and stand with me for the swearing in."

"We will be there, son."

Duncan said goodnight and walked into his old bedroom. He could sure use a certain head nestled on his shoulder tonight.

Before he could pull his boots off, he heard Ace whistle. Somebody or something was out there. He had not heard hoofbeats during the conversation. But the big blue roan was never wrong.

Duncan strapped on his revolver and picked up the Winchester. As he walked towards the door, he saw Angus there already, carbine in hand.

They walked out to see a beautiful brunette climb down from a black horse.

"Howdy. Miss me?" Miranda said as she removed saddle bags and her .32-20 carbine from Raven.

***

After Raven had been taken care of and put in a stall, Miranda told the Duncans she had called school off once she got the telegram and saddled up. At a canter, it had taken her what she guessed was ten or twelve hours to ride the good dirt roads from Wickenburg, through Prescott to the ranch.

Before Duncan said anything, she offered, "With the hat and coat, I looked like a boy or a man. I had two revolvers and my carbine. I was in no danger at all, James."

"Let me fix you something to eat," Ann offered.

"No need. I have ridden enough with your son to automatically drink water and chew jerky and biscuits while riding. I am quite full, thanks. The idea of a pillow under my head sounds pretty good, though," Miranda said.

"The bed is ready," Duncan said. "Give me a second to move my stuff to the bunkhouse." She gave him a face his parents could not see.

"No way I was going to miss the swearing in."

She set her rifle in the corner and picked up Duncan's and followed him out the door and into the bunkhouse.

As she laid out his belongings, he built a fire. Miranda went out to the pump and filled the coffee pot with water for the morning.

She stretched up on her toes and kissed him. "Soon, Sheriff. Very soon," and walked out the door.

***

Angus got up early as he was wont to do, dressed in his

church going clothes, which he seldom wore. He had stopped going to church many years before. As he hooked Bub up to the buckboard, he noticed a faint smell of cleaner in the bed but figured Ann had used it and cleaned a spill while he was away. He was right.

Duncan came out of the bunkhouse in his black suit, white shirt, tie and Stetson. He had his six-gun belted low so a quick sweep of the coat's skirt would clear it for a draw. Not perfect, but still faster than the heavy cover of the winter coat he wore on the trail.

Ann and Miranda came out in dresses and shawls against the spring winds. Both epitomized Western women. Duncan noticed Miranda's purse seemed a bit lopsided. He chalked it up to the weight of a small revolver.

Duncan had suggested breakfast or an early lunch in town in lieu of fixing breakfast before leaving the ranch. It had not taken much selling to his mother.

He whistled for Ace, who came trotting over to him at the corral fence. The roan followed him through the open gate into the barn and was saddled and equipped with the usual carbine and several day supplies.

Duncan trotted the horse around to the buckboard and they left for town. He looked hard at the entry to the Hatton ranch and knew he needed to make an offer and begin construction of a house on it sooner than later. His parents had already suggested the bunkhouse for a temporary marital abode until the more final one was settled.

They tied the buckboard and Ace near the courthouse and walked in. Duncan led the way to the Clerk's Office and requested to see the judge in chambers, saying he was expected. The party was shown in within minutes.

Judge Jedediah Higgins was a small man in his late sixties. He had long white hair and a matching beard. Higgins was already wearing his robe.

"Well, young Duncan. I was already expecting you. And, I guess this must be your family?"

Duncan responded and introduced his parents and Miranda.

"We have two things today," Higgins said. Duncan looked at him with some degree of surprise.

"Governor Brodie had the Attorney General consult with me about dropping all charges against Aaron Piyah-gonte and five named other Yavapai Indians for leaving the reservation without permission. We talked about it and decided it was a criminal matter and not a military one. So, I have written a court order you can deliver to the Army to cease and desist in their pursuit of these young fellas. Immediately." The judge handed the order, signed in duplicate, to Duncan.

"Thank you, sir," Duncan responded surprised but pleased.

"Now, let's get on with the primary reason for your visit. Mom and fiancée, please hold the Bible."

They did and Duncan put his left hand on it and raised his right. One minute later, he was the Sheriff of Yavapai County, Arizona Territory.

The judge shook hands with all and excused himself to deal with what he referred to as the circuit's "recalcitrants".

The party left the court and walked a block to a café and had breakfast. Passing a newsstand, Angus picked up copies of different newspapers after seeing the frontpage articles.

The picture of his son must have been taken during the impromptu speech outside the hotel after Duncan had rescued Miranda, recovered the bank robbery money and decimated the bank and train robber gangs. It showed the governor, Rynning and Miranda clearly in the background.

The articles in all papers had the same photograph, probably provided by the Governor's Office, and the announcement about James Duncan, formerly Arizona Ranger Sergeant, being named Sheriff of Yavapai. Complimentary words about Roberts were followed by a biography of the new sheriff, including him saving Teddy Roosevelt's life twice during the charge up Kettle Hill and the San Juan Heights during the recent war. Brodie was a Republican. The Democrat-leaning papers added commentary about the new sheriff having the reputation of bringing in his prisoners dead instead of alive. And, so it began.

Following breakfast and some congratulations from citizens, the two women did some final shopping for items, including food for the upcoming wedding. Angus dropped them off and went to the livery to speak with the blacksmith, and Duncan rode Ace to the Sheriff's Office and tied him out front.

Apparently, word of the swearing in had preceded him. Ev Masters shook his hand, as did the several deputies who were in the office.

"Ev, I am going to have to depend on you for guidance now every bit as much as when I was a wet-behind-the-ears deputy starting out. I'm sure glad I have you here to keep me straight." The message was sincere, but also a signal to Masters his job as Chief Deputy was secure since he worked at the pleasure of the Sheriff.

Roberts had come in and was sitting in his small office long enough to speak with Duncan and give him the gold star. He looked relieved to be out of public contact and updated Duncan briefly on what cases were going on, including a missing Easterner whose father had sent a private detective from Richmond to Prescott. Duncan asked the missing man's name and did not give a "tell" by hesitating, blinking or looking away when Riley Hancock was mentioned. He just nodded and said he would talk with the detective as soon as he could.

Roberts said the village near his ranch was growing and though he wanted to step down as sheriff, he asked the governor if he could remain a deputy on full deputy salary and cover his area on an as-needed basis. He said the governor had agreed. So did Duncan, who considered Roberts too much of an asset to lose and said as much.

With the brief conversation done, the old sheriff gave the new sheriff a shiny gold star, some keys and pointed to a pile of papers he should sign. He arose, nodded at Duncan and walked out. Duncan knew the man's strengths and eccentricities and nodded back, taking no offense. He pinned on the badge and began to read the paperwork and sign the ones. All but a few made sense to him. He would ask Masters about the remaining ones later. The missing ex-husband worried Duncan. A lot.

Duncan inspected the jail from a perspective that was new for him. He was now an administrator, a strange and new function for him. The chief walked around and gave him suggestions he had not been able to clear with Roberts. All were reasonable. Duncan agreed to prioritize them with Masters and study the budget to see what would be done first.

He spent a long time studying the Wanted poster board in the public area. Apparently, the private detective, from some agency other than Pinkerton's, had printed up Missing Person posters with Hancock's face and description and the detective's contact information. It was the man he had noted getting off the train. And, had some concerns about. There was a reward. Duncan wondered if it was Dead or Alive. He smiled to himself. Dead would be so much better, knowing what Miranda had told him about her former husband.

Duncan and Masters sat in the sheriff's office and discussed strategy briefly. Duncan said he wanted to walk around town and "show the flag", then over the next several weeks, ride by the larger ranches and do courtesy calls on the ranchers. He would visit any small ranches or mines along the way for the same purpose.

"You gonna wear that suit you got on like Bat Masterson did?" Masters asked.

"I think so. I believe it shows respect for the office. Maybe not on the trail. And, I am sure as hell not going to wear a derby hat like Bat did."

"Hmm...would not be the first sheriff here to wear one if you did," the chief said, referring to Roberts, who generally wore a derby with his white shirt and tie shoes.

"No, but I guess my Stetson will represent going back to the old way for Western lawmen. I think I will save this old Gus-creased one for the trail and get a silver belly one with a cigarette curl for in town."

"Damn, boy. You are gonna be a dude," Masters said, then reddening as he realized he was now talking to his new boss.

"Ev, let's get something straight up front. You are my mentor and friend. I expect you to always be. It's 'Ev' and 'Duncan' or 'James'. You can and should say anything you want to me. Anything you would have said when I was a deputy who didn't know shite from Shinol'A," referring to the soon-to-be simplified shoe polish name.

"Ha-ha. When you're wrong, I will just say 'Shinol'A.' and you'll know what I mean," the chief offered.

"Aye, my friend. I surely will. And, I expect no less of you. I'm going to head out and walk around town a bit. See you later."

He walked past Ace and had a few words with him.

The horse snorted in reply and shook his head and the sheriff walked on. He had the new badge pinned on his vest. It was partially covered by his suit coat. Several people stopped and congratulated him. He would speak awhile, then move on.

Duncan was a known quantity in Prescott. Indeed, throughout the county. Nobody who lived here needed to take his measure as the new sheriff. His reputation for fairness as a deputy and for his gun as a ranger were well-known.

He saw Miranda and his mother come out of a general merchandise as he walked up the sidewalk.

"Out patrolling, Sheriff?" his fiancée asked.

"Yes, Ma'am. See anything I ought to know about?" he asked.

"Not a thing. Hmm...maybe one. Do you have to take over any unsolved cases from Sheriff Roberts?" she asked. It was the same question his mother had asked. His intuition and a private detective in town worried him. But he was not going to show it.

"Pretty much the way it works. If I solve the case of the Lost Dutchman mind, you will be the first to know. It's the only open case I know about for sure," Duncan said.

She did not appear to him to see the humor in his answer. She put her arm in his and they walked down the street, greeting people, as he kept his eye peeled for any threats.

Later, they heard Ann call from behind them and Miranda turned and went to her to finish their shopping. Duncan continued on.

***

Earl Royston had been a Baltimore detective. An unfortunate situation regarding false accusations about some missing evidence had interrupted his career fifteen years before retirement. He had drifted south to Richmond and opened up a detective agency and quickly became successful.

He had a good sense of how criminals worked.

Royston had fixed some issues for Riley Hancock's businesses.

The senior Hancock was mean and pompous and a poor excuse for a human. He was not beholden to anyone. Royston knew . But his accountant paid on time and the checks did not bounce.

The money was enough reason for Royston to continue to work for a man he neither trusted nor liked.

This case looked like a good one from the start. Hancock's son had disappeared three weeks ago. A visit to Richmond's Main Street train station ticket window had revealed he had bought tickets to Arizona. So did Royston. He could charge by the day, bill some good expenses and probably find the bum drunk in a saloon or beating up his ex-wife in Arizona Territory. He knew the history from trying to buy off victims and witnesses before the Pinkertons got to them. The buy-offs had not worked out well for Royston. The Pinks were just too thorough in their investigations. The old man had not blamed Royston. He knew full well what his son was like.

Riley Senior was not much better, just different. He curbed his lust for liquor and hourly lovers in favor of using his malevolent hubris by being a demanding and underhanded businessman.

Royston had picked the best hotel in Prescott, knowing the rich boy would pick only the most expensive, and questioned the day front desk clerk. The man had not wanted to talk, but a ten-dollar bill lubricated his vocal chords.

"Have you seen this man?" Royston asked, handing him a poster.

"I have been hired by his father to locate him. He has not responded to wires for several weeks now, actions very much unlike him. He and his father are real close," Royston lied.

"Yep. He had room 210. His stuff is still there. If he's not back in a day or two, I am going to have to put it in a locker until I find out what to do with it."

"When did you last see Mister Hancock?"

"Coupla afternoons ago. He had come in from lunch and asked me about two women who had just ridden by in a buckboard."

"Who were these women?" Royston asked, confident he knew who one of them was.

"I think one was Missus Duncan. Her husband is a rancher about three miles up the road in front of the hotel. To the right."

"Did her name seem to ring a bell for Hancock?" the detective asked.

"He kinda lit up when I said the other woman was the school marm from Wickenburg who was gonna marry the Duncans' son," the man told Royston.

"What happened then?" Royston asked.

"Mister Hancock went up to his room, came back down and went out the door," the clerk said.

"Did you see him after?"

"Yeah, I saw him ride by a while later. Mebbe after getting something to eat. He was heading out of town." The clerk said, "I figure he had gotten a horse from the livery stable and was riding out to the Duncan ranch."

"What day did you say that was?" Royston prompted, knowing the man had not yet mentioned the day.

"It was Wednesday afternoon."

"Did he return anytime Wednesday?" Royston asked.

"I went off duty before seven. He didn't come back before then. I think I'd a heard if he had come back any time after, since I talked with my relief and the manager about what to do with his stuff in the room."

"I'll need the key to search his room. You can go with me if you want. The items there will need to be packed for shipment back to his family if he doesn't show up in another week or two."

They went to the room and Royston searched it thoroughly in the desk clerk's presence. It did not look like a room the resident had permanently vacated. The suitcase, clothes in the wardrobe and no money or guns, suggested Hancock had left with the full intention of returning later. Or, Royston wondered, was it a setup for a disappearing act. Was he going to kill his ex-wife and disappear? Or, had he committed some other crime—probably against a prostitute—that necessitated faking his death?

"Which way is the livery stable? I might need a horse anyway," Royston asked after the room search.

The man pointed left out the door and told him it was about a hundred yards down the street.

Royston walked down to the livery stable and identified himself. He gave the owner a copy of the Missing poster.

"He wanted the best horse and tackle I had, so I got him Crook, a black. He rode out. It was late Wednesday. The horse came back the next morning without a rider. I went over to the sheriff and let him know. He sent a deputy out to look for him and could not find hide nor hair."

"Did he have a bedroll or saddlebags or canteen, anything suggesting he'd be gone several days?" Royston asked.

"I wouldn't know. He rode out of here with just the

saddle and bridle. Whether he picked up gear, I couldn't say," the liveryman said.

"What was the condition of the horse when he got back? Any injuries to the horse or signs of blood on the saddle?" Royston asked.

"None at all. Crook didn't look any the worse for wear."

"I guess I might need a horse to ride out the direction Hancock took. Is the same horse available?"

"No, he's out for a week on a hire. I have a good dun mare I could give you."

"Okay, saddle her up. I will come by in about an hour to get her," Royston said. He was going to change into better trail clothes and modify his gun before riding out towards the Duncan ranch and questioning everyone there.

But first, he thought he needed to drop by the sheriff's office and see what the yokels thought about Hancock's disappearance.

Ev Masters was the only one in when Royston entered.

Royston had questioned a younger deputy and left the Missing poster with him yesterday.

"I'm Detective Earl Royston from Richmond. I spoke with one of your deputies yesterday about a missing man I'm trying to locate. His name is Riley Hancock. I see you have my Missing poster on the board over there with your Wanted posters."

"Yep. It's over there all right. He went missing Wednesday and you arrived the next day. Pretty quick isn't it?" Masters asked.

"He actually left Richmond with no notice to his family three weeks ago. I have trailed him this far since," Royston said in response.

"I sent the deputy you talked with out Thursday morning after his livery horse showed up without a rider. My deputy rode and cut sign for a full twenty miles. He did not see any sign of Hancock. No sign of a fall, blood or a scuffle. Nothing. It's like he got kidnapped or just disappeared in thin air," the chief said.

"I have reason to believe he might have been heading to the Duncan ranch. His former wife is, or was, a visitor there."

Masters looked him in the eye without a waiver.

"The Duncan son who is to marry Missus Hancock was in the office this morning. He did not mention anyone coming to the ranch. The poster was hanging there. I told him about the case. Not a blink," Masters ended.

"Why would he have been in here?" Royston asked.

The look the lawman gave him did not leave any doubt he resented the question. Instead of saying anything, he picked up today's newspaper from his desk and slid it across the desk to Royston.

"Here, keep this. You may want to read it before you go pushing young Duncan too hard."

Royston left the sheriff's office and stopped at the café. He ordered a coffee and sat down to read. Reading page one, he realized the chief deputy's warning was valid. He had been given the Democrat paper, the one opposing Brodie and everybody on his team. By the editorial page, Duncan sounded like a stone-cold killer. And, he was the senior law enforcement officer in the very large county.

Royston had not lived this long by being stupid.

He decided to ride out the road like the deputy did and look for clues. Royston knew he was not a tracker. But he had certainly seen enough crime scenes in his career to recognize one more. He had to do due diligence. And, he had to bill the older Hancock for as much as he could.

Royston stopped in the hotel and changed to riding clothes and a less formal jacket. He took off his shoulder holster and removed the Merwin & Hulbert .44 with the three and a half-inch barrel he generally carried. Reaching into his bag, he removed a seven-inch barrel and replaced the shorter one with it. He also took out a longer brown leather holster and gun belt. The changeable barrel revolver was as close as a gun could come to a Swiss watch.

Mounting the livery horse, he rode out of town. He looked for the world like he belonged in Arizona. Royston was good. He always fit in and looked like he belonged. He was neither handsome enough nor ugly enough that anyone took particular notice of him. Just an average size brown haired man who could change into whatever clothes everyone where he was wore and disappear into the crowd.

He did not see any overt signs of a fight or robbery. He did not see blood signs. Or, a body. He did not see anything. Royston rode for two hours. He looked over the edge as well as he could on the parts of the road had cliffs. When he came to parts with woods, he dismounted and walked through them.

Hancock had left in the early evening on Wednesday and the horse was at the livery stable the next morning. Did the horse get back at nine at night? Or, six the next morning. If he knew more exactly, he could figure backwards to where the horse left from and where the likely scene of the crime, or riding accident was. But there was no way to compute when the horse got back. Whenever it was, it was likely before townspeople would be awake.

Royston went over alternative situations in his mind. Hancock could have fallen off the horse and rolled over a cliff. He could have been robbed, shot and pushed over a cliff. He could have been kidnapped and put in a wagon instead of riding on his own horse. He could have met someone and ridden off in a wagon with them. But, then, he would not have left his belongings at the hotel.

Other than something unexpected happening to Hancock, he would not have left his belongings in the hotel. Unless, it was a set-up and he had planned his own disappearance. The left belongings, the horse returning without him could have been planned.

Royston settled on the robbery and murder as one probability and the possibility Hancock planned his own disappearance as another.

But, why in Arizona Territory? Why Prescott? Because he wanted to see his ex-wife one more time before he dropped off the face of the earth? But he did not know she was going to be in Prescott. She lived in Wickenburg, a long ride away, he mentally answered himself.

What would have caused Hancock to want to disappear? Gambling debts? Had he gotten in so deeply the old man would not bail him out this time? Had he committed some heinous crime? Royston knew Hancock liked to rough up women. Had he killed a hooker by mistake? Maybe on the way out to Prescott...

Royston felt murder and disposal of the body was the most logical. But it presented him with problems. The senior Hancock would marshal his substantial assets for a search of the entire road, probably for fifty miles. And, there was always the possibility the son had doubled back around Prescott unseen and ridden south to whatever befell him. Royston might be along for the whole search. A lot of billable days. But no real solution unless they found him, which seemed unlikely to Royston.

Royston rode back to the hotel and took up pen and paper. He wrote to the senior Hancock and told him he had done a detailed search of the area his son had last been in and found no signs of wrongdoing.

He carefully asked the old man if he was aware of any

reason his son would wish to fake his own disappearance, because the evidence strongly suggested it.

He went down to the dining room and ordered a steak and bottle of wine.

Duncan went back to the sheriff's office and the chief deputy briefed him on the private detective's visit.

"What do you think, Ev?" Duncan asked.

"Well, I sent Bob Wilson out. He rode twenty miles and didn't see a thing. Now, mind you, he ain't the tracker you and your dad are. The damn fool either fell off his horse and rolled down a cliff or was robbed, killed then was tossed off a cliff. Nothing else makes sense to me."

Duncan thought for a minute.

"Could there be some plan we cannot imagine? Somebody after him and he wants to disappear for a while?"

"I 'spect so, Duncan. But I can't figure what or why?"

"Well, we have access to the best white tracker in the whole West about fifteen minutes up the road. Maybe Pa and I will take a ride out there and see if he can find something."

Both men had bad feelings about this. Neither mentioned those feelings.

Duncan rode Ace back out to the ranch. He found his father in the barn and told him about the detective and Hancock.

"Something may have happened here we aren't being told about," Angus said, pointing out a dried drop of blood in the bed of the buckboard. "The bed has been cleaned out, but I'm thinking this spot of blood was missed."

"Ma and Miranda both asked me at different times whether I was going to investigate unsolved cases from Roberts' tenure. I thought was odd. Especially with the only one being the disappearance of Miranda's former husband," the sheriff said.

Continuing, he asked, "Pa, do you have a few hours to ride with me for a spell up the road to look for sign? Whatever happened, we have to do this right."

"I think we need to. You going to wear the monkey suit?" the senior Duncan asked, nodding to his son's apparel.

Duncan shook his head as he headed to the bunkhouse to change into trail clothes.

He came out five minutes later looking more like himself, though with a gold star replacing the silver ranger badge.

They mounted up and rode, eyes to the dusty road, up into the hills.

"If I was going to hide a body, I'd dump it at old prospector cabin about fifteen miles up," Angus volunteered.

"Me, too, Pa."

When they got to the turnoff for the cabin without seeing anything suspicious on the way, Angus dismounted and studied the road and the path to the old cabin.

He looked up at his son with a worried look.

"It appears a buckboard about the size and type of ours turned off here. The tracks are several days old, but otherwise, nobody seems to have been up here for a long time," he said.

Both men rode, bent down to examine the path, until they got to the cabin. It was log, with a caved in roof. There was a well in the front.

Duncan dismounted and walked over to the cabin. The door was long gone so he stuck his head in the one-room structure.

"Nothing here, Pa," he called. He walked around back.

Angus heard a shot and pulled his carbine from the scabbard and strode around the cabin.

His son was reloading one round into the Colt's revolver. A headless six-foot rattler was still writhing on the ground in front of him.

Angus looked down.

"Good shot, Son," he remarked.

"Nothing here either," was all Duncan said as he walked back to where the horses were.

He bent over the well and sniffed. Nothing. There was an old rotten rope on a crank leading down into the well. He wound it up carefully to keep it from breaking. He leaned over and sniffed the water in the bucket as his father watched.

"Water is clear. No bodies down there. They'd smell to high heaven if there was a dead body. But, look at this."

He removed a Webley-Fosbery revolver with a perfect finish from the bucket. No rust at all. He broke it open easily, with the barrel tilting downwards. It held a full cylinder load of cartridges. None had been fired.

He put it back in the bucket.

"I'm thinking if we searched the bottom of the well, we'd find other items, maybe with Hancock's name on them," he said.

Father and son stared at each other without speaking.

Deciding, Duncan took out the Sheffield Bowie knife assigned him by Rynning and with a wide swing, slashed the bucket rope. The bucket fell to the water below with a splash, probably to stay there for eternity.

The two men mounted.

Angus looked at his son.

"There are some things in life best left alone. I think this is one. Something happened and the women are part of it. If they want to tell, they will. Otherwise, I reckon we better keep our thoughts and our findings to ourselves."

Duncan nodded.

They mounted and rode back to the ranch. Both women

looked at them questioningly. Both men smiled pleasantly and said nothing.

Duncan rode back into town and to the office.

"Pa and I rode quite a way out the road looking for signs of Hancock. Nothing on the road at all," he told Ev Masters.

"Well, if the two of you can't find something, it ain't there," the chief remarked as he tacked a couple of new Wanted posters on the board.

"Any of those of immediate interest to us?" Duncan asked.

"Doubt it. A couple of Nevada notices."

They heard the door open and Detective Royston came in.

He nodded at Masters, and introduced himself to Duncan, who he recognized from the photograph in the newspaper.

"I came in as a courtesy call to let you know I have recommended to my client the case be put on hold. I believe Hancock engineered his own disappearance to evade the law for a crime we don't know about yet or for gambling debts his father would refuse to cover. He will likely turn up when he thinks things have blown over, or he may never turn up," Royston said.

"I just looked for sign along the main road for two hours north with the best tracker around. There was nothing we could find on the road to indicate foul play," Duncan said. "I am inclined to agree with you. Officially, this office will close the case file unless other information comes up in the future, which I doubt."

"Thanks, Sheriff." Royston turned and left. By late afternoon, he was on the train, with Richmond as his ultimate destination. He had not heard a response from the senior Hancock but did not care. As long as his bill was paid...

Duncan was more sure than ever the only two women he had ever loved were involved in the death and removal of Riley Hancock's body. He knew neither were murderers. Hancock had to have initiated something and one of them had shot in self-defense. He knew both were capable of it, beyond the shadow of a doubt. It would be interesting to know what the senior Hancock would say to Royston about this case being closed. It was something he suspected he would never know.

18

ARIZONA TERRITORY
1904

At dinner, Duncan announced the closure of the case regarding the disappearance of Riley Hancock II, both by his office and the private detective.

He said evidence suggested Hancock had probably engineered his own disappearance to avoid retribution due to high gambling debts or some uncharged crime, possibly against a woman.

He had told his father privately he planned to do this at dinner, so Angus listened with casual interest. The women took it silently and managed not to exchange glances.

As far as the Duncan men were concerned, the matter was over. There was no proof. If there was, neither wanted to know about it.

On the following Saturday morning, the Governor and First Lady would arrive on the train to Prescott. So would Captain Rynning and a Presbyterian minister of Scottish descent from Phoenix.

The marriage service was scheduled at the Highlands Ranch, with all members of the public invited. Due to the unknown number of attendees, box lunches and cups or mugs were encouraged for those who wanted to eat after the noon service. Several large kegs of beer and pitchers of sweet tea would be provided by Angus.

In the several days before the weekend, the couple rearranged the bunkhouse to live in it until their house could be built. Duncan and Angus moved the bunks to a storage area of the barn. Miranda drove the buckboard into town, and they picked out a bed and mattress, a wardrobe, linens and things like a pitcher and bowl set, dishes, and towels.

By Saturday morning, everything was in place for the wedding. At noon, it went off without a hitch and Sheriff and Mrs. James Duncan and his parents entertained guests. The Territorial Governor and his wife represented Miranda's family.

In a conversation in the ranch yard with his former boss, Duncan learned Rynning had a history in construction. His company still existed, though owned by a former partner. He promised to write the man and have him contact Duncan about building the house once Duncan had settled on the purchase of the Hatton property.

Later in the night, after the crowd of well-wishers had left, birds were singing in the trees near the bunkhouse and Miranda came to Duncan in the way both had dreamed about since the cabin in the Hualapais.

On Sunday morning, they rode over to the Hatton's and made an offer. It was accepted at a price leaving sufficient money to build a small house. Duncan and Angus would build a temporary shed and corral like in Wickenburg for little money and several days' sweat.

By Tuesday, a local lawyer had drawn up the deed of sale and Duncan and Hatton had met at the bank, money was tendered, and the deed signed. They then walked to the courthouse and filed it.

Sheriff James and wife Miranda Duncan now owned three hundred twenty mixed acres on the road outside of Prescott. Their livestock consisted of two horses, a big blue roan who seemed to understand English and a black quarter horse whose language skills were not fully known yet.

Several weeks later, the new sheriff received his first paycheck and was pleasantly surprised at the amount. With the salary and his portion of fines, it was far larger than the pay of an Arizona Ranger sergeant. A joint demand deposit account was opened at the Bank of Arizona.

Duncan had posted a letter to General Delivery, Kamloops, British Columbia for Aaron Piyahgonte the day of his swearing in. In it, he advised his friend he had a pardon signed by a territorial circuit judge. The original would be in the hands of his father and a copy would be personally delivered to the commanding officer at the Army fort outside of Prescott well before the letter arrived in Kamloops. He could return to Arizona at this pleasure for a visit or permanently, as could any of the five braves who accompanied him.

He ended by describing his wedding and asked if a similar service had been held for Aaron and Wenonah. He took some money from his new pay and included enough for two round trip tickets by train from British Columbia to Phoenix. Several weeks later, he would hear a positive response.

In the meantime, he scheduled a trip to the spring camp of the Yavape with Angus to deliver the original to Noah Piyahgonte and a trip to the Army post.

By late April, Duncan had settled comfortably into the role as sheriff of a large, rural county. He tried to split his time between the office, visiting populated centers and patrolling, with or without his deputies. He wanted to be a working sheriff, not just an administrative one.

He had also received a return letter from Aaron, appreciative for the pardon and the travel funds.

Aaron said he and Wenonah had married with the ceremony of the Nlaka'pamux tribe, but he would come soon to introduce her to his family and have the Yavape Band of the Yavapai Tribe marriage ceremony performed also.

Aaron said he wanted the two Duncan couples to attend the ceremony.

Duncan shared this with his father, who said it was a singular honor for whites to attend such a sacred Indian ceremony and one he would relish seeing with his family.

***

Duncan sat at his desk signing warrants and reviewing new Wanted posters from around the Territory and beyond. His coat and silver belly, pencil roll Stetson hung on the wooden stand in the corner with his suit jacket.

The long gun rack was on the wall to the right rear of his desk. All deputies had a key to his office and the rack, which held six rifles, five .30-30's and one was a Winchester 1895 like he carried in the rangers, but in the brand new .405 WCF caliber. It had a knock down power of over thirty-two hundred pound feet of energy. The final three guns were short barrel shotguns in ten gauge.

All the guns were kept loaded and were secured by a chain through either the lever or trigger guard. Boxes of additional cartridges were stacked on a shelf beside the rack. The key to the gun rack also unlocked a steel box welded to the bars of the lockup which held additional handcuff, or "nippers" keys and jail door keys.

Duncan had asked the blacksmith to craft and install window bars on all windows and both the front and back doors of the office. The blacksmith also installed a steel bar to swing into place and block the inward opening front door. Duncan considered the jail impenetrable to about any attack other than explosives or fire.

Since the new dress vests Duncan wore in town did not have pockets of sufficient size to carry his .38 S&W break open revolver as a backup, he traded it. The new model .38 Special Hand Ejector had a slightly longer four-inch barrel and he wore it in a small inside holster clipped on his left hip. The gun's round butt and its frame were largely hidden by the vest .

Duncan checked the Elgin pocket watch on its chain in the vest pocket. He told the time by the sun on the trail, but almost daily court appearances required more precise timing.

He had ten minutes to meet Miranda at the Hotel St. Michael dining room for a late Sunday breakfast. It was a celebratory one. Just after the marriage, they had returned to Wickenburg with the buckboard and picked up belongings and she had resigned as teacher. It had taken the ensuing weeks to finalize a teaching job in Prescott. But, college-trained teachers were few and she had just been confirmed in town.

He strapped on his usual gun belt and donned his suit jacket and hat.

"See you in a while, Ev. Lunch with the boss," he said as he walked through the office towards the door.

"Say hi to Miss Miranda for me," came Master's rejoinder.

Duncan walked down the street, doffing his hat at people, but still searching from side to side for threats.

He walked into the hotel and to the dining room entrance.

"The Missus here yet?" he asked.

"Not yet, Sheriff. Want me to go ahead and seat you?"

"Sure."

Before he could take a step, he heard a shot outside.

Duncan spun and pushed his coat back behind both his Colt's .45 revolver and the backup on his left.

He carefully stepped out of the door.

The first thing he saw was Miranda standing at the edge of the street, a hundred yards away. She saw him. Even before identifying the threat to himself, he nodded to her left and she moved away onto the sidewalk and into the doorway of a shop. Once he knew she was safe, he looked to Gurley Street in front of him.

Next was the threat. Or, threats. It would be there in the street, based on the sound of the shot.

A tall man was in the street, gun in hand. A window in the hotel had been broken, apparently by one of the shots Duncan had heard.

Flanking him on either side were two more disreputable looking armed men, neither with drawn guns. Yet.

The midday sun was bright, but not in Duncan's eyes.

He stepped out into the street. Miranda watched safely from a doorway. Citizens scurried for cover and a watch point.

The man with the smoking gun was former Army lieutenant Nicolas Smoot. A man who had sworn to get him.

"Duncan, I warned you I'd kill you. Now's your time," Smoot said.

"Drop the gun and throw up your hands. You and your friends don't have to die here today," Duncan said clearly, but not loudly.

Duncan had quickly analyzed the situation. One man,

an enemy, with a gun in his hand, two aching to draw and moving away on either side.

Duncan knew the only way he would survive this was to act first.

Smoot did not give him the chance. Duncan saw Smoot begin to raise his gun hand.

Duncan drew, his left hand only a millisecond slower than his right.

Two shots to center mass of Smoot, a right and a left hand shot to the men on either side as they drew.

Smoot staggered forward and tried to raise his gun. Duncan extended his right arm and shot him between the eyes from forty feet.

A bullet whistled past Duncan from the man on Smoot's right. The sheriff heard the "thwack" as it hit some part of the façade of the hotel. He aimed the round butt, four-inch Smith & Wesson .38 and fired at the man's center and he fell, hit hard a second time.

The other man was on the ground rolling around. He raised his gun in Duncan's direction.

One more time the Colt's .45 spoke, and the man ceased to move. His gun fell to the ground. On his back, he raised his legs straight up towards the sun. It was as in he had been sitting position on his butt and rocked back onto his back, legs in the air. They stayed pointing upwards for a moment, then gently settled to the dirt of the street as he passed this life.

Eyes on the three men in the street, the sheriff ejected empties from the .45 and replaced them before moving forward. He had holstered the S&W, but kept the single action, smoothed by the great Chris Madsen, in his hand as he walked carefully toward the three in the street.

There was no doubt whether Smoot was dead. Either torso shot would have killed him within minutes. The head shot killed him instantly.

The man on his left's eyes were locked open staring sightlessly into the bright sun. No doubt there, either.

Duncan walked to the third man and kicked his gun out of his hand. He bent down. The man was blinking, and a pink froth was at his lips. He jerked several times then stopped. Duncan took his fingers and gently closed the man's staring eyes.

He stood and looked around the area for a full three hundred sixty degrees. Prescott had come alive again and people were coming out of the doorways and alleys to which they had retreated to watch safely.

People approached slowly. They were curious to see up close what would be recounted frequently over the years, as the legend of the lawman grew. Duncan recognized most and knew none represented danger. Ev Masters approached and picked up the guns laying near the bodies. The two lawmen looked at each other. Both nodded.

The sheriff looked up and scanned the windows of buildings for any backup shooters Smoot may have positioned. Duncan did not see any. A couple of curtains were pulled open, but only women and men who did not appear to have rifles, peered out, interested in the goings-on just as the people in the street were.

A beautiful woman walked towards him, a revolver in her hand. It was pointed downwards, beside her leg, as she approached. She was not a threat.

Miranda Duncan stopped ten feet from him, knowing he might have to react to something unseen in the flash of a second, but Duncan holstered the smoking .45 and let out a breath.

Tears began to roll down her cheeks and she tried to shake them away with a toss of her long brown hair. "This time, I was scared for you. Three against one. Standing apart in the open. Even for you said..." She stopped. There was no need to discuss it again.

They stood and looked at each other as if they were the only two people on the earth. She moved closed to him and stood there, bodies touching.

They did not speak. He smiled at her and she smiled back through her tears.

No more words were necessary.

Duncan and Miranda heard a church bell begin to chime in the distance.

Civilization was coming to Arizona Territory.
But the sheriff knew one thing for damn sure.
It hadn't gotten there yet.

IF YOU LIKED THIS, CHECK OUT THE JACK LANDERS WESTERN MYSTERY SERIES BY G. WAYNE TILMAN

INTRODUCING MODERN LAWMAN JACK LANDERS IN THIS FOUR-BOOK BOXSET!

Special Agent Jack Landers is a young Oklahoma state investigator and a Western lawman who would rather have been chasing down the Doolin-Dalton Gang in Indian Territory in the 1890's. The thirty-five-year-old lawman has several gunfights under his belt and the scars to show for it. He has dealt with tough cases and tougher crooks with no problems.

When multiple murders occur he finds himself heading a serial sex murderer task force that is statewide. Jack is divided between enforcing the law and vengeance, and things spin beyond his control—almost.
Jack has to decide between right and wrong in order to determine what to do about it…

AVILABLE NOW ON AMAZON

About the Author

G. Wayne Tilman is a full-time author. He retired from the Federal Bureau of Investigation several years ago. Prior to the FBI, he was a Marine, bank security director, deputy sheriff, investigator, and security contractor.

He holds baccalaureate and master's degrees from the University of Richmond and has been an adjunct faculty member there, as well as the University of Phoenix, St. Petersburg College and Florida Metropolitan University.

He wrote his first novel over thirty years ago and has now written thirteen novels. Genres include espionage thrillers, mysteries, and Westerns.

G. Wayne Tilman's impetus to write in those genres comes from both personal experience and heritage.

Find more great titles by G. Wayne Tilman and Wolfpack Publishing, here: https://wolfpackpublishing.com/g-wayne-tilman/

15695658R00189